SECRETS OF THE CITY

OTHER BOOKS BY ANNE ROIPHE

Novels

Digging Out
Up the Sandbox
Long Division
Torch Song
Lovingkindness
The Pursuit of Happiness
If You Knew Me

Nonfiction

Generation Without Memory
A Jewish Journey Through Christian America
Your Child's Mind (with Dr. Herman Roiphe)
A Season for Healing: Reflections on the Holocaust
Fruitful
1185 Park Avenue
For Rabbit, With Love and Squalor
Marriage: A Fine Predicament

ANNE ROIPHE

SECRETS OF

THE CITY

A NOVEL

SHAYE
AREHEART
BOOKS
—
NEW YORK

Published by Shaye Areheart Books, New York, New York.
Member of the Crown Publishing Group, a division of Random House, Inc.
www.crownpublishing.com

Originally published in serial form by *The Forward,* December 14, 2001, to March 28, 2003

SHAYE AREHEART BOOKS and colophon are trademarks of
Random House, Inc.

Printed in the United States of America

Design by Lauren Dong

Title page photograph © Lynn Saville/Photonica

Library of Congress Cataloging-in-Publication Data
Roiphe, Anne Richardson, 1935–
    Secrets of the city : a novel / Anne Roiphe.—1st ed.
    1. Mayors—Fiction. 2. New York (N.Y.)—Fiction. 3. Terrorism—
Prevention—Fiction. 4. Hostages—Fiction. I. Title.
PS3568.O53S43 2003
813'.54—dc21   2003011640

ISBN 1-4000-4945-8

10 9 8 7 6 5 4 3 2 1

First Edition

To Harry Chernoff,
father of Violet Malka.

ACKNOWLEDGMENTS

I WOULD LIKE TO THANK J. J. Goldberg and the staff of *The Forward* for their kindness in finding a place for *Secrets of the City* for so many weeks.

CONTENTS

1 The Demon Foiled *1*

2 The Angel of Death Is Hovering *6*

3 Don't Print, Don't Plead *9*

4 All the Birds in Heaven *12*

5 Body and Mind, Pocketbook and Health *15*

6 The Cardinal Swoons, the Ducks Die *18*

7 A Man Will Sell His Soul for His Grandchildren *21*

8 A Heart-to-Heart *24*

9 Things Unseen *28*

10 Good Food Goes Bad *31*

11 City Dwellers Head for the Hills *35*

12 The Imp of Darkness Ducks for Cover *38*

13 Maddie Miller's Late-Night Tip *42*

14 The Mayor Is Shafted *46*

15 A Slice of Trouble *50*

16 Down and Down We Go *55*

17 Ruth Seeks the Truth *59*

18 In the Laboratory *63*

19 Acceptance and Assumptions *67*

20 Thousands of Men, No Regrets *71*

21 Emptying the Vials *75*

22 The Death Count Grows *79*

23   Methods and Madness   *83*

24   Meet Neil Maguire, Parking Commissioner   *87*

25   The Spinner of Holy Tales Tells All   *91*

26   A Seder Night Different from Other Seder Nights   *95*

27   The Unkindest Cuts of All   *99*

28   The Solace of Sound   *103*

29   Dirty Work and the Evil Inclination   *107*

30   Law and Order in the Real City, Not the TV City   *111*

31   Neil Maguire Goes Down to the Docks   *115*

32   A Dark Day for the Caseworker's Shadow   *119*

33   Ina and Brooke Put Both Feet on the Wrong Path   *126*

34   Brooke's Eyes Glitter for Sequins   *130*

35   Sergei Crashes the Hadley Party   *134*

36   The Truth About Neil Maguire   *138*

37   A City Inflamed   *142*

38   A Family Killed, a Man Repentant   *146*

39   The Mayor Is Spat upon at Firefighter Billy Finnegan's Funeral   *150*

40   Brooke's Secondhand Life   *154*

41   The Price of Silence   *158*

42   Strike Central   *162*

43   Greasing the Buses' Wheels   *166*

44   The Truth Behind the Shower Curtain   *170*

45   Gimpel Stops *Don Giovanni*   *174*

46   Lilith's Spawn on the Loose   *179*

47   Is the Mayor in on the Take?   *185*

48   On the Trail of a Sugar Daddy's Sugar   *189*

49   Fisticuffs on the Boardwalk   *193*

50 Mel Comes Under Fire (and the Eyes of Apollo) *197*

51 The Mayor and the Lions of Judah *201*

52 The Parking Commissioner's Moving Violation *205*

53 Hate Him if You Can *209*

54 A Critique of Robin Hood as an Economist *213*

55 A Lightbulb Goes on over Leonid's Head *217*

56 A Snowstorm Hits Hard *221*

57 Ina Tells Sergei Her Secret *225*

58 Leonid Becomes a Capitalist *229*

59 Kibitzing from a Front-Row Seat in Heaven *233*

60 Leonid Asks for a Loan *237*

61 A Journey in Search of Justice *241*

62 Push Me and I'll Push You Back *245*

63 Are You Cain or Abel? *249*

64 Cold Comfort in Cold Times *253*

65 A Conversation About Uncivil Things at the Civics Club *257*

66 Brooke Crosses a Bridge *261*

67 Maddie Makes Her Move *265*

68 A Confession That Changes Everything *269*

69 A Business Deal Is Sealed *273*

70 They Lost It at the Movies *277*

71 It's All Hollywood's Fault, or Is It? *281*

72 Food, Glorious Food *285*

73 Everyone Loves a Parade *289*

74 Awards and Rewards *293*

75 The Bell Tolls *297*

76 A Story Needs an Ending *301*

SECRETS OF THE CITY

1

THE DEMON
FOILED

The new mayor of the city was Jewish, which didn't mean he wouldn't celebrate Kwanzaa. Also Christmas Mass at the Cathedral of Our Lady of the Sea, which spread solid and squat across two blocks of prime downtown real estate. He would appear at the food kitchen serving the homeless a meal of turkey and cranberries, and sing along with a gospel choir. The camera would find him at a shelter for abused women dressed as Santa Claus some weeks before the actual birth date of the significant baby. He had been elected by a mere hair and was quite sure that many felt he was not up to the task, too inexperienced, too much an outsider, not a man of the people at all. He was aware that the schools were rundown and class sizes too large and the bridges in need of overhaul. For months now he had been worrying about bottom lines, the appearance of favoritism here or there, the failure of those he had appointed to stem the tide of disarray. He knew that the taxi drivers might strike along with the elevator operators and sanitation workers and at least half the libraries might have to close because the funds were not there. He knew that the prisons were so crowded that riots were imminent but the citizens still felt unsafe in their neighborhoods, that the police sometimes behaved like warlords, and that the minorities in his city did not trust the particular minority that had nurtured the mayor himself. All this gave him a headache, the kind that two aspirin hardly touched.

The mayor's wife had prepared for Hanukkah as she always did. The children and the children's children would come for supper. There would be presents for the younger children, and then they would light the candles; this year they would do so for the cameras. His aides had thought it would be helpful to show the mayor to his fellow citizens as a man who respected his tradition, a man of God, a family man. The mayor's wife had purchased a larger, more elaborate silver menorah than they had ever had before. This one had an eight-inch Lion of Judah at the base and grape leaves and pomegranates engraved on the cups that would hold the blue and white candles. The mayor's grown daughter, Ina, had placed red velvet ribbons in her own baby daughter's hair and had insisted her three-year-old son, Noah, wear his jacket. The mayor's son, Jacob, who privately felt that his father was a bit old for the job and should have let a younger man take his place at the top of the ticket, shaved so thoroughly that he cut himself and arrived with his five-year-old twins, Kim and Kelly, at the mayor's house with a bit of bloody tissue pressed to his cheek. He reminded his twins not to say "Merry Christmas" to their grandparents. In silent pluralism lay unity was his policy.

This year the mayor's wife did not make the potato pancakes herself. The cook made them and burned them and made a new batch. The children did not eat them because they did not like them and never had, although each year the mayor's wife offered them. The cook had to make them pasta with butter instead. They also did not like gefilte fish, rugelach, brisket, matzo balls, or apples with honey. So be it. They could always have pasta. The mayor wanted to tell the children how his own mother had grated potatoes and added onions and fried them on her old stove, and the smell clung to his clothes for days. But he had told them all that before.

There was nothing new to say. For the cameras he had prepared a speech. He had rehearsed it as he dressed in the morning and added to it during the day in the seconds between appointments. He had thought of the ending in the five minutes before his luncheon guest, the CEO of a major firm who was thinking of moving the company's offices out of town and was angling for some tax concessions (also tickets to the opening game of the baseball season), had arrived. He had polished it while waiting for his internist, who had dismissed his stomach ailments as an occupational hazard and suggested a week in Florida, which could not and would not be fit into the schedule.

The computer games his wife had purchased for the children seemed to be accepted with pleasure, but then one of them was lost in the pile of blue and white and silver paper on the floor. The new owner of the game wept and stamped her feet, and the mayor's son had to fold each piece of paper before it was found. The baby whimpered and howled and would not be comforted. "The room is too hot," said the mother of the infant. The windows were opened. "It's too cold," said one of the twins, who wrapped herself in the mayor's wife's velvet evening coat. The stuffed mouse and the soft elephant were greeted with hugs but then forgotten behind the couch. The daughter and the son made polite conversation, but the mayor saw ice floes forming as they spoke. It had always been that way. Their conversation was strained through the sieve of years, through the small resentments and the larger ones that formed a toxic plume snaking its way across the living room rug. The mayor preferred to ignore these particular hostilities. The mayor of such a city knew all there was to know about jockeying for personal advantage, about the petty adversarial words of one for another, and wished with all his heart that he had not been persuaded to invite the press to his home for the lighting of the candles. But he had.

The time came. The party assembled around the now cleared dining table. The TV cameras moved in to show the glorious menorah. There was a moment of quiet. Then the mayor's wife said the prayer, which was not so short because it was the last night of Hanukkah. The mayor's son helped his daughters take the match to the large candle and light it, and then he lit all the candles, one after another. The TV cameras rolled, and the children's faces in the candlelight glowed, their cheeks were pink. The picture was picture perfect, and the mayor cleared his throat, ready to give his speech, when suddenly the candles that had been lit went out, one by one, just as they had been lit, each leaving behind a little wisp of smoke that curled upward toward the ceiling. It must be a draft; it must be the open window. "Cut, cut," said the mayor's campaign manager, Moe Alter, to the TV cameramen, who did not stop their cameras. The mayor's son picked up the matches and relit the candles. The mayor's wife said the prayer again, not sure if that was the right thing to do or not. The candles burned for a moment and then again, as if the wicks were made of river water, sank into darkness. The mayor's daughter tried, and the mayor's son-in-law, Sergei, tried, and each time the candles flamed up and then died as if a great breath had blown on them. Everyone in the room turned toward the mayor. He would have to explain this. He would have to explain the failure of his menorah to light to all the citizens of the city who would see it on the evening news.

The mayor was mute. His eyes were frightened. He could find no words for this strange, unnatural occurrence. His wife had tears in her eyes. His daughter was sulking her terrible sulk. His son was not entirely dissatisfied. What was this? The mayor searched his mind. Was it a sin of his? Was it sign that God had deserted his people? Was it a sign that he had gone too far in calling the cardinal "Your Excellence" the week before? What had he done that his candles would not light?

Behind the drapery the Spawn of Lilith, the Demon of Political Turmoil, had waited, stamping his little feet and hugging himself in malicious delight. Now, unseen by human eyes, he floated past the mayor, a tip of his scaled hoof brushing across the forehead of the sweating politician. There was noise in the room. The aides were trying to spin the situation: "cold air, bad candles, damaged wicks, sabotage by the other party." Then the mayor raised his arms and spoke. He understood the reverse miracle, which was itself a sort of miracle. "This was a year for darkness, for lights that would not light. This is a promising sign, a menorah in rebellion against taking things for granted. Clearly this is a hint of good things to come, a positive miracle, because," said the mayor, although this was not the speech he had rehearsed at all, "out of darkness creation began, out of the void there came a new beginning, and this darkness will be the beginning of all our people of our city living together not in a grim truce but in mutual respect and true affection one for another. The darkness of this menorah is the beginning of our new light. It is our opportunity to create a better world than the one we live in now. Take a moment, everyone, respect the darkness cast by the nonlighting candles. Out of the void the beautiful world was once formed. These candles are not burning, and in their not burning they leave us in darkness, and this darkness tells us that light will surely return, spring will come, that men are brave and nations can defend themselves against evil-doers. We are not afraid of the dark."

The Demon, hearing these words, knew he was defeated. Depressed, deflated, he left the mayor's house disguised as an uneaten potato pancake. Before he departed he hid the computer games in the bag of a cameraman who would not find them until long after Easter.

The mayor shot so high in the polls that there was talk of his running for president. After all, someone has to be the first Jewish president.

2

THE ANGEL OF DEATH
IS HOVERING

Ruth Rosenberg woke up with a start. Mel was snoring, but that was not what had broken her sleep. Without waking he rolled over to her side of the bed and pulled his woman to his side, pinning her down among the tangled sheets. The snoring subsided as he tangled his legs around hers. She stroked his back and put her lips on the bald expanse on the top of his head. The dream that woke her was slipping away. Something horrible about invisible spores, visible to the dreamer, heading in V formation like geese on a flight through the window of her daughter's apartment and settling on the bars of the baby's crib. Her heart was still racing.

The night before she had heard Mel talking on the phone to the commissioner of health. "How long would it take for the smallpox vaccine to be flown in from Washington? How many lives would be lost in the first hours of contamination?" Mel was scratching his face. "Goddammit," he said, "I want more information on my desk in the morning. I want to know about cholera and bubonic plague and Ebola and TB and what you're doing to protect us."

"Why did I go to law school instead of medical school?" he yelled at Ruth, who had a few answers for that one, concerning but not exclusively a failed chemistry exam, but held her tongue. After he got off the phone he looked very pale. "I don't know what to do," he said to Ruth. "We can't seal off the city, no buses, no trucks, no strangers, no boats. We can't tell everyone to go to the country for a month or so." In his mind's eye he saw carts carrying the dead, bodies in the elevators of office buildings, the sick calling out for water in the parks. Ruth said, "Maybe it's an empty threat; we've had them before. Perhaps nothing will happen." "When," said Mel, "has nothing ever happened?"

Later while Mel was shaving in the bathroom the phone rang. It was their daughter, Ina, whose voice was low and cloudy. Ruth knew the tone. "What?" she said. "What's wrong? Is the baby sick?" "No," said Ina, "it's just something I tried in the lab. It didn't work out." "Sorry," said Ruth. "It's months of work, wasted," said Ina, who despite her higher degrees could whine as well as any six-year-old in town.

An imp sat on the breakfast table. His smile was broad but not kind. His teeth were badly in need of orthodonture. He smelled of burned rubber, which was not his fault. That's the way imps smell. He knocked over the coffee in the pot, and the liquid spread languidly across the table and down onto the rug below, which Ruth knew was the property of the people of the city and should be respected as such.

"Do you smell burning rubber?" the mayor asked. "Must be the toaster," said his wife as she went to unplug the offending appliance. The mayor remembered his father, in his bathrobe, close to the window, greeting the day with prayers of gratitude. What were those words again? Time and indifference had scrubbed his memory clean, but traces remained buried deep down like long-forgotten arrowheads resting under the cement streets. The mayor couldn't catch the words, but he heard the echo.

In the neurons and synapses of the mayor's mind fear melted like ice cream in July. "Have courage," he said to his wife. "Plagues come and go. We'll outsmart the bugs, just watch." The imp break-danced on the mayor's eardrum. "There's something in my ear," he said as he went out the door. The Angel of Death hovered high above the city, making a gray day grayer still.

3

DON'T PRINT, DON'T PLEAD

The mayor was sitting at his desk crunching numbers. They were not crunching easily. They escaped his columns, they dripped down the sides of his yellow legal pad, they added up but not the way he wished. The budget bulged in certain places, seemed shrunken in others. If only he had a counterfeiting machine in the basement of city hall. If only money were on the grief standard— x number of dollars equaled x number of woes. He drank his third cup of coffee. The police chief was waiting in the outer office. The lights on the phone blinked one after another. There was a banging on his door. In came Maddie Miller, a velvet skirt, a black angora sweater, wobbling on high heels that made her left ankle turn in toward the right one with each step forward. Maddie Miller, Miller the Killer, his legal staff called her. She was the city hall reporter for the *Daily World,* the biggest paper, the most serious paper in town. She leaned over his desk, and he closed his eyes so that he wouldn't look where he shouldn't. "Mr. Mayor," she said. "I need your help." What now? he thought. Alarm stiffened his arms, and he pressed them against his sides. "Don't worry. I'm not going to touch you," said Maddie. Mel blushed. There was no need to be afraid of Maddie. At least not physically. "There's a little something I overheard in the elevator that I need checked. I need you to confirm or deny." Maddie looked him in the eye. He blinked. She was not, as everyone knew, a particular woman. She had been seen with men of letters, men on boards of Fortune 500 companies. She closed bars. She attended every charity ball. She chased movie stars and made them lovers until she tired of them. It was not easy for Mel to believe, but several people had told him she wanted him, body and soul. A mayor is surrounded by flatterers, by intrigue, by nitwits, no matter how hard he tries to avoid them. Maddie confused power with sex. What worried Mel was that while he too enjoyed power, relished it, dreaded its absence, sex he preferred with Ruth. Except there was something about Maddie—a burning flame lit her face, an awkward and speedy fling of her arms as she spoke, an invitation just behind every sentence. "I heard," she said, "that we may have a terrorist alert. Is it true? What are you doing about it?"

Mel's personal assistant, also his liaison to the gay and lesbian community, Harold, opened the door. "Your son is calling, says it's urgent." "Leave the door open behind you," said Mel. He pressed the lit button before him and put the phone to his ear, waving to Maddie, a just-a-moment, what-can-you-do wave. "Jacob," he said, "what's wrong?" "Dad, you have to find someone on the board of Duncan Academy. And now. We need a reference with clout. You find time for everyone else in this rotten city. Find time for Kim and Kelly. Get us a board member. You have the list on your desk. You've had the list for a month." Mel said, "Couldn't you and Brooke consider using the public schools?" There was a rude sound on the other end of the line. Mel made soothing noises. He didn't suggest a Jewish day school. He hung up. He pushed the papers around, searching for the brochure he hadn't seen for weeks from Duncan, a school so desired its very name made butterflies dance in the brains of hopeful parents.

"There's no terrorist alert," he said to Maddie. "There are rumors, and if you print them we'll have panic." "And if they are true?" said Maddie, breathing some sort of fresh mint into his face. "Print rumors," he said, "and you'll have egg on your face and a lot of explaining to do." "Poached egg or fried?" she asked. "Don't print," he said in a manner that he hoped wasn't abject. Don't plead, he reminded himself. "Want to have lunch with me at my apartment?" she asked. He did, he really did. "No," he said. "We'll order in, then," she said. "Ham with mustard on rye for me," she shouted to Harold. "Tuna for his honor."

The brochure from Duncan was on the floor under the mayor's desk. He saw it, touched it with his left foot, and left it there.

4

ALL THE BIRDS
IN HEAVEN

The mayor spilled tuna on his pants. Maddie tried to wipe it off with her napkin. He stopped her. "What are you doing to protect the subway riders from nerve gas?" she asked. In fact he was doing nothing because he didn't know what to do. "I'll let you know," he said. "The car's waiting downstairs," Harold said, interrupting the intimate lunch. "No," said the mayor, "I don't need it." He never liked sitting in the plush dark back of the car with the tinted windows and the driver in such a funereal suit, and while it was a well-intentioned perk of his office, it always made him uncomfortable. He was no socialist. He believed in wealth and the signs of privilege. He just preferred them in other people. He also didn't like the driver, who called him "boss man" in a tone that implied he wasn't.

On the sidewalk near the hot dog vendor's cart he saw a green bird lying on its side. Its small body was heaving. It seemed too cold for green birds to be hanging around. He'd never liked birds, mostly because of Alfred Hitchcock, but still his eye was caught. The creature seemed to be struggling to get to its feet. He bent down and scooped it up. He could feel its beating heart beneath the ragged feathers. It was a parrot, an escapee, a doomed creature from another clime. Its eyes were blank, no message there, but its heart was thumping with a desperate fear that Mel could not help but recognize. He was on his way to the Board of Education. He would bring the chancellor, with whom he was quarreling, the parrot as a gift for a classroom. Beware of Jews bearing gifts, he thought. Sooner or later he was going to get rid of that chancellor. His granddaughter could do a better job.

Three security officers accompanied him down the subway steps. One of them had lost his pass and was flashing badges at the clerk in the glass booth, but the others following the mayor jumped on the train that had pulled into the station. Mel sat down and absently smoothed the feathers of the parrot, now in the deep pocket of his blue overcoat. Can a man comfort a bird? Can the bird begin to know the man whose hand is being very careful not to press against the small head, the tiny orange beak? Nature shows were Ruth's pleasure. He found them boring. The subway rattled. The dark tunnel curved, and the train wheels made harsh metal noises that were, once you knew them, comforting, like the sound of waves at the beach. The mayor's fellow passengers did not seem to recognize him. They stared like zombies into space. Mel pushed away the pall of sorrow that he saw in the faces around him. He was not a man of sorrow.

Suddenly a drunk—was it a drunk?—lurched toward the mayor. His guardians were up on their feet instantly. The man had a small head, and he smelled of things uncivilized. "See, see," he screamed in anger, "the handwriting on the wall." They were pulling into a station. Only the usual graffiti spread across the tiles behind the heads of waiting passengers. "My bowels, my bowels! I am pained. At my very heart: my heart maketh a noise in me. I beheld and lo, there was no man and all the birds of the heavens were fled," shouted the man, and he fell on the mayor's lap. It was over in a minute—his guards had pinned the man down in a seat. "Take your medicine," some woman who looked like she knew what she was talking about shouted at him as she tried to kick him with the toe of her boot. On the station platform a blind saxophonist was playing "When the Saints Go Marching In."

It was a few minutes before the mayor realized he had a dead bird in his pocket. He threw it in a trash can as soon as he emerged onto the street. How could he protect the subway riders from poison or bacteria released in a small airless container like a train? He couldn't even protect one small bird. He arrived at the Board of Education filled with regrets, as if he had known the parrot a long time, perhaps shared a childhood together.

Way uptown a man closed his refrigerator door gently. The precious vials were carefully placed in a stand next to the milk carton. When the door was shut the light went out and the contents of the vials swam about invisible to the naked eye. On the window ledge outside the chancellor's window a pigeon collapsed. Its mate pecked at its lifeless body.

Gladys, the chancellor's assistant, buzzed her boss. She whispered into the phone in a voice filled with mock respect, "The first Jewish president of the United States of America is here."

5

BODY AND MIND,
POCKETBOOK
AND HEALTH

Mel wanted to fire the chancellor. He wanted him brought to the edge of town in a police car and told never to show his face again across the border. What Mel wanted to do was run the school system himself. He wanted the head of the teachers union to bake him cookies and agree to a major vacation cut. He wanted the schools open all year long. He wanted the janitors who littered, the teachers who yelled, the ones who lost control of their classes, and the ones who barely could read themselves strung up like the traitors they were, traitors to common sense, to the children who needed books, computers, smaller classes, hot lunches, and dentists. At first he had liked going to schools and reading *Green Eggs and Ham* or *The Little Engine That Could* with a group clustered around his legs. But now he could hardly look the kids in the eye. What had he done for them? Exactly nothing so far. What he said to the chancellor was, "I'm not as opposed to vouchers as I used to be." The chancellor blinked nervously. Mel's stomach growled. He hoped it was his stomach. It might have been a sound in his throat. In the same way a cat puts out his paw to touch the trembling mouse, Mel put out his hand and offered it to the chancellor, who had no choice but to take it.

The mayor's own children had gone to the Solomon Nachman Day School, a few blocks from their home. In their teens they had transferred to the elite academic high schools for which they were, if anything, overqualified. Ina in particular had been able to beat her father at chess from a very early age. She was a serious little girl with a passion for labeling, cataloguing, collecting stones. When she discovered the microscope the shape of her life took form. It made Mel proud when she won the science prize at graduation. He did ask Ruth if his daughter was normal, quite normal? Ruth did not answer. She obviously thought his question beneath contempt, or else she was worried, too. When Ina met Sergei at grad school Mel had breathed a deep sigh of relief. When their son, Noah, now three, was born Mel had overeaten at the bris and paid for it the night after but didn't care. Nothing spoiled his belief at that moment that he and his kind had a special dispensation from the Holy One or at any rate were tapped by fortune for success. What Mel meant by success was everything: body and mind, pocketbook and health. He remembered what had happened to Job, but at least at the moment when Ina appeared in the living room, the mohel ready to perform, with the baby in her arms, her contact lenses in, her dark hair falling forward over the baby's head, he believed that Job probably had done something wrong the chronicler had over-looked.

At the same moment Mel was beginning his conference with the chancellor Ina settled herself in a chair in Dr. Bergen's office. She sniffled. "I couldn't sleep again last night," she said. "I watched the late late show again. I saw a movie in which an alien creature falls to earth and catches a cold and dies horribly. It was in black and white. It made me cry." The thought of it made her cry. Dr. Bergen tried to imagine Ina in her lab, pulling out slides, dropping liquid solutions into petri dishes, keeping notes, reading journals. "I want," said Ina, "to stay home with the baby. I hate going out each day. My son looks at me as I leave like I'm a drunk off on a binge again. The baby turns her head away from me. And I put on my coat and I go out the door. I bite the inside of my cheek—in fact, I bit a bloody hole in my cheek as I waited for the elevator. I don't want to do it anymore. It isn't fair." "What isn't fair?" said Dr. Bergen. "Oh, everything," said Ina, looking at him as if he were last week's Chinese food sitting in the back of the refrigerator. "What are you working on now?" said Dr. Bergen. Ina paused. She was paying for this. Should she tell him, or should she tell him it was none of his business? She sighed. "It might be," she said "that one day we could develop a bacterium that would prey on other bacteria, yet do no harm to the human body." "But you don't want to work on this? You want to be home with the baby?" Dr. Bergen wasn't sure what was going on with his patient. Was this a serious depression, a somewhat delayed postpartum response, a regression to her own childhood need to be with her mother, a real need to be with her baby? As he puzzled this, Ina began to wail, "I want to be in two places at once." "Well, that makes sense," said Dr. Bergen. "Who doesn't?" He himself wanted to go salmon fishing in Alaska when the kings were running up the river and a man in waders standing in the icy water had a chance, a real chance, of landing one. "Besides," said Ina, "my mother has always loved my brother more." "How unusual," said Dr. Bergen. "And in a Jewish family. I can hardly believe it."

Quit, quit now, said a voice in Ina's mind. Not yet, said another voice. There were reasons, hard to explain to a rational person, that Ina loved Dr. Bergen.

6

THE CARDINAL SWOONS,
THE DUCKS DIE

Augustine had killed a bird and carried it in from the garden. The cardinal called for his secretary to come and remove the bird, a starling perhaps, from the doorway where it lay. The cardinal sat in his favorite chair. "St. Francis was perhaps too much of an idealist," he said. "I'm a realist," he added. "I know," said the mayor. Augustine sat on the cardinal's lap, shedding white fur that floated up into the air and settled down on the oriental carpet below. The mayor, who had quit smoking ten years earlier, was having an urge that made his fingers curl and uncurl in his pockets. The cardinal was a man in whose eyes no trace of condescension showed. The cardinal was a man with a gift for politics, which is why he was not a parish priest. "In what way can I help you this afternoon?" said the cardinal. The mayor's heart was beating loudly. Nothing to worry about, the cardiologist had said. Why were pictures of torture machines running through his mind? Every time he visited the cardinal at his residence, which was very Gothic, with stone arches and mahogany staircases and massive chests pressed against each wall, he thought of secret staircases and dungeons and grand and not so grand inquisitors, and every time he thought of exile and inquisition his blood boiled, a Jewish boil, a useless boil, a boil about things done long ago, things that still rankled and wounded but could not be expressed, not one reasonable man to another. The cardinal was not, after all, the man who had tortured Jews for lighting candles or eating matzo. The cardinal was a man who was always careful to ask the mayor how Ruth was feeling—well, he hoped. He always referred to the Judeo-Christian tradition, and it was impossible to think that this man, who could multiply vast numbers in his head (Mel had heard him do it), would ever condone a pogrom or encourage his followers to boycott Jewish stores or allow blood libels to spread across his domain. Nevertheless, Mel was not entirely comfortable.

"We have spaces," said the cardinal. "We could make more. Our schools are for all the citizens of the city. We do a far better job than you do. It is the lack of values, discipline, purpose that affects your students. I know you know what I mean," said the cardinal, scratching Augustine behind the ears, bestowing on the mayor a smile that seemed to Mel an anointing of the favored, almost an embrace. "I believe that we have the votes in the city council, you and I. We should issue a joint press release expressing our confidence and pride in our parochial schools, don't you think?"

The mayor had no intention of inflaming the anti-voucher lawyers and columnists and concerned parents by such a press release. He also was not happy at the thought of public schools abandoned to all but the particularly inept, the near dead, and those about to be imprisoned. Also he believed that, pledges aside, Catholic schools would produce Catholics as Jewish schools produce Jews, and while there was nothing wrong in that, it made him squirm to think of impressing on young minds things that were, after all, not so certain. "No," said Mel, "no press release. It wouldn't help." "Wouldn't it?" said the cardinal. "No," said Mel, but he didn't look the cardinal in the eye. He looked instead out the window.

There was a slow, hollow sound in the room. It was the cardinal falling forward. Augustine jumped to the carpet carefully, out of the way of his master's flailing legs. There was a strange gurgling sound. There was a bump as the cardinal's head hit the floor. The mayor wheeled around, reached for the cardinal to steady him, lost his grip, and slipped to the floor. The two men lay there for a terrible instant. The mayor stood up. The cardinal didn't. The mayor rushed to the outer room and called for help. The days of man are as grass, he flourishes as a flower in the field—the wind passes over it and it is gone and no one can recognize where it grew. How lucky he was that it was not his own heart, thought the mayor, and was ashamed of this thought.

At St. Mary's Hospital the mayor paced the waiting room. Reporters gathered and jostled each other and camera lights shone. The doctor appeared and took the microphone. The cardinal had recovered consciousness. Tests were being done. The press would be informed when there was more to say. "What were you and the cardinal meeting about?" asked a reporter. "Life after death," said the mayor. "The cardinal believes in it, and I have my doubts." "Really?" asked the reporter. "No," said the mayor, "not really."

"Why," asked a woman reporter, "are the ducks dying in the pond at Middle Park?" "I hadn't heard," said the mayor. "All the ducks in the park are dead," said the reporter. "This administration will not tolerate dead ducks," said the mayor, looking straight into the camera's eye. "I promise you that."

7

A MAN WILL SELL HIS SOUL
FOR HIS
GRANDCHILDREN

Get me Al," the mayor said to Harold. "Now," he added as Harold stood there as if he had something more to say. "Jump Up is really upset," said Harold. "Oh, them again," said Mel. "Well, it's my group," said Harold with a sulk and a reproachful glare combined. "They need to meet with you. I promised I would arrange it." "Schedule it," the mayor said with a sigh. He loved Harold like a son, which meant there were times he wanted to strangle him. "Get me Al," he shouted at Harold's departing back. Al Nussbaum, the mayor's friend from the old neighborhood who had made it in cyberspace, handheld guided missiles, and electronic parts for elevators—all offshoots of his father's men's clothing store, where Mel's own bar mitzvah suit had been purchased.

"You played like a blind quarterback," Al said as soon as the mayor picked up the jangling phone. He was referring to last week's poker game, in which Mel had bluffed when he should have folded, folded when he should have stayed in, and lost enough money not to mention it to Ruth. His concentration had been shaken. The feds had notified him, not for the first time, that they had information about a credible threat. But where, when, what precautions should he take? Al had donated a new gym to Duncan Academy. He had endowed scholarships for less fortunate children. He had bought the entire sixth grade tickets to the Broadway hit *Dogs.* He had taken the eighth grade on vacation to his home in St. Croix. His grandchildren were scattered all through Duncan's lower, middle, and upper schools. Al's stretch limo picked them up at the end of the day because his driver took them to their dance, tennis, and skating lessons. Al was on the board. Mel had allowed Al to contribute to his campaign, but within bounds. The contribution was not to be considered an investment in anything. Al had slapped him on the back and smiled. The mayor should not have taken that particular gift. But he had. And now, in addition, he was asking a favor, a most humiliating favor.

"Al," he said, "my twin grandchildren were turned down last year for Duncan. Yeah, I know, how could they turn the mayor's grandchildren down? It seemed they didn't do so well on the interview, whispered to each other or something. Anyway, you know how kids can be." Mel attempted an easy laugh. It came out as a cough. "Yeah, a little cold, that's all. Anyway, could you put in a good word?" "Sure," said Al, "what are friends for?" The little toad, the wart-covered Sprite of Corruption sprang up from between the Mayor's toes, and his feet began to itch. Was it the socks? Long ago Greed had looked into the eyes of Ambition and told her she was the most beautiful of all the earth's creatures. Mel hung up the phone. Mel had gone to schools named after presidents or Cabinet members, not obscure Shakespearean characters. His crowd, including Al, had been a million galaxies away from those whose fathers could pick up the phone and alter destiny. And now it was a generation later, and some other clueless kid was sitting in a school named for a president, and Mel was picking up the phone waving magic wands made of money. Mel was sad. He had switched teams, and that was something he regretted.

The commissioner of parks was in the outer office. Hernando Ruiz was a slight man. His doctorate was from Harvard. His political connections were through his wife's family. He was the sweetest soul that Mel had appointed to his administration. Mel hoped he had the grit for the job. "Hernando," the mayor said as they walked into his office, "do you know why the ducks in the park have disappeared?" "One of my crews found them lifeless on the grass in the early morning. They seem to have been chewed on," said Hernando. "An informant tells me their corpses have been sold to restaurants in Chinatown." The mayor called his commissioner of public health, Dr. Ahmed Jamal. "Any rise in hospital admissions, any unexplained illnesses?" he asked. His scalp was prickling. Oh, God, he prayed, keep me out of the whale's belly. "We have," said the commissioner, "gunshots, cancer—colon, breast, liver, brain—pneumonia, eczema, asthma, food poisoning, stab wounds, the usual. I think," added the commissioner, "I will resign soon and go to an island and fish." "I like fishing, too," said the mayor. "But not yet, my friend. We can't go yet." The mayor called his daughter at her lab. "Oh, Daddy," she said. "I'm too busy to talk." "One thing," he begged her. "Can you think of a reason that the birds might be dying?" "Are they?" she asked, her voice sharp. "They might be," he said.

Harold was standing before him, his purple shirt blazing like the colors of a brave knight of old riding to combat. "The cardinal has died," he said. "You need to issue a statement." "I hate funerals," Mel said, covering the phone with his hand. "If they had told me I would have to go to so many funerals, I would never have run for office." "Jump Up is going to protest in front of the cathedral," said Harold. "Tell them to cool off," said Mel. "What will that look like at a time of grief? Bad taste." Mel scowled. Harold smiled. "That's the point, sir," he said. "No one pays attention if you're not rude." "Believe me," Mel said, "it's not a good idea to get every Catholic in the city mad at you."

8

A HEART-
TO-HEART

Early in the morning a boy, a wool cap pulled low over his ears, staggering under the weight of a cardboard box, made his way through the winding streets of the city's Chinatown. In the pale light of dawn the child stopped and rested his burden on the fender of a parked car. Above him the signs with Chinese writing creaked on their hinges; a red banner floated in the slight breeze. A turquoise and pink paper fan lay in the gutter, torn in half. In front of the store windows the iron grates were pulled closed. A man in a stained apron emerged from a doorway and took the box after passing an envelope to the boy, who ran off as if the *Yetzer hara,* horns, scales, bad breath, and all, was chasing him.

As the sun hit the middle of the sky Ruth Rosenberg, with her own protective detective first class, Brian Peaks, sitting at a nearby table, was having lunch at the Dangling Noodle in Chinatown. Her old friend Toby, a companion from the days when the children were small and their mothers were stranded in playgrounds, animal crackers crumbling in their laps, Band-Aids, bottles, and pacifiers in plastic bags hanging from the back of strollers, was sitting opposite her. "My God, look at those ducks," said Toby. There in the window hung a black wire strung from one side to the other. The wire pierced each of the long necks of the birds, plucked and lifeless, flabby and pale, that swayed in the draft of the opening and closing door. "Duck?" asked the hovering waiter. "Fresh duck, come in this morning, specialty of the house, you want duck?" "No," said Ruth. "Peking style, but New York duck," the waiter added. Ruth hoped he had a green card. She wished she had bundles of green cards in her pocket and could pass them about like hors d'oeuvres at a cocktail party. The hanging ducks reminded her of the famous picture of Mussolini, although Mussolini had been no sitting duck. Anyway, she had no appetite for the bird, with or without hoisin sauce. Neither did Toby, and they ordered the lo mein. Detective Brian Peaks, however, ordered the duck, one of which was promptly removed from the wire and whisked off to the kitchen.

Ruth sighed. "What?" said Toby. "It's Ina," said Ruth. "What?" said Toby. Ruth was not a woman for crying in public places. The worst that happened was that her nose turned red, which it did now. Ruth had her doctorate in public policy from City University. She was still working at the Rothman Foundation giving away money to worthy projects, although now she had to be very careful to avoid any grants that might seem political; the truth was that all grants were political, and she was thinking she might have to quit. She was one of those women who had always believed in *tikkun olam* the way other people believed in diversified portfolios. She was small and now in her middle years round, rounder than she liked, but she still knew how to make a head turn, how to send a vibration out into a room, how to make her husband glare fiercely at some man she was talking with, how to wave her hand in the air in a gesture of helplessness that was in fact an invisible ordering of the universe.

"All I wanted—well, not all, but almost all—was for my children to have no pain." Toby giggled. "Come on, Ruth," she said. "It's me you're talking to." Ruth smiled but not widely and not genuinely. "I mean I wanted them to have great jobs and think big thoughts and love someone and reproduce and feel good when they woke up and when they went to bed and have more than we did." "You had a lot," said Toby. "More calm, I think," said Ruth. "More security. More safety. Less doubt. I wanted them content. Why is it so hard for anyone to be content?" Ruth asked her friend, who shrugged. "I feel," said Ruth "a shadow over Ina, a grayness that comes between us whenever I look at her, as if she were walking around in a cloud of ashes."

Toby giggled. "Come on, Ruth," she said. "She's just like everyone else." "What's the point," said Ruth, "if the next generation is trapped, strapped down, caught in an invisible net?" "Hey," said Toby, "what exactly is the problem?" Ruth blinked. "I wish—" she said. "Me too," said Toby, and each knew what the other wished. It had something to do with paths not taken. "I should have made *aliya*," said Ruth. "That old song," said Toby.

"I think," said Ruth, "that I tried hard, but trying is not good enough. I think that something went sour in Ina, something between the time I was reading *Goodnight Moon* and the morning she left for college, six packs of cigarettes in her backpack." "Did you read her diary?" asked Toby. "Of course not," said Ruth, "at least not often." Toby laughed. Detective Brian Peaks looked over. He felt left out. It wouldn't be right to ask what the joke was. He tore the last bit of meat off the bones of his duck. He gulped his sparkling water.

Detective Peaks sat in the backseat with Ruth on their way back to her office. Detective Ross, who had waited in the car outside, was driving. As they approached the building, weaving through the traffic, Detective Peaks suddenly turned white as a blank page on which bad news was about to be printed. He bent over. He leaned forward, the seat belt supporting his body. He fainted. Ruth, her

heart pounding, her own hands shaking, told Detective Ross to use
his police siren. They headed for the emergency room at St. Mary's.
"Call ahead," she said. She patted the detective's back, wiped his
forehead. She had seen pictures of his daughter and his wife. She
leaned over him and began to blow air into his mouth. She tasted
duck.

9

THINGS
UNSEEN

Mayor Mel Rosenberg did not lack for commissioners and deputy commissioners, liaisons and assistants. He had mountains of memos and back-to-back meetings, and he thought of the phone as a bump on his ear. He knew that the baggy circles under his eyes gave him the look of a basset hound. What he lacked was a divining rod. He needed to discover oil in Middle Park. He needed a diamond mine to be unearthed under the Upper Rotterdam section of town, where chips and holes and gates and grates decorated surfaces, Dorito bags and syringes clogged the drains. Amid the cleaned-up brownstones, the shiny new senior citizens' residence, the health care center he had visited the week before lay dozens of storefront churches, broken hinges, boarded-up buildings, cats hiding their kittens behind the wheels of rusted cars, sirens moaning up and down, projects that looked like prisons looming above, dead-eyed kids in wool hats and big pants roamed and every last soul was waiting for him to deliver more than he could pay for. Not vouchers but smaller classes, that he had decided. But where was the money to come from? The papers spilled across his desk. He had mixed them up—sanitation was mingled with parks, parks had pages from hospitals, and four hundred pages of itemized budgets for hospitals had fallen to the floor. Transit wanted more cops. The contracts were out for bidding on a new subway line that would connect to the airport. If only he could triple taxes. File clerks wanted longer vacations; everyone wanted health benefits increased. If only he could tax vice and virtue alike, collect from the people entering churches and synagogues and mosques, collect from the nannies in the playground for use of the swings. If only he had a toll booth at the entrance of emergency rooms and at the doors of the big stores. What if doormen collected a dollar for the city each time a resident entered or exited a building? But the facts, he reminded himself, were simple. Short of printing it in the basement of city hall, the money wasn't there.

He really ought to get to the gym. His belly was extending over his belt.

Across the river in a small apartment on Pacific Avenue with a big TV on a stand in the corner and unpacked suitcases lying at random angles across the floor, several men lounged on a faded red pullout couch that had a pattern of bright fall leaves spilling across the upholstery. They were drinking diet Cokes. One of them was simply not very bright. He was with his older brother, who had a degree in engineering from the university. The other two had been friends for most of their lives. Their fathers had been friends. They were not comfortable in the cold weather. They were soldiers. In this they were proud. They were agents of God. In this they were certain. They missed their mothers, their uncles, their cousins, their food, their streets, the music at the corner bar. This you could see in their eyes. The new images of lampposts and tall buildings, highways and dogs with strange shapes on leashes and women with high heels and their hair blowing free, the moon coming up and then disappearing again behind high buildings, all things strange, jumbled in their minds. Sinful, voluptuous thoughts plagued their nights. It was hard for them to remember that once they had been little boys whose mothers cleaned the dust from their eyes and carried them to bed when they fell asleep at the table or on the floor.

The pilot of a plane loaded with bombs knows that harm will come when he releases the lever. This is his job, and he imagines nothing as he dips and rocks with the wind that blows under the wings of the plane and he checks his instruments and he looks out at the vast sky and thinks very little. This is manhood. This is war.

So the four men in the room lay about, hardly talking. This one said he liked the new toothpaste that he had bought at the drugstore. That one said he found it too sweet. Another said he wanted to take his shirts to the laundry down at the corner. The engineer said he could do so. "Ah," said the third as an ad came on the television for a car that could climb to the top of a mountain ridge and balance there. "I like that," he said, "very much," and smiled.

Ina looked at her husband, Sergei. His hands were stained with blue. He, too, was a scientist. They had met during her first postdoc. He put his blue hand on her face. Lately they had both been too tired. She had been with the baby each time he had wanted her. She had turned her face away from him when he shifted toward her the night before. Now he looked at her. His beautiful wife, who knew what he knew about the multiple crawling, swimming, floating things unseen that invaded and coupled and divided and threatened the human body each hour of every day. Ina worried if he loved her still. She needn't have worried. He leaned against her. She felt how warm he was. She was cold. He warmed her. "Are you glad your brother is coming?" Ina asked. Sergei sighed. He loved his brother, Leonid, but *glad* was not the right word. "Don't be mad at Leonid," Sergei said. "Why should I be mad at him?" said Ina. "I haven't even met him."

10

GOOD FOOD
GOES BAD

The usual crowd of reporters waited on folding chairs. Mark Washington, press officer for the Rosenberg administration, lover of opera, amateur flute player, strode to the podium. He glared out at the crowd. "We do not yet know what caused Detective Brian Peaks's collapse. The report from the hospital"—and here he rattled some papers and straightened his spine, a tall man who suddenly became taller. Certainty, calm, that was what he wanted to project—"says he has not yet regained consciousness. The doctors are suggesting a very severe case of food poisoning and the Department of Health has closed the restaurant where the detective had lunch with the mayor's wife yesterday afternoon. An inspection team is in there as we speak."

A hand rose, a dozen hands. A TV camera rolled forward, catching the very faint line of sweat above Mark Washington's lip. Maddie Miller rose and without waiting to be recognized shouted out, "Are there other cases of so-called food poisoning that you are not reporting to the concerned public?"

Mark Washington's ankles ached. He had been ice skating in the park with his daughter that morning. There were five other cases of food poisoning in the city, but none as serious as the one that felled Detective Peaks. "We are looking into that," he said. "There is absolutely no reason for panic in the city. People get food poisoning all the time." Maddie Miller wrote down his words, but she caught the slight flare of his nostrils, the exaggerated way he shuffled his papers, and was not reassured at all.

"I have to see the mayor immediately," she said to Harold a half hour later. Harold was not afraid of Maddie, but he knew that it would not do to make an enemy of her. She opened the mayor's door to find him struggling to his feet. He had been searching for the name of the director of the zoo, which he was convinced was on a blue piece of paper he had let slip to the floor. He wanted to know what the zoo director knew about the habits of ducks. A passing wind pushed open a window, and Maddie's skirt rose above her hips and sank down like a sail in a summer squall. Papers blew about. Mel laughed. "Maddie," he said, "is that your personal ill wind we have here?" He closed the window. "I'm working," he added. "I saw," said Maddie. "I'm curious," she added. "Is something happening here that you are not disclosing?" Mel got up and grabbed Maddie by the shoulders. This was a mistake. She shook him off angrily. He had felt her flesh and was blushing. He said, "Don't spread rumors. Don't create panic. What we have here is a detective with food poisoning who seems to have eaten some bad duck. We have a few other people around town showing up at emergency rooms with something as yet unidentifiable. We have a few million people in perfect health going about their ordinary business. That's what we have here." He smiled at her. She looked so irritable, and in looking irritable she reminded him of his daughter. He raised his hand to touch her hair but then thought better of it. "Off the record," he said, "what do you think of vouchers?" "Not much," she said. "But then I went to Catholic school, twelve years, and I wouldn't do that to an innocent child."

The zoo was nearly empty on a weekday afternoon. There were a few mothers pushing strollers along the path. There were the usual homeless pushing their shopping carts through the monkey house, letting the warmth soak through their bones. There was a family of tourists from Paris. There was the balloon vendor, recently arrived from Bombay, who also sold peanuts that could be fed to the goats and the llamas. At the entrance gate a young man carried a sign that said WEAR YOUR OWN SKIN—DON'T TAKE HIS; above the lettering there was a picture of a fox with a tear in his eye. "Schmaltz," Ruth had said when she first saw the sign, taking Ina's son to visit the seals. "What is schmaltz?" the child had asked. "It's when," said Ruth, "you pretend you don't know that everything in the world eats something else smaller and weaker and preferably tasty." Her grandchild had clutched his stuffed lamb closer to his heart while temporarily ejecting his grandmother from her privileged place there.

In the tropical bird house there was silence. The toucan lay on the ground, his orange beak faded and flat. The cockatiel (*Nymphicus hollandicus*) and the horned parakeet (*Eunymphicus cornutus cornutus*) had fallen on the dirt below their boughs. The albatross, his huge wings spread for his final flight, had fallen behind fake ferns. The keeper, who was pushing his cart of bird feed, seeds, and bits of corn through the aisles of the indoor cages, was sweating and breathing heavily. He didn't feel well. He was dizzy. He noticed his charges, his beautiful feathered companions, his obligations, his reason for getting up in the morning, on the floor. He smelled death. He pulled out his cell phone and called for help, and then he collapsed.

About ten blocks away as the pigeon flies Ina's baby was being rocked by the nanny. The infant watched the afternoon light slipping away. She opened her fingers and tried to catch the dust that danced in the rays that entered through the window and ran across the room. Across from the park, the mayor's daughter-in-law, Brooke, was waiting for the mail. The school admissions would be announced soon. She closed her eyes and willed, with all the desperation of Sarah praying for a child, the arrival in their mailbox of a fat envelope from Duncan Academy.

In the winter afternoon the steel beams of bridges to the city tossed orange bouquets into the water below. The fierce glow of the dying sun caused the windows of buildings facing west to become a chorus shouting "Glory, glory" to the sky. Rows of double-parked taxicabs waited along the avenue while their drivers went in to pray to Allah at the white marble mosque by the highway that circled the city. In the dusk the downtown theaters lit up their marquees. The subways carried rush-hour passengers home. The Imp of Imperfection chipped and peeled and crumbled and littered everywhere, and was ignored by all.

Mel and Ruth Rosenberg were going to a benefit for a charity that gave college scholarships to deserving youngsters. It was going to be a boring evening. Very boring.

11

CITY DWELLERS HEAD
FOR THE HILLS

Cassandra Appleton, director of admissions at Duncan Academy, had an appointment with the head of the board of the school. She had come to his office on the top floor of a downtown building in the heart of the financial district to discuss his concerns about excessive diversity at the school. He was a busy man. He had his assistant order lunch from a local Chinese restaurant. Cassandra Appleton had requested duck. The head of the board had the orange-flavored beef. By midafternoon Cassandra Appleton was feeling ill and went directly home.

Uptown at the zoo someone called 911. Only hours later men covered in white suits with plastic face masks and hoods that made them seem like an exotic species of dodo bird were swarming out of vans and police were closing off the zoo and escorting the few remaining visitors out of the cordoned-off area. The zoo restaurant was closed, a police banner plastered across the entrance. The short-order cooks, the illegal dishwashers, and the boy whose job it was to fill the ketchup and mustard bottles were all told to get out as fast as possible. The vendors abandoned their carts and left for home. The press was not allowed in, although some, carrying their cameras, made an end run around the hippopotamus house and got as far as the wide moat in front of the polar bears before the police very politely, trained as they had been in First Amendment issues, removed them. The air did not smell of alien chemicals. The seals took long, graceful dives from one end of their pool to the other, not knowing that their dinner would be late, very late. The head of the animal keepers union was threatening to sue the city council, the mayor, and the moon for all they were worth. The employee who had been in the bird house was on a respirator at St. Mary's. Mel promised to visit him there as soon as he could. The Centers for Disease Control in Atlanta had dispatched its investigative staff. Every TV station carried news of the emergency at the zoo.

"Daddy," said Ina in a small voice, "what is it, what's happening?" "Stay calm, baby," said Mel. "I'm not a baby," said Ina. "Of course not," said Mel, and hung up. The police commissioner paced the floor. The head of the Department of Health and Hospitals was complaining of a migraine. The phone was ringing and ringing. "Gastrointestinal illnesses, even fatal ones, occur naturally and have since man has dropped from the trees," said Dr. Morton Newbold to the members of the press who had cornered him in his office on the top floor of the J. Edgar Hoover Cancer Institute. "We share the world with several billions of unloving life forms, and some of them enter our cities and do us harm. This harm is natural." "Do we know what this illness is?" the reporter from Channel 12 asked. "Not yet," said Dr. Newbold. "But we will. Modern science will catch this bacteria or virus, find its DNA, and smear it across a scanner, and it and all its relatives will be driven out of town." "Can you tell us," said the reporter from National Public Radio, "is this illness caused by an evil axis or is it working on its own behalf?"

People with summer houses near the beach or in the mountains were on the roads. Traffic had virtually stopped on the more commonly used highways. The train stations and the airports were overflowing with citizens who had suddenly decided to visit relatives and friends in other parts of the country.

Meanwhile Detective Peaks breathed his last without ever regaining consciousness. On hearing the news Ruth lay down on a sofa and tried to calm herself. The *malach ha'mavet,* the Angel of Death, had passed over her table and taken the detective, who was still a young man, whose family needed him. He should have taken her instead. Ruth felt most sincerely that the Angel of Death had made a mistake in her favor. She judged herself guilty, guilty of not dying. On the other hand, this was a guilt she could live with.

Later the young widow, Larissa Peaks, several months pregnant, stood next to Mel on the improvised podium in the lobby of the hospital. She was wearing a blue dress with a little violet ribbon pinned to her collar. She gave a similar ribbon to the mayor, who stuck himself in the thumb with the pin as he was attaching the ribbon to his lapel. He sucked the blood from his finger, which caused him to look somewhat undignified before the camera.

The young widow, holding next to her breasts a picture of her husband on their wedding day, leaned over into the microphone and asked in a sweet, high, trembling voice, "Mayor Rosenberg, who is responsible for my loss? Will you find out, punish those who did it as they have punished me? Will you promise me, here on this podium, that you will send them to their deaths, as they deserve?" Mel had always been against the death penalty. Everyone in the city knew his position. Some had cast their votes for him on this issue alone. There was a pause. Mel said, "I will do everything in my power to honor Detective Peaks. That I promise you." It was a bad moment. Not the last.

12

THE IMP OF DARKNESS
DUCKS FOR COVER

A letter came to Mr. and Mrs. Jacob Rosenberg from Duncan Academy. It was flat. It was small. Brooke held it in her hands for a full half hour before she was able to open it. It was not a rejection. It was a note from the admissions department saying that due to an unexpected departure of one of the staff, the admissions notifications would be delayed by several weeks. Relief, joy—the feeling was so strong that Brooke wept, although she had nothing to weep about yet.

Ruth was wearing her black dress and black coat, and pinned to her lapel was the little violet ribbon that said to all the watching world that she was very sorry that Detective Peaks had fallen in the line of duty and that she supported the police. In the car she phoned her son. "Jacob dear," she said, "why don't you call your father? He would like to hear from you." "Would he?" said her son. She chose to ignore the tone. "Yes, he would," she said. She sighed. It was that way in families; the same words were spoken again and again. The same raw spots were rubbed till they bled, and if they should heal, they would be opened again in time. Ever since Jacob's voice had changed he had been using it in less than winning ways. At moments like these Ruth would remember her son in the bathtub, his small limbs thrashing about, his wide, excited eyes and the damp hair hanging over his forehead, and the beautiful shoulders so skinny she could count his vertebrae, the sweetness of the smell of the soap, his smile at her as she wrapped him in a towel. To love like that is to love forever, no conditions, no exceptions. "Jacob," she said, "your father needs you by his side. There are pressures, there are reasons. He would want your advice." "Sure," said Jacob, and she could see him twirling his pencil between his fingers. "Jacob," she said, "I mean it." "I'm working," said Jacob. "Oh," said Ruth. "Yes," said Jacob, "I have my own fish to fry, or at least the firm's fish to fry." "Fried food is not good for you," said Ruth firmly, and clicked off. She immediately called back. His assistant answered the phone. "He's not available," she said in her honeyed tone. "Oh," said Ruth. "Give him a message for me. It's all right to eat fried food in moderation."

Mel was meeting with the Reverend Benjy Crick, who was the self-appointed representative of the African American community, or at least some of it, or at least so he said. At the meeting was the head of the Moravian Church and the Evangelical Heart congregation, also the ever-present lawyer Alan Semolvitz, who although not a person of color was on the scene wherever a scene could be found, staring the TV camera right in the eye and giving expert legal opinions, explaining to the ignorant public the value of their Constitution, the perfidy of their leaders. This was a man who knew he was never wrong. Mel, who had no such conviction, admired him along with despising him. There were cookies on platters on the table. The police commissioner was at the table, his face stony cold, not a muscle moving—the look of a man who hopes to fool the approaching snake into thinking he is a tree. The Reverend Crick was warming up: "Like the children of Israel, waiting on the shores of the Red Sea, fearing abandonment, we in the African American community look up to the sky and find it empty and see no kindness coming our way. We look to the offices of the mayor to ensure our safety, to provide for us all that has been provided for others and we fear—yes, we fear, we tremble—that once again the peoples of the city will suffer while the others will slide away, will receive vaccinations against the coming plague, and we and our little children will wait in vain." "Reverend Crick," Mel interrupted, leaping to his feet, shouting at the top of his lungs, and banging his fists on the table. Anything less would not have stopped the waterfall of words, the lyrical swooping song that the reverend was beginning to unwind. "Reverend Crick," said Mel, "we have no vaccine, and if we did, we would not, I assure you, hold it back from anyone living in our city or visiting our city. No person of any color or religion or ethnicity would be denied access. I promise you that." The minister of the Evangelical Heart congregation interrupted. He spoke in a deep, gravelly voice. "Ah, but the Jews, the Jews will get the vaccine first. It is said that already there are doctors and nurses arriving at homes and protecting the children and the mothers. It is said that in the synagogue basements they are vaccinating now, and it is said that Jewish doctors are supplying the vaccines at the singles dances while we have nothing." "There is no vaccine," said Mel. Reverend Crick stood up. "We expected you to say that," he said.

Semolvitz, who loved cameras and microphones equally, asked for a diet Coke, and when it was brought to him he said, "My clients and I are prepared to sue this city for wrongful death if any child of color dies. Is that clear? We are prepared to bankrupt this city if you do not immediately release vaccines into the communities served by my honorable clients." "There is no vaccine," said Mel. "We don't even know if there is a big problem. We have had a few incidents. We have a few mysteries to clear up. The zoo, the birds in the park, other reports are coming in. We have asked people to avoid eating birds. We do not know if there is or is not a danger to the public, and we certainly have no vaccine." In a very sad voice, a world-weary voice, Reverend Crick said, "We voted for you in large numbers. We have a right to expect that you will not betray us. We will picket. We will ask the African Americans in this city to strike, even perhaps to throw a stone or two—a small riot might bring you around." Reverend Crick smiled. Perhaps he was joking, perhaps he was not. Alan Semolvitz put his hand on the reverend's sleeve. "We don't want to make a threat here, of course," he said. "Good," said the police commissioner, "because I can handle any riot you might plan. We too are prepared. No riot will catch us with our pants down." Through Mel's mind rushed the image of the entire police force, their trousers around their ankles, waddling forth to do combat. This was funny, but when the meeting was over and he was alone in the room with the police commissioner he threw his chair against the wall. "God, God, God," and he swallowed the rest of the phrase. The Imp of Mischief, the Imp of Darkness, the Imp of the Perverse cowered under the table, so fierce was the mayor in that troubled moment.

13

MADDIE MILLER'S
LATE-NIGHT TIP

Ina had an early-morning appointment with Dr. Bergen. She wore her lab coat over her black slacks. She loved her lab coat, the thick starched white of it, the promise of a germ-free surface, the uninterrupted glacial space at her back. She settled down. Dr. Bergen knew immediately she was pleased about something. Beneath the surface change was approaching. He could feel it coming the way the groundhog signals spring. Sometimes he was right, sometimes he was not. Ina started. "My brother," she said, and the room filled with Jacob, his commanding ways, his testosterone, his bare knuckles in her ribs, his way of holding forth so she could hardly get a word in, the way his mother looked at him as if he were Moses himself eating his brisket at her table, all the money he got for his bar mitzvah, his cruel smile, his mistreatment of her hamster. Ina had just begun. The fern plant on the windowsill drooped, signaling a desperate need for water. Dr. Bergen, who was prone to allergic sneezing, began to sneeze. He reached for one of his own tissues. Ina paused. "Oh, grow up," said Dr. Bergen. There was a shocked silence in the consulting room.

Meanwhile Mel sat at his desk and drank his third cup of coffee for the morning. The papers were spread out before him. A man killed his girlfriend, who loved somebody else. The son of a real estate developer with close ties to the mayor had punched the bouncer of a downtown disco in the nose at a hotel because the bouncer didn't have any cigarettes to offer him. Detective Peaks's widow, on national television, had warned that the mayor was ignoring the arrival of a plague in his city.

The zoo was closed indefinitely. The sanitation workers were refusing to enter zoo property, which was causing a pileup of banana skins, among other items. There had been a drug bust. The police claimed they had a big haul of little dealer fish, caught in the middle of the night selling their wares during a panty raid at a local college. The five worst-scoring elementary schools in the city were named and their principals' pictures had been taken and hung above the article like mug shots. For all the good that will do, thought the mayor. Harold arrived and asked the mayor if he wanted more coffee. The phones in the outer office were ringing. The mayor was considering action, some action, what action, against whom—that's what he was considering.

Maddie was there. The mayor could hear her cajoling Harold. She was kissing someone. He heard the sound of lips against flesh. She was wishing the receptionist, whose name he thought was Latisha, a happy birthday. He heard giggling. The door opened. There she was, wearing heels that made her ankles wobble and a leather skirt that was probably too young for her. "Mutton dressed like lamb," Ruth had said of her, and she was right from a fashion point of view, but there were other points of view a person could take. Maddie sat down on the couch and ran her hand through her hair as if she were petting a horse. "I had a call at home last night, three in the morning," she said, "a confidential call." The mayor grunted. What could she be wanting? he wondered. "I have nothing to tell you," he said. "The press knows everything that we know and probably more." She looked him in the eyes and blinked. "You look tired," she said. The mayor grunted again. "Ordinarily," she said, "my tips are mine alone, and only a jerk would go running to the mayor, but . . ." "But what, Maddie?" The mayor was thinking about his first girlfriend, whose father was a car salesman, and so his daughter had keys to a new Buick and they necked in the backseat while the car was parked in the lot. The smell of new leather always did something to him after that.

"I picked up the phone and this high voice, a woman or a girl, said, 'Maddie Miller, if I were you, I would go right now to the McDonald's on Avenue P and Tenth. You would find it worth your while,' and then she hung up. Of course I rolled over and went back to sleep. Ten minutes later she called again. 'It's important,' said the voice. 'I can't call again. Go—I'm begging you.' So I got up." Mel wanted to ask if she had been alone in her bed, but visions of sexual harassment suits danced through his head. He said nothing. "I called a car from the paper and it took about an hour to get there." The phones were ringing. Harold was waving in the doorway. The fire commissioner wanted to talk about increasing recruitment among minorities, a matter the commissioner loved to talk about as long as no action was required. The morning was passing and he wasn't doing anything useful to anyone. "Maddie," he said, "we can talk about this some other time. Call me." He stood up. Maddie didn't move. "When I got to McDonald's the place was dark and closed. By the front door there was a homeless woman curled under a blanket. I stepped up to look in the window and she grabbed my ankle. I bent down to take her hand off my leg and she handed me this. She ran off around the corner. I couldn't run after her. My shoes—" Maddie shrugged. The mayor nodded. "A reporter should always wear sneakers," he said. Out of her bag Maddie pulled an envelope. The enclosed letter said, *Birds first, people second, more will die, next we make the rich walk. We are going to continue until there is peace in the Middle East.* "In other words," said Mel, "forever." He sighed. "We have to turn this over to the FBI, to the police, right away." He dropped the letter on the floor. "I shouldn't have put my fingerprints on it. Maddie," said the mayor, "let's keep this out of the newspapers for now." "What the hell do you think I am?" she said. "I went straight from McDonald's to the city desk." "Oh," said Mel, and sighed. "And then to you," she added. "Thank you," he said.

While Mel and Maddie were waiting for the FBI and the police to arrive at his office the elevator man at 734 Forest Avenue felt he needed a break. He went down to the basement and headed for his locker, where he kept a bottle of scotch for just such emergencies, but he felt the ground tilt up at him, and his knees buckled and he collapsed. The residents of the AB section who were attempting to leave their apartments rang and rang, but the elevator did not come. There on Forest Avenue, where all the big, smooth, impressive apartment buildings lined up like soldiers in a war against irregularity, uncleanliness, where buildings were discreet, awnings provided shade, brass poles, marbled lobbies, Art Deco silver-inlays across the mirrors, there where doormen in white clothes and captain's hats and braid on their uniforms opened the doors of chauffeur-driven cars, there where all the world knew you dwelled when the gods had favored your designs or the spoon in your mouth at birth had been silver—there something terrible had happened.

As Icarus fell from the sky into the waters unnoticed by the toiling peasants in a painting by Brueghel, so the death of the elevator man, whose name—Serbian, or was it Croatian?—did not make the evening news.

14

THE MAYOR IS
SHAFTED

Moe Alter didn't like the idea. The chancellor was offended and threatened to resign. The head of the teachers union wouldn't even let him finish explaining before she hung up on him. His own rabbi laughed when he told him what he planned to do. His old friend Marty, a regular in his poker game, told him he would end up with cement boots at the bottom of the river. The mayor was the sort of man who took advice when he could, which wasn't always. He called a press conference for noon. He straightened his tie, brushed back what hair remained on his head, and walked out to the podium. "I called you here to talk about the schools. Education is my priority. The fate of this city depends on our improving our schools for all our children. But frankly, nothing is going to improve in the near future. Our efforts are too small, too late, and constantly undermined by two factors. The first is the entrenched way of doing things. The unions, the contractors, the teachers have rules and devices that favor their own pockets and disfavor the children, that work against change. The second cause for our failure is the children themselves, or rather the families and neighborhoods that produce these children. Yes, we used to be able to take all children and give them an even break, but we can't anymore because too many of these children come to school damaged by the chaos in their homes, wide-eyed but not ready to learn, to sit still, to grow up. Poverty, a parent in prison, malnutrition, drugs, make for homes in which little children fall behind their more fortunate brothers and sisters before they have reached the age of five. We can't change this with a test, with a reading specialist, with an art or music program, which we can't afford anyway. Year after year, mayor after mayor has stood before you promising improvement, and the truth is we can't do it. We can't afford to do it. We don't know how to do it. We can't buck the force that tells some kids in some neighborhoods that school is for fools. We can't make mothers read books to children at bedtime. We can't prevent some kids going wild with anxiety or boredom or fear of the dark. We need smaller classrooms, really small classrooms, and we haven't the money or the space to create them. So nothing is going to get better, not on my watch. The test scores may go up or down, depending on cramming and screaming and maybe a little cheating here and there, but the real thing, the child's learning, that isn't going to get any better. So I'm announcing that we are going to fail. We're going to fail our kids this year and next year and the year after.

"Of course, we could do something real that might work. We could break up the big schools into small units, maybe one-room schoolhouses like those that served the prairie. We could start programs for mothers with babies right out of the hospital that teach about stimulation and love and how the two work together, and we could give every parent a course in parenting, and we could have school days that last until six o'clock, and we could make every school as good as our best private schools. We could turn religious buildings into live-in kibbutzim that would take in all families with small children in a five-block area. We could have mentors for all our children. We could allow each school to be adopted by a company that makes money in this city, and those companies could pay for computers and tutors and music lessons, and their employees could assist teachers and inspire and run school newspapers and arrange soccer games and tennis lessons. The only way the schools are ever going to improve is if the citizens of the city decide they must and if they will do it themselves, one kid at a time. I can't do it. The teachers can't do it. The budget is too small, our buildings too old, our children too needy, our imaginations stunted. I'm a failure and I admit it." The mayor stopped. "Any questions?" he asked. Pandemonium followed.

As the mayor was giving his perhaps less than wise education speech, the residents of 602 Forest Avenue were ringing downstairs to the doorman. *Where's the elevator, for God's sake? I have an appointment with my doctor in a half hour, my hairdresser, my accountant, my mortgage broker, my agent, my shrink, my dentist.* The calls were coming fast and furious. Inside the elevator cabs, both in the front and in the back of the building, the elevator operators were lying on the floor, legs spread out, hands reaching up for something, eyes rolled back in their heads. The super called the police, who called the fire department, who forced open the doors of the elevator cabs and found the bodies. The cabs were fully automatic; the elevator operators were simply a relic of older, slower days, a courtesy to the owners of the apartments. Two more buildings, 448 Forest Avenue and 301 Forest Avenue, put in calls to the police within the next fifteen minutes. Their elevators, too, had stopped rising and falling at the whim of the residents. By midafternoon the fire trucks were coming from districts across town because so many buildings had summoned them. Reporters and TV cameras were there when the elevator operators were discovered dead, blue around the mouth. The evening news had the story. The mayor's speech was overshadowed. "Shafted" was the tabloid headline the next morning. At first blush it seemed as if all the elevator operators had suffered fatal heart attacks. The union called for its members to stay home. The doormen walked out in sympathy if not terror, and Mel turned to his wife in bed that night and asked her, "How many funerals can a man attend before he goes mad?" Ruth rubbed his back. "You won't go mad," she said. "Insanity is no excuse," she added, because she wasn't a lawyer.

15

A SLICE OF
TROUBLE

Even though you bellowed out that you can't save the schools, they love you," said Ruth. "That's what the polls say," said Mel, a pleased smile stretching across his wide face. Now he looked like a basset hound that smelled supper. There had been the usual voices raised in mock horror. "The mayor has abandoned the children of our city," Reverend Crick had roared into a microphone. But most in the city just shrugged, laughed, or nodded in agreement. If a man's car had slid off the road and was floating in the swamp, alligators chewing up the upholstery, salamanders posing on the steering wheel, he would do just what Mel Rosenberg had done and call it a day. Ruth had qualms. "I'm going into P.S. 138 this morning and I'm going to read *Green Eggs and Ham* to the second graders," she announced. "I'll send the photographers after you," said Mel, "so wear your blue suit. I love you in your blue suit." "It's at the cleaners," said Ruth. "It's always at the cleaners," said Mel. Ruth had no intention of telling him about the ten pounds that made that particular suit no longer a viable contender.

As soon as she left the room Mel called his health commissioner, Dr. Ahmed Jamal. "The elevator operators—what happened?" "We did a toxicology screen. We found pizza in their stomachs and a concentration of some chemical we have not yet been able to identify but which is most likely the killer here." "Why would anyone want to knock off elevator operators?" said Mel. "Maybe," said the health commissioner, "they did it to show that they can get our transportation system anytime they want." "What?" said Mel. "Up and down," the commissioner responded. "That's travel, too."

Mel hung up and rang through to police headquarters. The police commissioner was locked in his office with his priest and had put all calls on hold, but his assistant told Mel, "The guys are checking all the pizza joints on Lippman Avenue within walking distance of the buildings that lost elevator operators. We're closing down all pizza places today. Original or copies, their doors are going to be locked."

Mel called the not-yet-fired schools chancellor (how many people on the board had to agree before action could be taken?). "We are sending emergency peanut butter to the schools that are offering pizza in their cafeterias," the mayor was told. "Fine," said Mel, who knew perfectly well that the city was not fine at all. The city was like a young girl walking home after dark, an ill wind blowing her skirt back against her knees as she turns the corner, ready to take the shortcut through the alley in which the rapist waits. The mayor sighed.

He let Detective Loew, whose grandparents had been born in Prague and who was a descendant of the famous rabbi who had brought the golem to life, put his blue bubble on the top of the car so they could move through traffic at the speed of light. Was it *beshert* that had brought Detective Loew to the mayor's side? Unfortunately, the detective himself was unfamiliar with the essentials of the Jewish tradition, because his mother was a farm girl from Idaho whom his father had met at a Jehovah's Witness meeting, and while he had heard the tale of his ancestor and the famous golem, he confused him with the Antichrist, which was natural enough.

A few well-chosen words to his press secretary, and the word was out over the radio—*do not eat pizza today.* Imagine how the owners of these struggling small businesses took the news. Think of the little they had—the small change they received, the wages they had to pay, the upkeep of their stores, the cleaning materials for their ovens, the turnover of help, the service they did for the neighborhoods. Imagine how they felt hearing that something in their product, something in the gooey cheese, in the thick tomato sauce, in the anchovies or the sausage, was responsible for the death of the elevator operators along Forest Avenue. There was talk of suing the city for libel; there was talk of appealing to the federal government for disaster relief; there were tears when one pizzeria owner used the calamity to fire his teenage waitress, who he suspected had her hand in the till.

"Your father's here," said Jacob's assistant, who had blushed red as a stoplight at seeing the mayor in the flesh before her eyes. "Here?" Jacob asked. "Yes, here," said his father, pushing through the door. "What's up, Dad?" Jacob asked as his father let his weight down into the soft chair reserved for clients. Jacob didn't mind the partners in the firm observing the mayor visiting his son. He also didn't mind his father seeing his office on the twenty-third floor with a spectacular view of the cathedral and the river and the bridge that curved like a rainbow over the waters. "Jacob," said Mel, "in confidence, under attorney-client privilege, I want to tell you we've received a warning that the city will be under siege until there is peace in the Middle East." Jacob looked at his father; the bags under his eyes could have contained the entire lachrymose history of the Jews. His father seemed older, not as healthy as he should be. "Peace in the Middle East?" Jacob repeated the words. "That again. I've heard enough about the Middle East to last a lifetime." Mel wondered if a mistake by the hospital had replaced his real child with another man's offspring, a man whose ancestors had a box at the opera and owned land granted to his family line by the English king.

It didn't come as a surprise that when Jacob was in law school he'd brought home a girl from a big empty state in the north of the country, a girl who had learned about Jews from Woody Allen movies and thought they were charming, at least before she met them in significant numbers. Mel wasn't the sort of Jew to pull out his hair because his son was marrying a stranger. He knew the statistics, he knew America, he accepted Brooke with open arms, but there remained an ache in his heart for the disloyalty of the thing, a regret for the line of history that would continue without Jacob, without his children. Mel was an American mayor, and he knew that the Jewish story, ripe and full, stormy and brilliant as it was, might not light the soul of his son as it had his. While such a regret does not make a man love his own son less, it makes him less content with his son. It was as if his only male child had been tarnished, crumpled, dented, stained, but simultaneously remained as dear as ever, dear but damaged. Naturally the contacts between father and son had become prickly, taut, and even the smallest of matters contained hidden messages of mutual displeasure along with certain yearnings that a woman might have seen but left a man keenly perplexed.

So it was a remarkable and unusual moment when the two men, young and middle-aged, emerged from the office building into the street, followed of course by Detective Loew, and began to walk downtown. "The question on my mind," Mel was saying, "should I alarm the public by full disclosure. Should I tell them the elevator operators died heroes in the war against terrorism? Or should I wait until something else happens or we have some hard information, or maybe even get lucky and catch the culprits." Jacob was considering his answer. He was so pleased to be asked that he couldn't get his mind to work as fast as it should, when a disheveled and dirty man stood before them and blocked their way. Jacob stood in front of his father. He didn't like the red eyes he saw. He didn't like the man's posture, which was not obsequious, as one might expect of a beggar. He didn't like the way the man held out his arm to stop their progress. Jacob was ready to spring. The man spoke softly. "I have information that the mayor would like to have. I have something to offer the mayor." "Pay no attention," said Jacob, still standing in front of his father. "Follow me," said the man, while from his ancient down coat stray feathers rose into the air.

"Don't be ridiculous," said Jacob as his father tugged on his sleeve, pulling him after the man. Mel had an instinct, Mel had a hunch. Mel did not think this man was his enemy. Mel was curious. Curiosity might be bad for cats, but he was not a cat. Detective Loew followed at Mel's heels as he moved forward. In the middle of the avenue there was an island surrounded by a low iron fence, some plantings within. The subway tracks lay beneath. The man lifted a grate and disappeared down the hole. Jacob, who was wearing a good blue suit with a white shirt and a fine tie given him when he joined the firm, shook his head and refused to move further. Mel peered down into the dark hole. He saw the ladder on the side of the hole, he saw a flicker of sunlight below on a track. What was there to lose? He had always wanted to explore down there. The mayor climbed down, followed by Detective Loew and then Jacob (who loved his suit but couldn't leave his father to prowl the underground of the city with only one police officer by his side) followed down the ladder, trying in his head to justify this foolish act, this absurd act. He didn't even have his cell phone, having left the office without it. He did have his Rolex watch, which he slipped off his wrist as soon as he reached the ground and saw, in the dim light from the grates above, his father walking on a narrow platform just behind the man who had stopped them on the street. "What the hell are you doing?" screamed Detective Loew, who was a medium-sized man with no magic tricks up his sleeve.

16

DOWN AND DOWN
WE GO

Mayor Rosenberg was not afraid of the dark or of pipes or tubes or tunnels that carried trains or served as ditches where rain could run and old papers turn to rot, where waste human and nonhuman pressed itself into the dark dirt. He knew that beneath the city, far under the neon lights, the tall buildings, the green park, electrical equipment, tools for repairing wires waited. He knew that the city contained in its gut places where rats nursed their young and where nematodes, roaches, and slugs bred in pools of water by rusted tracks and blackened beams and exposed rock. He knew that under the city there was a continuous stirring, a murmuring of the not entirely pleasant, just like the murky, bitter subconscious of a man's thoughts. The citizens of the city gave little thought to where the sewers ran and what smells they contained, and what floated, rested, and nestled there all invisible from the streets above.

Mel, however, familiar with the reports of the firefighters and the subway, sanitation, and phone company workers, considered the long tunnels that united the streets of the city with the river at its edges no more malevolent than his own intestines, large and small, which had served him well enough, if somewhat irritably, over the years. His mother had escaped the Warsaw ghetto through a sewer as a child of nine, following the barely visible back of her older brother, leaving behind—but that didn't matter here. It was not the sewer his mother had to fear.

Ahead on the side of the tracks a small group of citizens who might have better taken advantage of the city's generous if imperfect shelters huddled around a small fire. "You're not allowed to have a fire down here," shouted Detective Loew in his most belligerent voice. He was ignored. The man he had followed motioned to Mel to come closer. "Stay where you are, Dad," said Jacob. A bleary-eyed woman, grimy and in bad need of dental care, offered a piece of paper to Mel. "This is what we thought you ought to see." "Me?" said the mayor. "Someone else in charge?" called out a voice from the pack of less than good-smelling folk. Mel moved closer to the hand that held the paper. He reached out for it and held it up. "Anybody got a flashlight?" he asked. "Sit by the fire," the woman told him. Detective Loew was calling into his cell phone: "Backup, backup, location in byway of subway track near Fiftieth Street, left side, left side." Jacob said, "Why aren't you people in the shelter system? We have a fine shelter system." "I'd rather go home with you," said a young black man with a stud through his tongue.

Mel opened the piece of paper. On it was written a notation, numbers, chemical signs, and a single word printed large: *death.* "Look at the other side," said the man who had brought the mayor down under. Mel turned the paper over. *Ducks, zoo animals, elevator operators are just the beginning. We were testing. Soon we go for real. Prepare to die.* Mel felt his heart skip several beats. His medicine was supposed to prevent that, but the irregular thumping in his chest could not be denied. "Did any of you write this note?" Mel asked. No one replied. "Well, where did you find it?" "A white guy pressed it into my hand outside of Starbucks on Twenty-third Street," said a man who seemed blind. His hair was filthy and his face so lined with grease there was no telling his age or race. "Was he tall or short, fat or thin?" asked Jacob. "Want to pay for my cataract operation?" the man asked, and grinned, revealing blackened, toothless gums. Stupid question, Jacob admitted to himself as shame made him blush; he was grateful for the dark that masked his face from his father. "What do we get for doing our civic duty?" asked the man who had first approached the mayor. "You'll be well rewarded," said Mel. "Oh, yeah," said the woman, "we know how that works. You put in an application and you wait two years and then they tell you they lost the paperwork and then you apply again and at last when your teeth are all gone they deny the application." "I'll get you the reward," said Mel. "He will," seconded Jacob.

"Let's just take your clothes, all of them," said the toothless man. Detective Loew stuffed his cell phone in his pocket and pulled out his gun. "Put it away," said Mel. "We don't shoot people over a suit." In a moment he slipped off his jacket and his tie and his shirt. "Pants too, man," someone shouted. The detective raised his gun. "Put it away," said Mel. He took off his pants. "Underpants—look, little diamonds on the boxers." Mel took them off. The crowd turned to Jacob. "Dad," screamed Jacob, "this is ridiculous. This is a two-thousand-dollar suit." In a moment he too was naked. The crowd turned to Detective Loew. "Cop duds too." They left the gun, the bulletproof vest, but took the officer's pants, his underwear, his shield, and his shirt. "Look what I found," said the woman holding Jacob's jacket, who had seemed to be engaged in a conversation with an invisible child on her lap, She held up a gold watch. Jacob would have lunged for the watch, but his father put a restraining hand on his shoulder. Jacob noticed that his father had an appendectomy scar across his abdomen. It glowed in the reflection of the firelight on his body. "Let her have it," Mel said.

"Sure," said Jacob. "When I finish suing the city I'll buy myself a Patek Philippe."

There were fast-pounding footsteps coming down the tunnel, shouts of "Up ahead!" The band of nonsheltered men and women melted away into the darkness, through openings that seemed in the darkness to disappear like bubbles in water. When the police arrived they found their mayor and his son naked. They found their own officer naked, waving his gun in the air. Jacob had goose bumps on his entire body from the cold.

Through the tunnels laughter could be heard. The Imps of Malicious Intent howled with pleasure at this turn of events. The tabloids ran with the story: "Mayor Bares All," "Naked City," "Mayor Flashes Cops." Ba-da-bing.

17

RUTH SEEKS THE
TRUTH

Ruth was sitting in a doctor's office on a leather couch, glancing and not glancing at a fashion magazine in which all the models were thirty years younger than she and thirty pounds thinner and their eyes were larger and their noses were shorter and their legs were longer and despite that she desired all the clothes they were wearing, or was it the clothes she desired? She had been waiting for forty minutes. It was just her annual mammogram. There was no reason for her eyelid to be twitching the way it did when she was truly alarmed. She had no symptoms. The mammogram could not give her cancer. If it was there it might save her life, or it would make no difference, depending on which study you believed. In any event, the mammogram itself was not the threat, although every woman feels the thread of her life quivering beneath the sharp scissors of Fate on such an occasion. Any woman who would deny this fear—lump in the throat, tremble in the leg—is lying. The wait makes everything harder.

It would not be a tragedy if she were to die now—young, yes, statistically speaking, but not so young that her children would wake in the middle of the night and feel an unbearable absence that would seep through their days, changing everything, darkening everything. If she were to die now, Mel would feel broken; the half of himself that had become her would be gone, and he would turn over in bed and reach for her night after night long after she was dust and bone. But he would recover. She would want him to recover. Some younger woman with a light spirit and a love of travel (Ruth did not love travel) might join him. He wouldn't bury himself with her. Contemplating his placing his head in another woman's lap, Ruth felt the odd heat of sudden and irrational anger. But then she reminded herself that she too would not bury herself with him should his death come first. She looked through a celebrity magazine, reading the captions, searching for marital disasters. Something about the catalogue of those disasters fortified her for the ordeal ahead.

If she were to die now, it would not exactly be a comedy, but there would be nothing Shakespearean about it, either. She stared at the Lautrec print on the wall. She had never really liked the ballet, all that up and down and waving of legs and arms. She had gone to the *Nutcracker* with each of the children, but she had also taken them to the dentist and the dermatologist, which in retrospect was less of an ordeal than waiting for the curtain to come down on the Sugarplum Fairy and friends. Now time crawled. Time lay panting in the desert. Time had stopped. The watch had not merely melted; it had been carried away by a million red ants, to be devoured in underground passages suitable for bugs but unseen by humans. An hour more passed. She called her office. "Delayed," she said. What she really felt was betrayed by the icy receptionist, the overly friendly woman who printed out the bills, and the radiologist, who was probably having a second breakfast or checking stock market quotes.

At last her name was called. "Ruth Rosenberg." The technician did not look her in the eye. The technician did not smile. The technician was a cog in a wheel, a wheel that was getting set to grind her down. Ruth was led to a small closet in which she was expected to undress, waist up, put on a robe open in the front, and wait. Ruth waited in the closet, sitting on a small stool provided for patients. She knew so many breast cancer survivors. It might not be a death sentence, but it would not be pleasant. She heard herself grinding her molars. She stopped. She waited.

The technician reappeared. She led Ruth to a small room with a large machine. Ruth slipped her robe off one shoulder and felt the cold air blow against her back. The technician picked up Ruth's breasts as if they were made of Play-Doh, as if Mel had never leaned over them or her babies had never suckled there. She placed Ruth's breast on the plate of glass and mercilessly lowered pieces of the machine to press the breast as flat as once the world was believed to be. The technician left the room, pressed a button, returned, released the left breast, and began again on the right. Ruth recognized that flesh is just flesh, life itself lasts hardly longer than the buzz of radiation from behind the door. She was calm but hardly collected. Her thoughts scattered everywhere. It would have taken the entire Sanitation Department to have gathered them together.

Mel was having coffee with the commissioner of human services. "What's wrong with you people?" he asked. The commissioner of human services sighed. "I need money, more money, a lot more money." "I haven't got it," said Mel. "Print it," said the commissioner of human services. "In your dreams," said Mel.

The technician had left Ruth sitting in the room with the machine. She had left her magazine and her pocketbook and her jacket in the changing closet. There was nothing to do but try to meditate. She thought of her favorite spot in the kitchen of the first apartment they had. She imagined herself a young bride drinking coffee, looking down at the street below. The door opened, there was a bustle. The doctor was there standing over her. "Fine, fine," he said, "everything looks good." He looked her in the eye, shook her hand, and disappeared. Reprieved; joy leaped up and made her face pink. It was all ahead of her: her grandchildren's graduation, her work, her week by the sea in the summer, her hand on Mel's chest.

Later at the Korean store on the corner she would buy herself a bunch of red carnations with baby's breath wrapped in clear cellophane. Who could resist such beautiful flowers?

18

IN THE
LABORATORY

Ina sits in the corner of her lab that she has turned into an office. She stares without seeing at her computer with its screen saver of Sergei and Noah and baby Anna, frozen in time, floating in the blue liquid of electronic sky. She is not thinking about her next session with Dr. Bergen. She is not thinking about what catastrophes are befalling her children while she is at work, selfishly planted in her lab, accomplishing little enough. She is concentrating on the problem before her. What caused the death of the elevator operators, what killed the ducks in the park, what wafted over the zoo, what do those who mean to bring civilization to its knees have in their arsenal? All the labs in the city had been asked to stop whatever they were doing and give some time to the matter. They had all been sent tissue slides of zoo animals that had perished as well as organ matter from the elevator operators. It was urgent. It was crucial.

Sergei was analyzing the uniform of one of the dead men, who seemed to have some strange substance burning holes in his jacket. Ina was letting her mind drift over the problem, soaking it through the way a soft summer drizzle turns the sand dark, gradually, gently, while half-eaten sandwiches are tossed to the waiting gulls, umbrellas closed, towels folded away, with people happy to swim in wet oceans now eager to stay dry and hurry out of the rain.

Citizens legal and otherwise were on waiting lists for smallpox vaccinations, although no smallpox had been found. People were demanding anthrax vaccinations, although no cases of anthrax had occurred. People had packed evacuation bags with water bottles and animal crackers for the children and made plans with their loved ones. Train, boat, highway escape routes were considered and rejected at the most fashionable dinner parties. The mayor had asked the press not to spread panic, but panic, like fire, flares quickly and asks no one's permission to spread. Everyone thought the arsonists were believers in jihad, exports from a cruel center of the world where hating Americans, hating Jews, was the very breath of life, the spine that kept the body public erect. Whatever weapon these terrorists held, it was a monster weapon simply because of the implacable hands that held it and the will to destroy that protected it. It was a city filled with Jews that they had targeted, had they not? You can say "Never again" all you like, but in the end words are just words, creating no carapace and doing nothing for your immune system.

Ina looked at her slides. She studied them carefully. She wrote out some formulas on her coffee napkin. She wrote out some more. She looked at the chemicals detected on the slides. She soaked some slides in solutions. She looked some more. And then, as if a voice were speaking to her from outside her own head, she pulled down one of the textbooks that she kept in a corner. It was there, the thing she was looking for. Psychotropic drugs, used to hush voices in the head, to wash out hallucinations, to coat the synapses and the neurons with shields of tiny chemicals. These were not intended for small birds and hungry elevator operators on their lunch break. In concentrated doses, in amounts that might make an elephant go mad, these drugs were the weapons of bioterror. Ina called Sergei. They went over it together. They had it. Ina called the chief of police. Ina called her father.

The hunt was on. Where did the drugs come from—prescriptions hoarded by noncompliant patients, or a raid on a drug company's cabinet or psychiatric ward? This was police business. Ina had done her job.

The commissioner of police called the FBI, keeping them up to date. This was a pro forma act, signifying nothing. No sane adult would depend on the FBI to rush to the rescue. Their agents' shoelaces were probably all tied together. But this was a real breakthrough. Detectives fanned out to all the hospitals in the city. Several went to the hospital a few blocks away from the McDonald's where Maddie had had her late-night adventure. Calls were made to the big drug manufacturer whose hold on the patent would last another 100 years. How hard could it be to find the right madman or madwoman in the city? The commissioner of police, Wolfe Joyce, had not become commissioner because he had a faint heart. A lesser man in charge might have gone home to bed. This one went to work.

The mayor called Ina as soon as he received word of his daughter's discovery. "I can't tell you," he said, "how proud I am. You're my heroine," he added. Ina felt tears in her eyes. "Daddy," she said, "I just want you to love me." "I do, sweetheart, of course I do." Mel put the phone down. He put his head in his hands. How was it possible that his daughter didn't know his soul and her primary place there? Why was it harder to be a father than to be a mayor? What had he done or not done that she doubted him? "Send my daughter a dozen roses," he said to Harold. But then he changed his mind. Perhaps a rose sent the wrong message. "Send her a bunch of tulips," he said. Perhaps tulips were too ordinary, but what the hell—he wasn't a botanist.

Uptown several men wandered around among the empty beer cans that littered the floor of their rented apartment. Ashtrays overflowed with cigarettes. A browned plant starved for water sat on the fire escape in a rotting basket. A bottle of ketchup had slid under the TV. "We need toilet paper," said one of the men. "So get it," said another. Girlie magazines were stuffed under the cushions. They were waiting for orders. They had practiced enough. They were ready for the main act. They were counting down the hours.

19

ACCEPTANCE AND

ASSUMPTIONS

The letter arrived, fat, full, puffed up, Mr. and Mrs. Jacob and Brooke Rosenberg. Brooke went into the bathroom. She opened the window and let the warm air fall on her burning face. It didn't matter. Jacob kept telling her it wasn't the end of the world if the twins were rejected by Duncan Academy again. But she was of a different opinion. Her stomach was hollow, her breath was short, her eyes blinked nervously. Her children, out of her body, fed, clothed, read to, chastened, catching her spirit, absorbing her the way plants draw water through the soil—were they good enough? Was she to be judged wanting? Were her mind and her heart less than the minds and hearts of those who would be chosen? Was she a small and rotten piece of human matter to be cast out along with her offspring? The letter weighed in her hand. Its heft was promising. She slowly opened the envelope. She sat down with it in the bathtub, her clothes on. She pulled the shower curtain closed. This was as close to shelter as a person in an apartment can get. This was as close to digging a hole as she could come. She pulled out the pages. *Duncan Academy is pleased to inform you that* and she stopped reading. Joy. With joy came a wave of tenderness for Jacob, for his father, Mel, who had made certain phone calls, for his mother, Ruth, who had borne her husband, for the Jewish people, who thought so much of themselves, who had suffered so much. Joy.

Meanwhile, the arm of the law was reaching out. "We are looking for a Moslem, probably Arabic, mental patient or relative of a mental patient, or a Moslem or Arabic laboratory worker, possibly a scientist on staff at a research hospital." So said Wolfe Joyce, and so said his men to their subordinates. Everyone nodded, but no one was exactly sure how to start.

"And what," said Harold to his boss, "if the fellow with the Haldol, Zoloft, Paxil, et cetera, arsenal is not a Moslem?" The mayor had already considered the possibility. But how in fact could you search an entire population for those who had access to mind-altering substances, legal ones? It seemed likely that every other citizen had Prozac tablets on the medicine shelf. It seemed as though the city had more therapists of every stripe than tailors or drugstores or fire hydrants. There were more halfway houses with the sedated, the bloated, the sorrowful drinking Coke in the lobby than there were elementary schools. We have to start somewhere. Mel chewed on a pencil. There were addicts living in the parks, there were recovering addicts in every fifth home. He believed in civics, in politics, in improving lives with good government, but he knew that over all legislation, all administration, all departments of public life hung the nightmares of the soul that each of his citizens endured in one way or another and that dragged so many beyond the reach of good government.

The medicine to soothe or hold the madness of the mind had been captured by those who wanted to destroy, kill, bring the city to its knees. Idly Mel considered whether or not nicotine patches could be turned into lethal weapons, whether all that was curative could also destroy, what to do if the needle in the haystack (what a metaphor for a city, where haystacks are too rare and needles too common) was never found. At least they knew they were looking for an Arab. Reason told him so. That narrowed the field.

Uptown a man stood in front of his long mirror and admired his tattoos. There was the obligatory snake that wound around the bulging muscles of his upper arm. There was the werewolf on his chest baring its teeth just above the navel. There was a picture in the center of his back that he could only see by holding a hand mirror behind his head; it might have been of a woman's buttocks, but perhaps it was a mountain scene. It was hard to tell. The words *Home* and *Mother* were written on his thighs. His wrists were encircled with tattoos of barbed wire. Under his armpits, not visible unless intended to be visible, were the crucial tattoos. The ones that mattered, defined him, explained him, served in addition the purpose of keeping certain voices that howled in his head at bay. Those tattoos were swastikas; they rippled with his muscle, they were covered with sweat when he was, they were there to keep him company at all times, friends that would not betray. He had an important meeting that morning with his fellow resistance fighters. It was time for them to move forward. They had proved that ducks would die. They had shown that a zoo could be rendered into a morgue. They had showed that human beings could be turned into dust with sufficient heart-racing overdoses of the drugs that they had gathered over time so patiently, pretending to a madness they did not have. The madness they actually had was never discussed with the hundreds of intake psychiatrists, most of them interns, scared to death, trying to help, unable to tell one mental affliction from another, willing to write out orders for whatever was required. They saw social workers and filled out forms, and then with the drugs in hand they disappeared, false addresses never checked. They never showed up for outpatient care. They were carried off in the tides of the noncompliant, never again heard from, at least not until now. As he stood before the mirror, the Imps of Misfortune, the evil Spawn of Lilith tried to laugh, but even they were stunned. Their laughter sounded through the corridors of the universe, unreal like the coughing of a radiator.

That evening Brooke and Jacob shared a glass of champagne and sat next to each other on the sofa shoulder against shoulder, heat steaming between them. "Jacob," asked Brooke, "do you ever wish you had married someone else?" "No," said Jacob. Had he waited an instant too long before answering? Had he been sincere? He didn't know. Brooke noticed that the living room seemed cramped. There were toys in the corner. The cabinet in the corner was too big for its spot. "Perhaps we need a bigger apartment," she said. In fact, she was longing for a bigger apartment.

20

THOUSANDS OF MEN,
NO REGRETS

There were thousands of them spread across the country. The ones who lived in mountains or out on the plains. Their guns waited under burlap bags stuffed behind the front seats of their old Ford trucks, dogs barking in the back. Those who had grown up on farms with rusty pipes and bowlegged cows and bill collectors pounding on the door now wore heavy boots for climbing on the rocks, for wading through mud, for keeping feet warm, which was sometimes hard even in heavy wool socks. In these boots their feet were meant to look big, dangerous, like bears and not deer, hunters and not the hunted. The ones in the country had meetings in the back room of a local bar or the parlor of a friendly insurance guy, or in the school gym after hours when the sympathetic janitor let them in. Those born in the city leaned over their Web sites and learned the talk of gun shows.

They had joined to fight a war, and the war was against the impurities, the mongrel peoples, the women in high heels with cell phones and stock portfolios. Their war was against the swarms of slant-eyes, the smell of curry and cumin, the Jamaicans and the

Dominicans and the South Koreans and the Jews. Of course the Jews, whose ways were the source of corruption, the origin of all pollution, who in fact made the city what it was, a cauldron of color, a mockery of the simple and the true and the snakes in the temple had now become so numerous it seemed that the temple itself, the city of man, should be destroyed as God had once intended to destroy Nineveh. Why should man exhibit less of a temper than God?

There were no doubts, no lingering regrets, when they saw children swinging on the swings or old men playing chess in the park, or the apples and the string beans resting in their bins red and green, shining under the awnings above. They did not regret their plans or grieve for their soon-to-be victims. They felt like warriors with a just cause, outnumbered by the others, outflanked, a Christian David against a Satanic Goliath. Like David, their secret weapon was their passion, their mission. Destroy. A city with a Jewish mayor would make a fine example for the rest of the country. Come back, Jim Crow. Get out, kike. May your dead be as numberless as the stars in the sky or the windows on the buildings of your downtown. May nothing last but the memory of your crimes; your odor will linger, but you will be gone. So thought the group that gathered their backpacks, pounded and poured powders into little vials diluted with water. So thought the group: retribution was nigh; the Christian man would now serve his God, and no one would laugh, no one would mock, no one would ignore the message. The newspapers, the TV reporters, the magazines—those that still had staff after the day was over—they would have to pay their respects to the Aryan Lords, who didn't need college degrees, who didn't need rank or good credit ratings to stand tall and bring fear to all who would meet them. Let them beg, let them crawl, let them die in piles in the hospital corridors, in the streets, in the offices and schools and gyms. The Aryan Lords raised in the city— lost in the city, perhaps a product of city foster care, city courts, parents who couldn't or wouldn't, aunts and uncles who turned away, priests and ministers and ignorant teachers, classmates who smelled weakness and tore the heart out of a child who had no defense—these men, now grown, with minds that screeched and screamed and played music always out of tune, all harmony vanished, now wanted to kill the accountants and the feds, the police and the firefighters. Let the city be stripped of its people. Then it would be a clean and holy place. So the group had been told. So they believed. So they were prepared to act.

Green pills, blue pills, Lithiums and their pharmaceutical descendants, soothers of the neurons, stimulators of the neurons, MAO inhibitors, helpers of the synapses, drugs that sang lullabies to nerve endings that tingled and shook, sleep inducers, sleep preventers, things that made the hands shake and things that made the shaking less violent—it all went into their cocktail, hundreds and hundreds of pills and liquids now ready, gathered so carefully, so cleverly.

They had spread across the city and waited in emergency rooms hour on hour and described the symptoms of terrible torment and they had been unshaved and they had been dirty and they had seemed to be afraid or angry when they were neither and they had received their drugs and their prescriptions for refills and more refills and they had sometimes to endure a few weeks inside a hospital in which they actually had to take the drugs that made them vomit or shake or fall asleep on their beds for hours and in addition, they waited outside clinic doors and took the drugs and the prescriptions from those who wandered out, pushing them against cars, speaking softly into their ear while holding a knife to their ribs. They ate dinner at a McDonald's uptown and sometimes slipped into a seat of a lone diner, taking his supply, leaving him dazed and ashamed. Some of their victims knew who they were. Some knew what they were up to. There were a few who wanted to warn the city. They had called a reporter in the middle of the night. They had lured the mayor down to a private place. They had not dared to tell too much.

Mel was not sleeping. He felt it coming closer, the thing that would harm his city, that had no exact name but hung over him now. He doubted his power to stop it. He woke Ruth up. "Hold me," he said. She did.

21

EMPTYING
THE VIALS

Now was the time to distribute the fatal cocktail across the city. Their army was not large, not more than fifty, but each of the fifty who had held jobs for weeks as bike messengers, hot dog vendors with carts, clowns with painted faces, waiters at downtown restaurants, guys tossing pizzas, dog walkers, espresso makers at local Starbucks—and where isn't there a local Starbucks?—began to pour the contents of their little vials into drink and food about the city. One 200-pound fellow had obtained a job as a deliverer of precooked packages of macaroni and cheese purchased by some of the more elegant private schools in town. Yes, Duncan Academy was among them. Another pushed a coffee and Danish cart through the halls of office buildings. A few worked in the muffin company that supplied the lunch shops in the financial district. Three had obtained jobs as night cleaners in a complex of tall buildings that served the city's major law firms. They had found a way into the pipes that served the water fountains. They were the army of God, the haters of Jews and blacks and cosmopolitans and liberals and those who allowed abortions and those who had abortions and those who lent money and those who borrowed money and all the cogs in the wheels of capitalism and all the newspapers that fed the hunger to know and all the trash and filth that made up the city.

They were out there spilling their vials into pizza and soft drinks, into sauerkraut and mustard jars, into tap water served in restaurants, on top of arugula and goat cheese salads, and into the wafers of the Mass at several Catholic churches around town.

Their leader, a man whose real name no one knew, sometimes called Ahab by those who knew him best, followed his troops around town in a minivan with an American flag flying from the front antenna. On his radio he heard a talk show host call a woman a communist because she was whining that Medicare wouldn't pay for her cancer drugs. He hummed a tune—was it "The Itsy-Bitsy Spider Went up the Water Spout"? This was the song his mother had sung to him before she left him with her aunt. It was cool out, but he wore no sweater. He was heated up enough from excitement. His dream was coming true. Isn't that what you do in a big city—you make your dreams come true? In the back of the minivan he carried large containers of the mixture of drugs. Every now and then he would park by the curb and someone would open the back of his van and then glide away, lost in the motion of the street, unnoticed the bottle of water he was carrying or the jug he had placed in a backpack. Refills. His plan was brilliant. It would be successful. Zero hour had come.

At police headquarters Mel and Wolfe Joyce were standing nose to nose. "You have to find them," the mayor said. "You have to stop them. Our citizens are going to die of the cure for madness." "Poison is poison," said the commissioner, who had no brief for metaphors and a dead ear for poetry. "Check the mosques," Mel yelled. "Perhaps someone knows something. Find an informant." The commissioner's ears turned red. He knew his job. He knew his job was on the line. "My people are out there. Overtime's going to cost," he warned. "I don't care about the cost," bellowed Mel. "Can I quote that?" asked Maddie, who had poked her head in the door. Mel turned to look at her. Across his face came a wave of despair; he looked like a cat who had fallen into the bathtub. Maddie said, "I was just joking." Mel said, "I am not in the mood." "No," said Maddie, "I can see that. What's up? Any leads?" Mel shrugged. The police commissioner looked out the window. "We got units at the airports grilling visitors from Moslem countries. Of course I can't torture them," Wolfe said, the lilt in his voice exposing an unspoken question. "No," said Mel, "you can't."

Mel had lunch with Moe Alter. Mel was rumpled and there was sweat on his bald spot. "You wanted this job," Moe reminded him.

And then the reports started coming in. Four collapses at the Bell, Becker, and Winnicott law firm. Three dead at Duncan Academy, children having lunch. Fourteen dead on the children's ward of MetroCity Hospital, all of a sudden, right after the clown had been through entertaining the kids, making them animal balloons.

"Look for clowns," the police commissioner said urgently into his radio.

Downtown three artists lay dead in a gallery, the gallery owner, too. The lunch they had shared was on a desk in the back room. Several suburban women on an art tour thought the bodies were part of an exhibit. On the ferry ten dead people, coffee cups in their hands, filled the seats.

Ina bit her fingernails, which was what she always did when she was nervous. She passed up the muffin offered to her by the lab worker down the hall. That was a good thing. The lab had eight deaths in the next hour. Ruth was in her foundation office balancing figures that seemed just a trifle inaccurate when her assistant, a girl from the heartland of America, collapsed and died. Ruth heard the phones ringing and ringing and finally decided to see for herself what was wrong.

Mel went on local TV. "Yes, we are under attack," he said. "Do not—I repeat—do not eat or drink anything that you have not prepared yourself. These are dangerous days. The city is under siege, but we will find those who would destroy us, and we will punish them. We will make our city safe again—have no doubts. No one," the mayor concluded, "can bring us to our knees."

Certain baseball fans, disappointed by the previous season, snickered bitterly, but the rest of his audience took heart. His voice was so sweet and real and came from a place in his soul that was immune to image, posture, pretense. "Don't think I'm not scared," he said to his fellow citizens. "But we will survive this. Report all mysterious people or matters directly to the hot line. If we are all eyes and ears, we will save each other."

The number of the hot line, 4 TERROR, floated across the screen. A million people saw it.

22

THE DEATH COUNT
GROWS

At first there had been a run on the Korean markets as well as the chain food stores, but then no one wanted to buy anything fresh, arriving at checkout counters with jars and cans of nearly out-of-date applesauce. No one bought anything from the hot dog vendors who stood on street corners staring at passersby with the sad dark eyes of far-off places they now wished they had never left.

The entire city was hungry. Slim-Fast and Ensure sold and frozen food sold, but most of it ended up in the trash unopened. When it came right down to eating, most people preferred to go hungry. But the death count was rising: 64, 72, 89, 114. With each passing hour the number climbed. In neighborhoods poor and rich, victim after victim was found reeling around, passed out, beyond help. The media reported huge economic losses. Pizzerias rolled down their metal gates, waiting for graffiti artists to do their worst; restaurants kept the tablecloths fresh, but waiters had plenty of time to regret they had not won a part in a play, completed high school, taken a computer course.

Everyone who could was trying to leave the city. The airports were jammed with reservationless would-be passengers. The mayor had declared an emergency and closed the toll booths on the bridges and tunnels, and still the cars moved like reluctant snails, never more than a foot or two apart, hour after hour.

Mel gathered his family around him. Brooke wanted Jacob to take them away, anywhere, mountains, beach, the other coast, out of town. Jacob wanted to go. But Mel asked him to stay. He might be useful. The captain and the captain's family do not desert the sinking ship, Jacob explained to Brooke, who considered whether the entire incident might not be God's wrath against her for marrying out of faith. Ninety-five percent of her conscious mind rejected this conclusion.

Ina and Sergei, the children, Ruth and Mel, all the family were in the mayor's house, along with the police officers guarding the kitchen.

Mel was sitting in his favorite chair with a list of the identified dead. It was long. It contained names of men, women, and children, names that sounded Hispanic, Russian, Polish, Italian, Irish, Jewish. His eye lingered on the Jewish names and then went on. The Jews counted no more to him than the others; it was just an old habit learned at his father's knee. You looked for your own as the floodwaters rose around you. He considered his list. Who shall live and who shall die? If a tornado had hit the city, it would have knocked into this building or that because of the barometric pressures, the random shifts of heat and cold. It would have no one in mind and in its indifference would have smashed all in its path.

The Mayor listened to his own heartbeat, considered the fragility of the body, its millions of nerves, synapses, messages running back and forth from brain to muscle, its blood flowing through the veins, the lungs filling and emptying, the brilliance of the body, the genius of the body, the glory of it, the beauty of the human cell, the protein and the plasma and the persistence of nail and hair and the whiteness of eye and the soft pink tissues, and the skeleton that kept all the oozing, pulsing fluids in place, the miracle.

The mystery of it drained the color from his face. Why this one and not his cousin? Why that child and not her older sister? Why the old lady from 525 Narrow Street and not the old lady from Fourth Avenue and 154th Street? Mel had no time for this sort of question. He had thought all this through time and again since he had been fourteen, and yet he couldn't stop asking himself: Why him and not her? As if there were an answer, as if the sense of it all would come to him if he just repeated his question long enough. There was no answer. He knew in his bones that accident and fortune, Fate and its nasty handmaidens, turned one person left toward the shore as another headed for the shark's open mouth. He knew it was not up to him. He, too, was among the living—at least now, on sufferance, by something as random as a muffin placed in the front or the back of a tray. Humbled and afraid, he sat in his chair as his family gathered around and his grandchildren complained that they wanted to eat and his wife stared at him as if he were a stranger who had entered her abode. He could have used some Comforters, although he knew that Comforters were more apt to be false than true. He felt a cramp in his stomach. That was the thing about philosophy. It almost always led directly to indigestion: the last thing in the world he needed in the present emergency.

There were many people in the city's churches and synagogues and mosques. Many fine things were said about God's capacity to save his people. Confessions were made, silently or to others. Regrets were admitted. People kept washing their hands and taking showers as if cleanliness were a shield against evil or a shortcut to God's favor.

Sergei was glad that his brother, Leonid, had not yet received his visa.

The Imps of Misfortune, the Imps of Disaster Impending, the Imps of Selfishness and Fear were tumbling about the city like scraps of paper blown in the wind. They fell from tall buildings, they somersaulted over the fountains in the park and the cornices and columns and arches of buildings, they balanced on window ledges and leered into the glass windows of offices, they rolled on the wheels of ambulances. If you listened carefully, you could hear the unholy racket they made in this time of need.

Mel stood up. "We are going for a walk," he said, "all of us. The police are doing their job. We will go to the carousel and the children can ride and we will buy them balloons and Crackerjack." "All right," said Ruth. "Let's do it without a guard." Coats were donned, and Mel waved away the bodyguards, who didn't exactly go away but stepped back, and then the family went out. The day was not bitter, and the air felt good in their lungs. Ina took her father's arm, Sergei held the baby, and Brooke, who had found her courage, which had perhaps been hiding in her makeup case, smiled bravely. As they walked, calm followed them—not relief, just calm.

That night the mayor looked out his window and saw a sky in which stars floated through the galaxies and the Milky Way spilled down and light and time mingled, and he did not believe that God's eye could find him there at the window in his favorite blue and white striped pajamas.

23

METHODS AND
MADNESS

The president of the United States sent condolences, and the army sent a phalanx of reserve officers and the senators of the state appeared together on the courthouse steps promising justice and deliverance, and as they were talking two women who worked in the records department in the courthouse basement turned blue and died as the crowd parted around them. "At least they weren't tourists," said the mayor's deputy for economic opportunity when their identity passes were pulled from their purses.

As the mayor headed back to his office with the sound of ambulance sirens in his ears and the press at his heels, a baby stroller blocked his way. There was no mother in sight. There was no baby in the stroller. He was about to push it aside when he saw a rag doll with its stuffing coming out of a deep slit in its belly. Attached to the doll was a white piece of paper on which had been printed in block letters the message EXILE THE JEWS OF THE CITY OR TAKE THE CONSEQUENCES. SEND THEM OUT WITHIN A WEEK OR OUR ACTIVITIES INCREASE UNTIL ALL YOUR CITIZENS ARE DEAD. YOU JEW MAYOR, YOU GO, TOO. For a moment the mayor considered it. A long line of Jews walking out of town across the bridges, lines at the bus stations, pandemonium at the train station, airports leaking people into the nearby bays, Jews blocking the tunnels with their cars piled high with everything they could gather, picture albums, grandmothers' samovars, gerbils and hamsters, dogs and cats, cartons of school report cards, bank records, passports, golf clubs, potted plants. He saw the Jews headed out on the highways for other cities that might suddenly refuse to rent houses to them or give them jobs *(not welcome, don't settle here),* town fathers afraid that their homes too would be attacked if they sheltered the Jews. Mel pushed the image of that exodus out of his mind. It wasn't going to happen. No one was going anywhere.

Maddie Miller appeared at his elbow. She read the note over his shoulder. Her paper would lead with the item. Certain other people in the city would say it was the Jews' fault—*get them out before we all die.* Certain others would rally. The new cardinal would stand with the rabbis. Local ministers would attend services at their local synagogues. Mel was sure, or almost sure. The police would try harder. The FBI—well, he wasn't counting on them in any case.

Ruth was in his office when he returned. She had heard the news over the radio. Her eyes were watery. "In every generation," she said. Mel was impatient. "Now is now," he said. His eyes had turned hard and cold. He had given up on poetry. He stared at a map of the city spread across his desk. Harold had put pins in the map for every place where one or more people had died. There was no pattern to be found. It was random: a hand reaching into a muffin tray, a little sauerkraut spread on a hot dog roll, a bite of apple or a bit of broccoli. Mel himself never touched a green vegetable unless it was disguised in a sauce. He knew that was no reason to congratulate himself on his superior survival skills; on the other hand, certain self-righteous people who had always mocked his eating habits might possibly feel abashed under the circumstances.

Maddie went back to the McDonald's she had visited in the middle of the night. She looked around. Some children with their mothers, a guy eating french fries while gulping from a bottle in a paper bag, a girl twirling her hair while waiting for her boyfriend. A few loners, so lone that you could smell it a few tables away. Here were loners with eyes that glared, hair that was combed with a strange precision or left shaggy. Men with dirt in their pores and stains on their pants, men so immaculate that you felt they couldn't be real. Loners drinking large Cokes and staring ahead.

She sat down at the table of one. "Maddie Miller," she introduced herself. "I'm a reporter." The fellow did not seem to see her. "I was wondering," she said, "if someone else had picked up your meds lately." The man didn't answer. She repeated her question. He shook his head. "I don't take meds," he said. "That's because you don't have them," she said. "I was just wondering who you gave them to." "Didn't give them," he said. "I never had them," he said. "But if you had them?" she pressed. "They'd be taken," he said. "By whom?" said Maddie. "I never had them," said the man. "But if you had them?" Maddie repeated. "They'd be taken. The Collective for a Better World wants 'em. Buys them." Maddie was all nerves, like the hound that sees the fox straight ahead. "The Collective for a Better World has your meds?" Maddie asked another fellow she saw on the bench outside as she was leaving. "Yeah," he said, but he wouldn't say anything else. Under the El, where the old tracks of the subway rose above the second story and the trains rattled above, Maddie found a woman sitting with all her belongings and folding her things neatly into a shopping cart. "I'm from the Collective for a Better World," Maddie said. "No you're not," the woman answered. "They're men." "I'm the girlfriend," said Maddie. "I got a double dose," said the woman, and pulled out a pharmacy bag with her medications inside. "I said it wasn't working." She laughed. "It works all right." Maddie wasn't sure if she was supposed to pay. She waited. The woman said, "Don't hit me, I did good." Then Maddie knew how the meds were collected. She called police headquarters on her cell phone. "Put me through to Wolfe Joyce right now."

Brooke called Jacob at his office. "Would you be upset," she asked, "if I got some little gold crosses for the children to wear on their necks? It might be a good idea right now." Jacob paused. He was very calm when he answered. "No, don't do that. Please," he added. When he hung up he felt dizzy. Was he angry or was he about to die? After a few minutes the dizziness subsided.

24

MEET NEIL MAGUIRE, PARKING COMMISSIONER

Neil Maguire was a very portly man. His wife was always trying to put him on a diet, but he cheated at lunch where she couldn't see him devouring the moo shu pork at lunch or the second helping of lasagna with his poker buddies, and in the middle of the night he raided the refrigerator. He stuffed candy bars into the glove compartment of his Camry, and he often stopped at Yonah's for a small mushroom knish on his way home. He had two boys at St. Francis Academy and two daughters at St. Agnes, and the girls were both on the basketball team, which made him very proud. He had a third son, his oldest, named Kevin, who had just been released from Quaker State Hospital and was now living at home, obtaining his meds from the local outpatient clinic.

Kevin had threatened to murder one of his girlfriends because she had Satan's mark on her thigh. Neil did not understand how one moment a child could be throwing a ball in his yard and the next hearing voices that told him to slash his own arm with a corkscrew or cut up his sisters' underwear with a steak knife. The doctors who treated his son shrugged and looked down at their laps when asked for explanations. Could God understand? Neil doubted it. In fact, he began to doubt God. His roof had worn thin, and the roofer his wife had called promised calamity if an expensive repair job was not done immediately. The family needed both of their cars, yet one of them spent entirely too much time at the repair shop. Neil was a romantic man who brought his wife roses and kissed his daughters on their freckled noses every chance he got. He had ambition. He wanted to be admired, and more than admired, respected. He didn't want to die like his father, with ten people at the funeral, leaving behind not a trace, not a mark, as if a man were no more than a blade of grass. In the Rosenberg administration he had won the post of parking commissioner. He had a large office on the river side of a government building above the Motor Vehicles Bureau. He had his own courthouse to supervise, where sinners whose cars had been booted came to plead for the return of their vehicles and pay their fines. Money flowed through the building upstairs and downstairs, violators wept, pleaded sick children on the way to the hospital, but paid their fines in the end. At night Neil Maguire had money dreams: cash falling into his bed, cash stuffed in suitcases, taking the entire family to Rome to visit the Pope and bringing the Pope a barrel full of cash for the poor and the Pope spreading out his arms and healing Kevin. In dreams troubles begin, and in dreams the seeds of scandal are sown.

The mayor was particularly fond of his parking commissioner, who when they met had been a young district attorney; Mel had been his boss. Neil Maguire with his big arm draped around Mel's shoulders had been Mel's first real Catholic friend. When he and Neil had shared barbecues on the patio and gone to ball games together, he had thought, How great is America? How sweet is this?

Kevin was waiting for a place at a halfway house. His social worker was trying to hurry things along. At least Neil hoped so. Kevin's sisters locked their door at night. His brothers kept a baseball bat in between their beds. Kevin glared at them all. He had grown fat because of the medication and his long hours of inactivity. He groomed himself strangely but said little. He sat in a chair by the window all day, and when his mother tried to get him to go with her to the market he banged his fist against the wall. She left him alone. "Are you taking your medicine?" she asked. "Yes," he said. But he wasn't. His medicine was plucked out of his hands by representatives of the Collective for a Better World each week. He was hanging on, but barely.

Neil approached his son. "I want to see the medicine they gave you at the clinic this week," he said. Kevin shook his head and opened his palms upward. Kevin rose to his feet and seemed ready to attack his father. Neil stood his ground. Kevin told his father that the medicine was stolen. At first Neil thought Kevin was lying; truth is a victim of madness, and Neil had been burned before. But then there was something in Kevin's face, the expression he had had as a child wanting his father to believe he had climbed the tree or put away the bicycle when he had, when he still told the truth more often than not.

That night the phone rang by the mayor's bed, and it was Neil on the other end of the line. When Neil told him that Kevin was being robbed, Mel was very excited and said he was coming right over with the police, and how important it was and that Kevin could save the city. In the Maguire kitchen the plot was laid: When Kevin left the clinic, he would be tailed by undercover police.

Mel thought of what he would like to do to the prisoners as soon as they were in jail. He was ashamed of himself. A man should not even think of the things he had just thought of.

The next day Kevin went to his clinic, which, after receiving several urgent calls from the Department of Health, finally gave him his medicine, even though he had come in with no appointment. After waiting for three hours and being scolded for appearing without calling his social worker (who was on vacation), he left, his medication in his pocket. He was walking his usual slow heave-shuffle down the street when he was suddenly bumped by three men in leather jackets with spiked haircuts who pushed him around the corner, unaware of the police up and down the block. It was no more than a minute before the three men had the medicine in their own pockets and the police had them in a van and the first big break came. Kevin was crying when his father jumped out of a police car and came to his side. He'd lost his medicine again.

Meanwhile, the leader of the band, the one who thought he was making the world safe for his kind, purified of the garbage that spoiled the God-given glory of the earth, continued to ride the streets in his van, pouring lethal doses of combined drugs onto whatever foods were exposed to the air. He liked doing this himself. As he walked he rocked slightly from side to side as if he had just dismounted from his horse after a long trip through wild country. Women turned around to look at him. His confidence was like a halo. It marked him as one of the chosen. He did not yet know that the police had chosen him as well, chosen him as their culprit to be caught, questioned, tried, and tossed into prison for the rest of his life. For now he was free, a man above all other men, a man who was fired by a hatred of Jews that stemmed from some dealings his grandfather had had with a banker by the name of Cohen in the mythical past, or perhaps that wasn't it at all.

Flattened like pancakes, strewn across the pavement like litter after a parade, the Imps of Fear and Calamity feared a defeat no less painful for being less than final: the story of a man providing new opportunities for chaos on every page of the calendar.

25

THE SPINNER OF

HOLY TALES TELLS ALL

Y ou don't really have to torture anyone, Mel was thinking. You
just have to offer them a deal. Less time in jail, a last visit with a
girlfriend with a mattress on the floor, some help in securing a
bank loan for a mother looking at foreclosure. It wasn't hard to get
a criminal to turn on his colleagues. Even idealists, fanatics, and
lunatics had their price. In the end, Mel thought with some sorrow,
everyone does. Did he? This was a question he hoped he would
never have to answer.

Behind bars the Collective for a Better World consisted of one
man in bad need of root canal and another with a hatred of Jews but
a fear of blacks that brought him to his knees, willing to trade anything to be placed in protective custody. The other member of the
group believed that when the Jews were gone from American
shores all the banks would disappear and the television would play
only old Doris Day movies and God would see the wheat growing
and the corn high in the fields and he would be pleased and grant
some of his favored children great wealth. Or something like that;
his vision changed, it wobbled, it became more or less bloody
depending on his mood, but it always ended in redemption. This

man, who was the smallest and skinniest of them all, turned his head away from the detective who was politely questioning him. He let his voice drop low and told the story of Jesus walking on water, and he quoted the words of Matthew, Luke, and John in great voluminous paragraphs. When he talked about his childhood he invoked angels who guarded over him and angels who smacked him in the mouth when he profaned. He would have been a more plausible preacher if he had happened to have more of a chin. When the detective held his hand and prayed with him, the man responded to the kindness with the confession that he had always had a sinful preference for little boys, and when the detective squeezed his hand in response and didn't let go, the man gave addresses, locations, and a description of the van in question.

The police chief had to admit that like everyone else, he too loved a happy ending, especially the part when the children lost to their parents would return running into their arms. The police chief had buried a child, a victim of bone cancer, only two years earlier, and it wasn't easy for him to keep the spinner of holy tales and the murderer on the other side of the two-way mirror in proper perspective. But he did, and within only a few hours he knew they were looking for a sky-blue 1989 Ford and that the apartment where the group's members had been staying since their arrival was on Coughlin Street.

The dying in the city hadn't stopped yet; it would, but for now the people of the city were hungry and afraid, and many were angry. There was looting in some sections. There were demonstrations in front of police headquarters. A picture of the mayor with his body stuffed into a trash can was held aloft at a rally in front of the band shell in the park. The newspapers were calling for federal troops to enter the city. They were calling for the police chief's head on a silver platter with a presidential seal embossed upon it.

The Greek Orthodox patriarch, the new cardinal, the bishop, the pastors of four or five of the largest Baptist congregations, and the imam from the newly built mosque appeared together in front of the TV cameras to say that anti-Semitism was not God's word but a perversion that should be abhorred or something of the sort. They assured their co-citizens who might be Jewish that their neighbors would not let any harm come to them and under no circumstances would give in to demands to push them outside the city limits. This would have been more reassuring to the Jewish community if just before the cameras were turned off Reverend Harold Michael, whose congregation was mourning the loss of their choir master who had fallen victim to a drug cocktail that had been sprinkled on his chocolate chip cookie, had not said to Reverend Spain, "Have you noticed," he said in a voice loud enough for the microphones to pick it up, "that whenever there is trouble, the Jews are at the center of it?" Reverend Spain made a face and said, "They wouldn't be missed if they left, would they?" This little exchange headed the evening news and was repeated over and over again on the news stations all through the night.

On Ninth Avenue, Ahab, born Eugene Barr, turned the van around the corner and waited at the light. In the back the vials of lethal cocktail clicked and rattled in their cardboard sections of large wooden cartons. On the seat beside him was a rag to clean the dust off the window and the seat. The dirt in the city offended him, the way it rained down over everything. It made him feel unclean. On the seat beside him was the swimsuit issue of *Sports Illustrated*. What he did with that need not be mentioned. He was confident. He was pleased. His muscles were hard, and he flexed them again and again as he sat waiting for the light to change. The justness of his cause, the joy of his ideals, made him glow. The fury that led him to those ideals, the child's rage and its reasons, were locked away in the synapses of his mind, where memory could hardly find them. There was something beautiful about him; self-satisfaction can do that to a fellow. He didn't notice the unmarked police car that had pulled up behind him.

The police officer checked the van's make and year and then called for backup. He put on his siren and roared up next to the driver. After that it was all over, more sirens, some guns pulled by the police. The antihero had a smirk on his face when he was led up the steps to the police station. It was a chilling smirk. It implied that no one would ever be safe again.

There was a press conference on the steps of city hall. The mayor congratulated his police chief and the entire police department. He said, "I want first of all to send my condolences to those who lost loved ones in the killing spree we have just endured. I want them to know that the mayor of their city would give everything he had in this world to turn back the clock, to have caught the criminals before harm came to any citizen. Do not think these zealots are anything but common murderers, no matter how they pray or what scripture they hide behind," the mayor said. He added, "There is nothing good to be said about this incident except that it is over, really over." The senior senator of the state flew in from Washington to congratulate the city on its capture of those who would undermine everything that made America great, et cetera, et cetera, et cetera, till the words themselves were emptied of meaning and collapsed on the podium like so many pricked balloons.

The mayor's political enemies, who were legion, called for an investigation of the mayor's actions during the crisis. The mayor himself went home and went directly to bed. Exhaustion had set into his bones, made his knees ache. There was a strange pressure in his head that wasn't so much a headache as a foghorn sounding in the ocean mist. Ruth kissed him on his nose, ran her fingers over his bald spot, and curled up quietly beside him while they waited for what she called his "kangaroo bounce" to return.

26

A SEDER NIGHT DIFFERENT FROM OTHER SEDER NIGHTS

na was lying on the couch in Dr. Bergen's office. The fan was making its noise like a mechanical wind playing over the office furniture. She was talking about Passover. "We were all there," Ina told her therapist. "Dad with his white shirt, Mom with the rings under her eyes she always gets at this holiday. It was ordinary. Jacob asked the four questions with the twins chiming in. The table with Grandma's dishes was just the way it always is, nothing special. Sergei's brother, Leonid, had just arrived. He was with us. His English is terrible, although he thinks it isn't. We had the bishop, who has a great fondness for gefilte fish. We had Dad's assistant, Harold, who had never been to a seder before, giving Dad an excuse to explain everything at great length. But explaining is the point of the thing, I suppose. Sergei held my hand until I needed it to lift a fork. Everything was fine, which is why what happened is so—so—odd." She paused. Dr. Bergen leaned forward. He waited. "The twins went to open the door for Elijah. Dad took a sip of the wine from Elijah's cup to fool them, although they're not that stupid, even though they are Jacob's children. Mom reached down the table to pick up an egg that had rolled up next to the Miriam cup.

She knocked the cup over and the water spilled. Don't read any-thing Freudian into that—the water just spilled. Then the kids called out. They couldn't open the door. It was too heavy. Jacob said it wasn't heavy, they weren't trying. He got up to help. He pulled at the door. It wouldn't open. Harold and the bishop and Sergei got up and tried. No one could open the door. It was stuck. I thought about fire. I thought about the back door. I said I would go and open the back door, that Elijah could come in that way. I heard them pulling at the door. Mother's aunt was clapping her hands and urging them on. In the kitchen I smiled at the two women who were putting dishes in the dishwasher. I opened the door, and then I fell backward. A great force had knocked me down. I knew I had bruised my elbow. I looked up and saw a very large man coming toward me. At least from the neck down it was a man. He had on a blue striped suit and a white shirt and a gray tie with little red dia-monds on it. But above his neck there was no head. There was instead a silver platter balancing on his neck muscles. I could see his arteries pumping, and on the silver platter was at least a six-pound brisket floating in gravy. He, or it, seemed to step over me and go into the dining room. A second later he passed me again, and I saw his back just as I noticed that a pool of gravy had spilled off the tray onto my dress."

"You hit your head when you fell," Dr. Bergen suggested. "You must have lost consciousness for a second." "No," said Ina, "I didn't." "So what about this Elijah?" said Dr. Bergen. Ina was silent. "You know," he added, "last week at our session I was wear-ing my blue striped suit and my gray tie with red diamonds and a white shirt." "You're posing as a miracle worker?" asked Ina, somewhat abashed at this information. "No," said Dr. Bergen, "you're posing me as a miracle worker." "Everything is always about you," said Ina. "What about the silver tray and the brisket?" asked Dr. Bergen. "Perhaps," said Dr. Bergen in the face of her silence, "you think I am providing you, or should provide you, with nourishment. Or perhaps," he dared it, after a short pause, "you want to devour me." "For God's sake," said Ina, now really irritated. "I hate brown Jewish food." "Really?" said Dr. Bergen. Ina at that moment would have traded in her unconscious for a cloak of invisibility, which she knew would have proved to be a far more useful tool in her life. Ina continued her report. "Then the front door opened. The family came back into the dining room. When I stood up there was gravy on my skirt. It hadn't been there before." "I doubt that," said Dr. Bergen, who shook his very real head that was attached to his very real neck. "Elijah's cup was half empty," said Ina. "None of the adults at the table could have done that. They were all in the hall pulling at the door."

The hour was up, leaving Ina, who liked to measure and weigh and calculate, unable to take the measure of anything.

Sitting at their kitchen table, matzo crumbs covering his lap, Mel said to Ruth, "I am not a rich man." "No, you're not," the mayor's wife replied. "But the kids went to school. Everyone had shoes, not to mention expensive sneakers. We have a retirement plan with enough in it for a year in Key West. What more could anyone want?" "Sometimes," said Mel, "I think I shouldn't have gone into politics. I could have used my head to build a bank account. Capital—that is what we lack." "What brought this up?" asked Ruth. "Neil Maguire told me at lunch today that he's buying a new Mercedes for his wife, and when I asked him how he managed that, he said he had made a profit in some real estate that was left to him by his father." Mel sighed. "The leather in those cars has real quality. That motor is worth its weight in gold." Ruth interrupted. Car talk bored her. "So he has a Mercedes," she said. "What do you really care?" "I don't," said Mel, "not at all. Sometimes I just wonder if you would have been happier if I were a more private person with a portfolio." Ruth stared at him. "Don't put it on me," she said, "if you're suddenly yearning for a beach house or a private plane." Mel grinned. What he really wanted was several billion more dollars to balance the city budget, to build parks and schools and an aquarium down at the docks and to open training institutes and rehab centers and to tear down the ugly projects at the north end and replace them with town houses with gardens and day care centers and health clinics. What he really wanted was an enduring surplus of money, and what he had to do was cut everything: snip and snap and break apart the safety net because there was no money. "One of these days," he said to Ruth, "I'm going to buy you a mink coat." "Thanks," said Ruth. "That's the day I'll buy you your Mercedes."

27

THE UNKINDEST
CUTS OF ALL

I t's gotta be the branch libraries, it's the libraries or the pools. Mel sat at his desk, his toes itching (had athlete's foot returned?). The decision had to be made immediately. "What if you cut back hours on both?" he suggested.

"No," said Jake, his assistant budget director, a skinny young man with a nose like a toucan and an unfortunate herpes sore on his upper lip. "Because of benefits, start-up expenses, cleaning and insurance we need to cut a line here, a full line. Right now. Actually, we should close both down. This city is not a country club, and it's time some people understood that." "Some people" included Mel.

The weather was warming up. The carts piled high with hot dogs, sodas, and pretzels were multiplying daily. The ball fields were filled with kids in school uniforms, teams put up by the local hardware stores, the big chains, the local fast-food establishments; more were needed. At the lake in the park visitors rented boats and rowed under the bridge with their maps and their cameras held on their laps. The lake was filled with old soda cans, and an occasional condom floated by. More sanitation men were needed in the park.

Sometimes it seemed to Mel that no one in the entire city ever picked up a piece of paper or threw anything away in its designated can. Something about the city, the way no one could tell your mother what you did because no one knew your name, encouraged dropping and spoiling—each man was a royal prince assuming a flock of attendants to pick up after him as he made his way.

Mel thought of the children in the hot summer opening fire hydrants and the fire department sending trucks through the streets to turn off the water, to stop the children from splashing, to keep the streets dry in case of fire, to husband water while the children boiled.

He remembered himself on the steps of the house he grew up in. His mother had slapped his face because he drank the last of the iced tea in the cooler she kept at her side. The pools, he decided. We will keep open the pools.

Which is why that evening he went to the local library in a far-out-of-the-center-of-town neighborhood sprouting new immigrants, a babble of languages and enough children to repopulate Babel: children in their American-bought sneakers and their baseball caps and their mothers in saris and dashikis and jeans, dads in turbans and dads with long black beards, a neighborhood where a square foot of dirt at the base of a tree might have been planted with corn or a smokable weed that might thrive, smothered in soot and car emissions, and grow plump in the heat of the season. Religious symbols, pictures of saints, plaster sculptures of the Madonna, gurus in white beards and long robes sat in store windows along with Russian dolls painted in bright colors, dolls pregnant with other dolls, each in turn pregnant with a smaller replica of itself, in a comment on the fertility of life, also indicating that the past shrinks into a smaller and smaller memory until it disappears altogether.

In the local library the two police officers who had accompanied the mayor leaned their backs against the librarian's desk, keeping their eyes on the mayor just in case some assassin lurked in the children's book corner or over by the encyclopedias. The library smelled clean—not institutional clean, but good clean. The windows were open. The air conditioner didn't work, and the head librarian was getting ready to ask the mayor for new equipment for the second floor, which turned into an oven in the bad days of July and August. The heater also was defective; in January and February the visitors to the library had to keep their coats on, and the librarian and her assistant had both developed chest coughs last year.

There were only fourteen people in the library, including the mayor and the police officers and the librarian. It was almost closing time. An old man was sitting at a table reading the newspaper. Two mothers with children in strollers were reading picture books in whispers to their sleepy offspring. Story hour had been attended by five children and their mothers, the librarian proudly announced. "Only five?" asked Mel. The librarian ignored him. "We can get any book anyone wants through the central system," she added.

Mel glanced up the stairs. On the top step he saw a huge cobweb. Behind it he saw a small boy in knickers and a Dutch cap clutching ice skates to his chest. *"Hans Brinker and the Silver Skates,"* Mel said aloud. "What?" said the librarian. "Nothing," said Mel. With his paws up on the table, his unmistakable head lifted upward, a howl toward the moon, Mel saw a familiar wolf, or was it a grandmother? A second later, swords flashing, the Three Musketeers dropped from the lighting fixture and melted away. "It's time to leave," Mel said. A sorrow was upon him. Movies, videos, TV—who needed libraries?

The written word, paper itself, was on its way out. Things moved in electronic currents, stories had pixels and were revealed on DVDs. It doesn't matter, thought Mel. Only a sentimental man would waste money on libraries. Mel sighed. Long John Silver stood on the front steps of the library, using his knife to clean his ear.

"If only," he said to Ruth that night when they were settling down to watch *NYPD Blue,* "I could climb up a vine and sneak into the giant's palace and steal enough gold to make our treasury bulge, then I could keep the libraries open. A mayor of the city ought to be a billionaire," he said. "In which case I could just write out a check." "In which case," said Ruth, "you wouldn't be a billionaire for long and finally you would be bankrupt and the city would have to tighten its belt or find a new billionaire. Not such a good plan for reelection." "I know," Mel said, because he knew. "Money isn't everything," he added. "But it would be helpful if someone I had been kind to in childhood, maybe an escaped prisoner who went on to make a fortune, would die and leave me an inheritance large enough to keep the libraries open." "What?" said Ruth. "Dickens," said Mel. "Oh, Dickens," said Ruth. "You can rent David Copperfield at the video store for a few dollars." "Sure," said Mel, who felt guilty. "I closed the branch libraries today," he told Ruth. "I had to." "Shh," said Ruth, who had had enough, just enough of the real world.

28

THE SOLACE OF
SOUND

The city in July smelled. It smelled of old fish and half-eaten oranges. It smelled of heavy sweet drinks and chewing gum, mint candy and cigarettes and unpleasant things left in the wire garbage cans on the corners and noodles in dirty containers and chicken roasting and old diapers and sticky stuff that clung to the bottoms of sandals. It smelled of a thousand varieties of sweat and a million tons of deodorant. It smelled of cumin and saffron and soy and ketchup and cat food and curry and pickles, sour pickles. The entire city appeared to have bad breath, as if the heat had spoiled the stomach of the town.

Mel was walking in the early evening to the Tisha b'Av services, where he had made a promise to a very powerful, well-connected rabbi that he would appear. This rabbi had more votes in his pocket than most men had pockets, a lifetime's worth of pockets. What we need, Mel thought, is a wind, a cooling wind, a wind that blows from the sea, clearing the head. He wished he hadn't had to wear a shirt and tie and a suit jacket. He envied the men he passed in T-shirts, bandannas, and cutoff jeans, who could let the air cross their bellies when they raised their arms. He found his way to the appointed synagogue. He was greeted by several of the men, who introduced themselves, and he was seated in the front. The windows were covered in black crepe. He was given a small flashlight so he could read the text. There was no air-conditioning. The women were upstairs. He couldn't see them.

Ruth would not come to such a place. She didn't like being upstairs. Even for appearance' sake she would not go with him. Mel understood. She had her pride.

The service began. A long, lyrical sound came from the unshaved men around him, a deep sound as if from the bottom of a pit, as if he were hearing sounds from another time, filtering upward from the past, wrapping him in their insistent call. "How has she become a widow! She that was great among the nations, she weepeth sore in the night and her tears are on her cheeks. The ways of Zion do mourn—all her gates are desolate: her priests sigh, her virgins are afflicted, and she is in bitterness." The sadness of it, the sound of the sadness, the rolling, grieving melody, the congregation pausing as one or another of the men around him picked up a verse, let it rise from the depth of his heart, and sang to the others of the pain, so they knew his anguish. The temple was destroyed, the city was in ruins. The voices, tenors, baritones, maybe neither made him forget the heat, the place, the fact that he understood the words only partially. Mel felt a lump in his throat, and then a strange terror rose in his breast. The city had been sacked. The grief was now, the grief was not lost in the millennia. Was it Warsaw they were crying for? Was it Cracow or Lodz, for that matter, Troy, Carthage, Stalingrad, Dresden, or some other place where bodies had been piled and structures wrecked, and stones crumbled and windows had been smashed? Under the melody that filled the room the way the river fills its banks, there was a humble question, "Why?" and the why danced through the words like an invisible conductor, ducking and swaying with the sound. Could it happen to his city? Could the enemy come and ruin the shining stores and the great buildings and knock down the gargoyles from their perches and break the pipes that bring water and crumple the bridges as if they were made of sticks? He was frightened for his city. What happened once could happen again. He could hear it in the voices of the men all around him, devastation, siege, exile—this was not some tale of the past but an ever-present possibility. Was it sin that had brought this about? That was not the question that concerned Mel. The responsibility weighed on him. He must protect the city. The lyric consumed him. Tears flowed. He was a sentimental man. He hated the Romans, the Syrians, the Cossacks, and others. He loved his city. The Imp of Despair pulled at his tie. The Imp of Deafness would not make him deaf. He heard it all. "Turn thou us unto thee, O Lord. Renew our days as of old. But thou hast utterly rejected us, thou art very wroth against us."

Mel was not a man inclined to religious thoughts, especially not miserable ones. In high school he had known a Richard Roth. On the way home he began to wonder what had become of him.

Earlier that afternoon Neil Maguire had found himself downtown staring into the window of a particularly posh jewelry store, the kind that had a man in a tuxedo open the front door, where the carpeting seemed thick enough to swallow a small child, and the salespeople appeared to be on a luxury cruise, eyes fixed on the distant horizon, hair shining in the glow of the indirect lighting. They wore the too-bright smiles of people who ought to be enjoying themselves but were not. Neil was drawn in through the great oak doors with their golden knobs and drifted over to the counter on his left. He wandered through the glitter, staring at the necklaces and the rings sparsely displayed, each resting on a little velvet pillow in the locked case. He loved the discreet, admiring glances cast his way. Then his eye was caught by a bracelet, a diamond bracelet, cold and clean, silver shining between the diamonds. What would such a thing cost? It turned out to cost close to the parking commissioner's entire year's salary, more than all his credit cards held. The salesclerk put it back in the case when she saw the expression on his face. "Can you give me an idea of your price range?" she asked without a drop of judgment in her voice. Neil did not hesitate. This was the right present for his wife and their approaching anniversary. It would bring her to her knees before him in gratitude. She deserved this bracelet as much as any other woman. He had a savings account. He wrote a check. Why should everything in their life be mediocre, bought on sale, less than the top of the line? Why should he go steerage when others were laughing in first class? The chipped linoleum on his kitchen floor, the bathroom fixture that he'd bought at the neighbor's yard sale, the TV that no longer swiveled on its base—all these things galled him. He had expected more of himself. The bracelet and its black velvet box were wrapped in rose tissue paper with a perfect paper lily pasted on the top.

29

DIRTY WORK AND
THE EVIL
INCLINATION

Neil Maguire put the box with the bracelet underneath his socks, which were neatly arranged in color zones from brown to black. He thought of it there shining in the dark, waiting for the moment when he would present it to his wife, who wouldn't believe her eyes. She would ask questions, of course, and she might even threaten to return the bauble, which thought brought a flush to his cheeks, part relief, part horror. Neil was a man who ought to be able to give his wife an extravagant gift even if he wasn't exactly that man. His heart was up to it; his savings account would be emptied. That savings account was a college fund, an emergency fund, a foul-weather friend, a small nest egg that was never meant to give birth to a diamond bracelet.

In a big office with a window overlooking the harbor, he played with the gift his children had presented him last Father's Day, a glass snow globe with a tiny replica of the town square. He turned it upside down and watched as the beautiful pure white snow fell upon the miniature scene. He was supposed to be looking over bids from the towing companies that did the city's dirty work, picking up cars parked illegally and bringing them to a pound at the edge of town where their owners would arrive frantic, angry, bitter, and with plenty of cash to redeem the vehicle. If the owners never came, which happened more often than you thought, the cars would end up as property of the police department if they made it intact for over six months. The truth was that most were slid off the books and redeemed in the chop shops uptown, bits and pieces, fenders and wheels, transmissions and alternators, headlights and brakes waiting for resurrection. The fellows who worked in the pound were not known felons, had no arrest records to speak of, but were often the cousins or the brothers of someone who had met someone while incarcerated. The fellows who owned the towing companies were all members of their Kiwanis, Elks, or Lions Clubs and contributed regularly to the United Way. But they too knew people who would help them get a contract when the time was ripe. The time was now.

Neil was thumbing idly through the presentations, which were done up in three colors and had covers similar to the one he had used on his seventh-grade report for Sister Maria Alice on the products of Switzerland. Only his colors had not been machine-generated but were carefully handwrought with his younger sister's Magic Markers. He had, for the record, received an A.

Triple Tough had the lowest bid. Deals on Wheels was recommended by Father Mahony as well as his son's high school math teacher. Service to U had a beautiful diagram of a car showing how carefully their men worked so that the city would be spared lawsuits and save a fortune on insurance. Prix Fixe Towing had a small note attached to their figures. It said, *If you would like to have a private conversation with us, we would be eager to talk. We are always able to accommodate our friends, who make such sacrifices to serve the people of the city.* What was that? Neil felt a flush across his chest. Not so much a heart pain but a constriction of the breath. The way he used to feel as a boy just before diving into the school pool: terrified but committed.

Meantime Brooke was shopping in Manny's. Manny's was a store so fine that it often didn't put clothes in its window but rather showed art prints of exotic landscapes or small perfume bottles that rested on tall columns with Doric curls at the sides. Brooke was upstairs trying on a dress that was black as coal with a white star at the waist and a neckline that plunged perhaps too far but which reminded Brooke, as she stared at herself in the mirror, that youth was fleeting and one day she would be old and her middle would spread and her ankles would swell. Seize the day, she thought. She looked at the price tag. It was staggering. What was she thinking of? It wasn't right. She took the dress off. Jacob could afford it. He wouldn't be pleased, but he wouldn't go to debtor's prison because of the dress. Perhaps it was the Evil Inclination that wrapped itself around her quickly moving fingers, but in a second she had rolled the dress up, electronic tag and all, and stuffed it into her panties, which now gave her a pregnant look she had not had when entering the store. She left the dressing room and took the elevator to the first floor. She stood at the doors to the street but couldn't move. She shouldn't do this. She should go back upstairs and return the dress. She intended to go back, but something propelled her forward and she went out the door. The sensor screamed. She ducked around the corner and joined a throng of people moving across the avenue. She didn't look back. Once in the street she knew she should return the dress. But how to get back in the store without setting off the sensors? That she couldn't figure out.

Hiding inside her closet at home, she worked at the sensor with a little scissors. She got nowhere. She didn't want to rip it out, leaving a hole in the dress. She took it to her local dress store. As she went in a shriek of a machine screaming "thief" accompanied her. "Oh, dear," she said with a helpless lopsided smile that almost always worked, "Manny's left on the sensor. I hate to go all the way back. Would you remove it for me?" The shop girl, who was really a dancer waiting for a break, used her clipper and removed the offending tag. Tomorrow, Brooke said to herself. I will return the dress or I will pay for it, but how without admitting I took it can I do either?

The Evil Inclination was pleased as Punch and as full of fight as Judy. The day had been his.

30

LAW AND ORDER IN
THE REAL CITY,
NOT THE TV CITY

t was shady under the bridge. That's why the two boys who had been practicing their basic skills took off their well-worn baseball gloves and lay down in the dry grass. Dust got on their shirts and shorts, but they didn't care. The ball lay between them, inert for the moment, silent, as is the way with balls. But then one of the boys flicked it with his foot, and the ball rolled forward and down a slope and came to rest at the base of the steel pillar that formed one leg of the bridge. There was a cooler, a red-topped Styrofoam cooler which had stopped the ball from falling in the water among the discarded cardboard cups, abandoned plastic containers, and one brassiere (hopefully removed willingly by its owner). The boys opened the cooler. Treasure, cold drinks, beer—they had hopes. What they saw was a little girl dressed as if for her first communion, all white ruffles and tulle. Her face was bloated, dried blood on her skin. Her eyes were open, but one was blood-filled, the other seemed torn. "Wow," said one of the boys, "it's just like *Law and Order* but in real life." "Yeah," said the other boy, "and we've got bit parts."

In no time the police were there. The dead girl's picture was in the papers. The identification was made. It wasn't a mystery for long. The child was supposed to be under the watch of the Human Resources Department. The mother had been reported for abuse before. Her other children had been taken from her. This one had slipped through a crack. Some cracks are wide enough for a body of a five year old to fall through.

When Ruth read about it in her morning paper, which carried a picture of the two boys who found the body, she said, "Look at that. Art really does imitate life." "But," said Mel, "*Law and Order* isn't art. Not my idea of art." "You don't think it high tragedy, a little girl beaten to a pulp by her mother?" Ruth was not an elitist, something she thought Mel was. In his heart, he was.

"I don't understand it," Ruth said to Mel as they prepared to go out to a benefit for AIDS patients in Zanzibar at which Reverend Crick was prepared to make a long speech. Mel had been forewarned by Moe Alter that he might not like the speech but should applaud and smile anyway. "The social worker lost the records? The social worker faked the records?" "The mother fooled her. I think," said Ruth, "you ought to buy those people some up-to-the minute computers." "It isn't the computers," said Mel. "It's the numbers, the daze those social workers get into, like medical residents working forty-eight hours without sleep. Besides," he said, "there isn't any money for new computers."

Brooke and Jacob joined them at the benefit. Brooke was wearing a black dress with a white star at the waist. "You look so beautiful," Jacob whispered in her ear as he led them to their appointed table. Brooke blushed. Jacob took this as a sign of her love for him, which was just as well. As the dessert plates were being cleared, Reverend Crick was introduced. His speech went on and on. What he said was, "Is no one responsible for Amanda Rolland? Did the mayor shut his ears to her cries? Who heard this little girl call out for help as her mother stamped on her back? Who ignored Amanda? Who should pay for her death? Should the good people of the city not rise up and demand of their leaders responsibility? Go to jail. You have killed a little girl." The mayor was stolid. The expression on his face did not change. The cameras came close to his table. Brooke was glad she was wearing her new dress. Reverend Crick pointed his finger at the mayor. "Our children need better care. In Zanzibar they cannot save the helpless little ones, but here in our great country, in this great city, it seems as if we cannot save them, either." He shouted out these last words and was greeted with thunderous applause. "He's good," said Ruth. "You have to give him that. He's got everyone worked up."

As they waited for their car at the entrance to the hotel, the mayor turned to Brooke. "Great dress," he said. "I may look bad tonight, but you look spectacular." Brooke sneezed. Fortunately, not on her dress.

"Of course we can afford it," Neil Maguire told his wife as they sipped their decaf coffee at their anniversary dinner at the Oz Restaurant, which the Zagat guide had given a 28. Said Bettina Maguire, who didn't want to be rude when she had just been given such a gorgeous gift, such a sparkling bracelet, "I don't need a real diamond bracelet." "Of course you don't need it," said Neil. "But you should have it. It belongs to you. You have a wonderful arm, it could've been on one of those Greek statues they have in the museum. Perhaps it is one of those lost arms. We might have to return it." She laughed. "You have perfect wrists." He grabbed her arm and, drawing it to him, kissed it just above the bracelet, just where her vein pulsed. Her eyes were bright, and not just from the wine.

The children had worn her out. The horrible times with Kevin, the terrible ache of his sickness, the fear that never left her that it was her fault, that she had harmed him in some way, had eroded her face. His strangeness wore on her and made her forget to wash her hair or clean the bedroom. The way things just went on, the others talking to each other, not to her, the peculiar feeling she got each morning that she had been passed by—by what or for what, she didn't know—seemed now to disappear, wiped out by the glint of the diamonds reflecting the candlelight in the center of their table. Bettina felt girlish, like dancing. She once again was overcome with love for her husband. She was in seventh heaven, which is located very near hell.

When Ruth looked at the photo of the child's mother being hustled into the police station, she gasped. The woman looked like a scarecrow whose straw had been removed. There was a bald spot on the side of her head where she had torn out her own hair. There was law and there was order, but was there justice? Fade out. Credits. Forget it, Ruth told herself.

31

NEIL MAGUIRE GOES DOWN
TO THE DOCKS

Neil Maguire was the kind of man who was very anxious that no one should think him anxious, overeager, or near an edge, any edge at all. He looked everyone in the eye, and even if his palms were sweaty he shook hands, hugged, or patted a colleague on the back. Back in high school he had learned—when he hadn't made a team, or lost an election for class president, or received a mark one might not want to boast about—that all would be forgotten if he smiled or winked or shrugged.

Neil had discovered a certain basic masculine principle: never let anyone see your beating heart, your shaking guts, your sorrow. He had discovered that a deep laugh and an expression of concern for his fellow man went a long way in providing him with ample cover. The fact that he was a large man who carried too much weight in his stomach for his doctor's approval helped him seem like a presence, a force, a kindly soul. His daughters threw their arms around his bulky middle and clung to him and clamored at him until finally in exhaustion he would drop into his chair and pretend to fall asleep. His sons came to him for advice, insisted he attend all their games. His oldest son, Kevin, still dreamed that his father would discover the medicine that would cure his illness, despite the frequently stated fact that the elder Maguire had never pretended to be a scientist hot on the trail of a new cure for troubled brains.

There was nothing fraudulent about him. His smile was sweet. He had allergies to chocolate and strawberries. He was soft and spongy as a wetland in need of preservation. His eyes behind his glasses misted over at Disney videos. He whispered endearments into the ears of the family dog, who licked his face in return. If he had a problem, it had to do with ambition. Why, for example, was Mel Rosenberg the mayor when he himself was a more popular man, a more obvious choice? Why had it always been assumed that of the two men, Mel would climb upward and he would be an aide, a party functionary, a recipient of favors? He was disappointed in himself. He was, although he didn't know it himself, hungry for applause. Better things should have come his way.

Maybe this was why he asked his assistant to make a luncheon appointment with the owner of Prix Fixe Towing. They met in a restaurant near the docks, which not so long ago had been filled with cargo ships loading and unloading but now stood like gaping mouths, piers rotting, a spot for lovers and thieves to meet and greet, for the homeless to spread their blankets out in the sun, for adolescents to dream of civilizations lost in the rages of time.

The Three Kings Restaurant was a beacon of light next to a warehouse whose heavy aluminum doors were covered with graffiti. The walls were crimson, and the light fixtures might have come from a set in Transylvania. The waitresses wore tiny skirts and pink blouses. The mirror behind the long bar was decorated with Christmas lights despite the warm weather, and the bartender's hair stood up in spikes. Neil thought that it had been unwise to wear his good watch to such a place. He told himself that he was just doing his job, meeting with a prospective contractor whose bid seemed reasonable enough but whose character he needed to judge.

The owner of Prix Fixe appeared in a suit and tie and ordered a tomato juice. "AA," he confided to Neil. "One day at a time," he added. "Good for you," said Neil. "Found my higher power," said the man. "Right," said Neil.

Neil ordered the pasta special and a glass of Australian cabernet. His companion ordered a Caesar salad and sparkling water. "I go fishing," he said, "on my own boat. You like fishing?" Neil admitted he liked fishing. "You own a boat?" The man leaned forward, his tie in his salad. "No," Neil answered. "Not in your budget?" asked his companion cheerfully. "No," said Neil. "Could be," said his companion. "Don't think so—lots of kids," Neil said, and shrugged. "Oh, you could have a boat if you liked. One for each of your kids if you liked." The man from Prix Fixe put down his fork as Caesar dressing slipped down his chin. "I see for you a very prosperous future."

Neil laughed. His stomach turned. Sweat appeared on his forehead. Joy leaped in his breast. A boat. He had always wanted one of those big ones, with a canopy and a place for the fishing poles in the front and a chair he could swivel and he really would enjoy a big wake following him about the ocean.

Ina was holding Noah, who had called out in terror in the middle of the night. He had woken from a nightmare. His covers were tossed on the floor. His face was flushed. He held on to her arms so tightly she felt pain. She made soothing noises. She kissed his head, the tips of his ears. It was not right, she felt, that a boy, a mere child, should have in his head frightening images, savage images. Finally he relaxed in her arms. Something about a clock that had opened its mouth and devoured his stuffed elephant was all he could explain. She hadn't understood just what it was that he had seen but she knew it was awful. Why? she wondered. Why?

After he had fallen back to sleep, a serene calm restored to his face, she lay awake in her bed puzzling. What was in the child's heart that made his dream so bad? Was a dream really a wish? What terrible thought was plowing through his mind? Was there no such thing as innocence? She laid her head on her pillow and waited for dawn.

32

A DARK DAY FOR THE
CASEWORKER'S SHADOW

Mel pulled his chair up to the paper-flooded desk of one Susanna Marshall, CSW. She was startled, becoming increasingly alarmed as she noticed the two photographers aiming their cameras at her head. She wanted to reach for her lipstick but suppressed the impulse. The aisles of her office on the third floor of the Health and Human Resources Center were filled with police officers, men in suits wearing visitor's badges and press badges, a reporter in a very short skirt who seemed attached to the mayor's elbow.

The desks were placed inches apart. The bathroom key hung from a bulletin board in the supervisor's cubicle. There was a lone window at the end of the long room. It looked out on a brick wall. The linoleum floor was in need of a mop. A wastepaper basket overflowed with paper coffee cups. Despite a red-lettered NO SMOK-ING sign the office smelled of nicotine, also of mint chewing gum.

"May I introduce myself?" Mel asked. "I'm going to be following you around today. Think of me as your shadow. I want to learn about what you do." Susanna Marshall felt her heart race. Why her? "I do the best I can," she said. "I'm sure you do," said Mel. He was sure. He wasn't faulting her, not her personally. But he did need to know why children in his city were sometimes treated like stray cats. If it was his fault, it was his fault. But ignorance was no excuse. Mel had a conscience swollen and oversize, sore and easily inflamed. However, he wasn't the sort of man who lolled around in a bath of guilt. He charged forward. A mistake, even his own, could be mended. If he didn't believe that, he would have gone to bed and never gotten up. He would never have been elected mayor. No one votes for a man who convicts himself without a fight.

"Today," he told Susanna, "I'm all yours. You set the schedule. You tell me what to do. I'll carry your briefcase if you like." He smiled at her. Was he serious about the briefcase? In fact Susanna found the sheer weight of the papers she toted from place to place in a well-worn bag a reason to wish she had another job, perhaps as a prison guard.

"I have nine families to visit today," Susanna explained. "They are not in the same neighborhood. We could take your car," she suggested. "No," said Mel, "pretend I'm not here. Just go about your work as usual." "Sure," said Susanna. The cameras flashed. They caught a furtive look in the social worker's eye. The mayor was thinking about where he would find the money to replace the linoleum or perhaps move the offices altogether, into better quarters.

It was early in the afternoon when Mel, whose feet were beginning to ache, walked up the five flights to an apartment in a neighborhood known for the fine quality of its chop shops. The press was right behind him. Maddie was by his side. Susanna rang the bell. A woman was screaming inside. A man was yelling. A child was wailing. In the hall in front of the door a small boy wearing only one sneaker was curled up in a ball. There was a bad smell floating down the stairwell. "This," said Susanna, "is a family in transition." "What the hell does that mean?" Mel asked. Susanna said, "The man may be moving out." The door was opened just a peek. Susanna identified herself. "The social work jerk is here," the woman said. "Stay out," the man shouted from inside, and they heard a metallic thud against the wall. Mel said, "I'm Mel Rosenberg, the mayor of the city. Let me in." The door slammed, and then suddenly it opened. An arm pulled Mel forward. The mayor found himself standing in the middle of the floor. A little girl was weeping. Her face was swollen. Her foot was twisted. The woman was swearing. The man slammed the door in the face of the press, the police, and Susanna, who had leaped backward as the mayor was pulled forward. The man waved a gun in Mel's face. "I got the mayor," he shouted from behind the door. "I got the mayor. Don't you dare come in here or you got a dead mayor."

Mel crouched down on the floor, "Hello, sweetie," he said to the little girl. "We are going to help you." She pulled away from his touch but kept staring at him. "It's all right," he said. "I'm here." So he was.

When Ruth heard, she wanted to smack Mel, the way you smack a child who runs into the street without waiting for the light. "Take me there,"she said to the police officer who had brought her the news. "I don't know," he said. "Do it," she ordered.

Meanwhile Neil Maguire had taken the afternoon off. "Dentist," he told his assistant. In the local diner he changed into his jeans and a T-shirt. Neil covered his large face with suntan oil. He didn't want to get skin cancer. He wore his St. Cat's baseball hat. He met Arnie from Prix Fixe Towing at the docks for an afternoon of fishing. The boat, *The Long John Silver,* had a captain and a crew of two. It was headed out past the lighthouse, where the big blues waited, and sometimes a striped bass or two. "Yeah, it's mine," said Arnie. The boat's motor made a wide wake, and the sun dimpled on the white water. Neil stretched out his arms and took a beer when it was offered by his companion. There was no need for words. Everything was just perfect.

It took a while for the fish to take the bait. If it was easy, if it was just a given that you got a fish, there would be no contest, no sport, no triumph in the thing. The radio from the captain's podium reported the quietness of the fishing scene from other nearby boats. The boat rocked gently, and Neil had to fight off the urge to close his eyes and drift off to sleep. A seagull honked its unlovely call, and a plastic Coke bottle floated by. The rods were baited by a crew member.

Arnie was talking about a racehorse he wanted to buy a half share in. Neil was thinking of pulling out his wallet and showing Arnie pictures of his kids when there was a sudden downward nod of his line, a pull toward the bottom that meant only one thing: a fish. Neil was up on his feet, reeling and pulling and holding his rod high, as he knew he should. The thing at the end of his line was electric, fighting for its life. Blood rushed to Neil's head. His arms began to ache. The fish was not giving up. Neil leaned over the side of the boat. He smelled the salt of the sea. At last the fish came up to the surface, and a crew member hauled it in with his net. The fish was gasping for air, its eyes looking unseeing at its captors, its gills oozing blood. Another crew member took a club and knocked the fish on the head and it lay there, its life over. Neil was exultant. It was a big bass, over 20 pounds. Arnie slapped Neil on the back. "That was great. Wasn't that great?" Neil agreed.

"You want," said Arnie, "we could go out again next week." Neil wanted. And God, how he wanted a boat of his own.

Mel was not a veteran. This was not a sorrow to him, although like all men he had wondered how he would have fared on Omaha Beach, at Okinawa. Judging from his general belief in the worthiness of words, the uselessness of fists, a horror of guns, a fear of blood, a conviction that seemed to have come to him with his mother's milk that cowardice was not so much a vice but a survival technique, he suspected he would never have won a Purple Heart.

He had daydreamed, of course, of great warrior feats. He had a plan to blow up the Nazis as they moved down the streets of the Warsaw ghetto. He and a few friends had successfully wiped out entire SS battalions several times over during the summer before his seventh-grade year. But as for reality, he had not considered—

until he took political office, that is—that something skin-rupturing, brain-spilling might happen to him. He had directed his attention to his sometimes high cholesterol and occasionally obstreperous blood pressure. When he did think about his own death, he assumed it would come from the prostate or some other inner site that he could neither scratch nor see nor supervise in its daily task.

But now here he was. The man was screaming at the woman about her theft of his money. The child was whimpering. The woman was weeping and running about in circles, and the man was waving his gun. "Your baby is scared," said Mel. The man said, "That's not my baby. She belongs to the whore." "Did you hurt the child?" Mel asked, the way you might ask if a cook had put salt in the soup. "Goddamn," yelled the man. "She's the one who hurts Teresa." Curse words flew about the room as if they were birds in a crowded cage. Even the baby said something that sounded like "Fuck you."

There was pounding on the door. "What do you want? What can we do for you?" Mel heard the voice of the hostage negotiator shouting through his megaphone in the hall. The man turned up the television volume as high as it would go. On the screen it looked like a car was about to receive the rapture and be lifted up to heaven from the highest peak of a mountain. Music filled the room. Why, Mel wondered, would anyone want a car that could dangle from a cliff? You could take a plane if you wanted to be near the clouds.

The man had not put the gun down. He pointed it at Mel. He pointed it at the woman. Mel considered the possibility of diving for the guy, throwing him off balance, and sitting on his chest until the police broke down the door. If this were a movie, he thought, that's just what would happen. If this were a television show, we'd have a commercial break. Mel was not smaller than the man, but he was clearly less prepared for the encounter. His tie was in place. His jacket, although of an excellent fabric, did not seem to be made for jumping on a fellow human. He couldn't get his muscles to move. He looked at Teresa, who had crawled over to the side of the ratty couch that seemed to be crumbling into the floor. He saw what he hadn't seen before, a wide red burn mark on her back. He saw blisters on her thighs, round shapes just the size of a cigarette end. He wanted to yell out the door to the social worker, "Where were you when this was happening? Where was everyone?"

Mel was tired. Excitement did that to him. He sat down. The man with the gun yelled, "Get up, get up." "Why?" said Mel, and didn't move. "I want to talk to Mayor Rosenberg," said the hostage negotiator. "Let me hear his voice." Mel shouted out the door, "I'm fine." "Send up some beers," the man said. "I prefer iced tea," said Mel. "I'm going out that door," said the woman, and she put her hand on the knob. "Bitch, you stay here," said the man. He grabbed her by the waist and pulled her backward. In that moment Mel walked over to Teresa. "Hey, honey," he said, "how about I lift you up?" The little girl stared at him. Mel picked up the child. She smelled of unchanged diaper, of orange juice, of spit-up. She had big eyes with long lashes. Mel kissed her on the nose. The child turned her head away but clutched his shoulder tightly.

The television now showed a diamond bracelet turning around by itself on the screen. The shopping channel. That's what they were watching.

Sirens blared in the street. "Beer and iced tea, outside the door," said a voice. "I'm not opening this door," said the man. "Then the beer will get warm," came the answer. The man kicked the woman in her shin. She screamed. "Everybody stay calm," the negotiator said. Mel knew that sharpshooters would be perched on the nearby roof and the fire escape across the way. He knew that the police were packed like sardines in the hallway. "Stay calm," he yelled. "I'm fine, we're fine in here." The little girl began to sob. "No, no," said the mayor, "don't cry." He began to sing: "*Avinu Malkeinu*—" "Shut up," said the man. Mel stopped singing. Whatever had made that come into his head?

Time passed. Ruth's voice came through the crack in the door. "Mel, Mel, are you all right?" "Sure," said Mel. Teresa seemed to be glued to his chest. He rocked back and forth on his heels. "We're coming in if you don't come out," came an ultimatum from the police. "Wait," said Mel, but the police were in no mood for waiting. There was a pounding on the door. The man waved his gun. "The mayor is dead," he shouted, and turned toward Mel. At that moment Mel rushed to the open window and, looking down, he jumped. He held the baby up in the air. He turned himself over so that he would land on his back. She would be cushioned by his fall. It was only two stories. Not a jump a man would wish to make, but under the circumstances his only choice. He heard his leg crack before he felt it. There was a pain in his shoulder and a thumping in his head. He heard shots, and then he was surrounded by police, red-faced, panting, upset police. He was not dead. His back was bruised but not broken. His elbow was the size of a grapefruit.

Susanna Marshall swept Teresa off to what was intended to be a better life. She had to pry the child's fingers from Mel's neck. "What were you thinking?" said Ruth. "You could've killed your-self." "But I didn't," said Mel. The papers said the mayor had saved the child. He had also saved himself.

"Do you suppose," said Mel to his wife when she visited him in the hospital, "we could raise one more child?" "No," said Ruth. She brought the iced tea up to his lips so he could have a sip.

33

INA AND BROOKE
PUT BOTH FEET ON
THE WRONG PATH

Sisters-in-law are not necessarily birds of a feather. This was certainly so of Ina and Brooke. They had not chosen each other but were nevertheless (in some arrangement that seemed permanent whether it was or not) stuck together at family dinners, at public events, in gossip columns, in photo albums, as tablemates for the long haul of weddings and funerals, election nights and campaign dinners, graduations, benefits, and all major Jewish and American holidays.

They made an unlikely couple. Ina was a scientist above all. Things followed from premises; order could be discerned if you stared hard enough. Ina was small and dark and moved abruptly as if her mind was racing and her muscles following. Brooke, on the other hand, must have been a former homecoming queen, Ina thought, or if not exactly the queen, then certainly a runner-up. She knew how to smile at the camera and tilt her head so that her hair hung across her cheek like a movie star's. Brooke herself believed that she was no one, from nowhere. Brooke believed that nothing had ever happened of interest to her own family, whereas the entire twentieth century had happened to her husband's people. Brooke was always worried that she might miss the joke. Ina was worried that whether he admitted it or not, her husband, Sergei, would have preferred a long-legged woman like Brooke. Ina, of course, loved Jacob like a brother, which is to say it might have been easier if one of them had moved out of town.

So when Ina called to alert Brooke to the fact that Sergei's recently arrived from the FSU brother, Leonid, had come upon a truckload of designer shoes and would allow the two sisters-in-law to have their pick at seven o'clock that very night on a street near the unloading docks, Brooke was more than a little pleased. First of all, she loved a bargain. Second of all, she wanted Ina to like her. If she could make Ina like her, then all the rest of the family would follow suit. Also, she liked the idea of something that offered a whiff of the underworld and mob movies. She loved mob movies. "Where did Leonid get the shoes?" she asked. "Don't ask," said Ina.

The two women took a subway almost to the end of the line. "Do you think it's safe to walk around out here?" said Brooke as they emerged from the stairwell. "Leonid will meet us," said Ina, and sure enough, there was Leonid, a leather jacket, a red shirt, a tattoo of barbed wire on the back of his neck. "Does Sergei know we're here?" Brooke asked. Sergei didn't. Brooke was glad she had brought her cell phone. Ina had brought cash in her pocketbook. If you happen to have a brother-in-law like Leonid, you should at least have wonderful shoes, thought Ina. Brooke was worried. Was this illegal? Jacob hated her to do anything illegal. He wouldn't let her exaggerate on her taxes. He wouldn't let her hide her perfume from the customs officer when they returned from their honeymoon. He was a straight arrow. He was a member of the bar. Leonid took Brooke's elbow. "You are like a lioness running in our streets," he said into her ear. Ina heard him. She was sorry she had signed papers promising to be responsible for him for God knew how long—forever, maybe. She considered writing a letter. *Dear Immigration Officer,* it would begin. Of course she would never do that. Sergei said his brother had been his right arm, his strength. But for Leonid he might never have received his passport, his visa. Ina suspected that neither of their documents would hold up to careful examination, but that didn't matter now. "We walk a block to the warehouse," said Leonid, "and you will see I have made for you a private sale. Great deals," he said, patting Brooke on her arm and sending shivers up and down her spine. "I'm so happy to meet you, Leonid," she said.

Ina sighed. Leonid took out a cigarette and lit it in the dark, his lips moist on the paper. "You should stop smoking," said Ina. "I will," said Leonid, "when I find the love of my life." His eyes flashed. Brooke gasped.

A large truck was parked on a deserted street. Leonid's partner, Ari, an Israeli former moving man turned American entrepreneur, opened the back of the truck. There were shoes: high heels, designer shoes, Nicole Miller, Manolo Blahnik, velvets, patent leathers with rhinestone buckles, pink and blue shoes, dark boots with fur trim. "Ah," said Brooke. "Ah," said Ina. "We've arrived at Imelda heaven." They were deep into the truck when the sound of a car, or was it two cars, came down the street. There were bright lights, there was a siren. Leonid jumped off the back of the truck and ran off down the alley, and Ari streaked forward and jumped into the water at the end of the pier, which Ina thought was not such a good idea because the water was sure to be contaminated and he would get impetigo or worse. When the police climbed into the back of the truck they found no men at all, only two women in their bare feet, clutching three pairs of shoes in their arms.

In the back of the police car on their way to the station Ina looked down at Brooke's feet. She had managed to replace her own shoes with a pair from the truck. She was now wearing ostrich-skin pumps in a butter-colored beige. Damn it, thought Ina, who without thinking in all the shouting had put on her own three-year-old black flats with the worn-down heels. "I think I'm going to cry," said Brooke. "You would," said Ina. Sergei, she thought, is not his

brother's keeper. He was working late in his lab, a complete innocent, which was more than could be said for his wife.

Mel was considering the Atkins diet. When the phone rang he
was explaining to Ruth its main theory, that carbohydrates are evil.
It was Jacob. The news was grim. It was serious. It would be in the
papers. He was on his way to the police station. Mel said he would
meet him there. "Don't be an idiot, Dad," said Jacob. "Stay out of
this." Mel hung up the phone. He began to laugh. He laughed so
hard, he could hardly explain the catastrophe to Ruth, who wondered why she hadn't been invited along. After all, you don't stop
needing beautiful shoes just because your youth is over.

34

BROOKE'S EYES GLITTER
FOR SEQUINS

As of September first, we'll use Prix Fixe for towing," Neil announced to his staff. "But," said Geraldo, whose office had vetted the bids, "Prix Fixe is not the lowest bidder or the company with the best efficiency rating." "Ah," said Neil, "figures don't reveal all. Your ratings are arbitrary, done without a feel for the human element. I have personally spoken with the people at Prix Fixe and believe beyond a shadow of a doubt that they will perform far better than their nearest competitor. Performance, that's what counts." Neil smiled, his sweet big smile.

A small bead of sweat had formed near the parking commissioner's temples, but no one noticed. Prix Fixe it was. The other bids went right into the reject file. To celebrate, Neil took his son Kevin out to a steak house for a father-son dinner. Neil didn't mind that Kevin seemed uninterested in the challenges a parking commissioner faced. Kevin just stared at his juicy steak as if eel or octopus had been placed before him. Neil didn't mind that Kevin fell asleep in his chair before the dessert was served. He himself felt joyous, liberated, an aristocrat among the peasants, someone in on the joke at last.

He had just opened a deliciously fat checking account separate from the one he shared with his wife. At the bank he gave as his address his sister's home in the suburbs. It seemed to him as if some court case had been settled, some heavenly adjustment in the fairness scale had occurred, and all he had done was taken advantage of an opportunity. What could be more American than that?

The police were not truly interested in Brooke or Ina, and finally, after a much-photographed perp walk, believed Ina's story about meeting a man at the luncheonette, where she had ordered a tuna fish sandwich to go, and the man had invited her to a shoe sale and promised prices that were out of this world. A police car took the women home in the wee hours of the morning. Sergei was worried that Leonid would be caught and deported. Jacob was furious with Brooke because her picture, not a bad-looking one at that, was on the cover of the daily tabloid, with the headline "Mayor's Girls Well Heeled." Exactly the sort of publicity Jacob's firm abhorred. It made him look cheap. It made him look small. "For God's sake, Brooke, go to a department store if you want a pair of shoes," he yelled.

It wasn't shoes Brooke wanted when she went back to Manny's several days later. She wanted a sequined jacket that she had seen in a magazine while she was having her hair cut. It flowed in the back, it plunged in the front. It was silver and had a trim of white feathers at the neckline. The designer was so hot, you could burn three western states with his reputation. Everyone said that. Brooke made plans to capture the jacket the way industrialists plan to capture markets, and academics intend to capture prizes, and moviemakers intend to secure audiences, and TV producers scheme to get their ratings. In other words, she applied her intelligence to the problem at hand.

Brooke's cleaning woman had arrived not quite legally from El Salvador only months before and did not yet speak English. Brooke, who had spent her junior year in Madrid, was able to instruct Gloria to call the police from the phone at the public library, which was near the park where Gloria took the twins. She told her to say two words, *bomb,* and *Manny's,* and then hang up. Gloria mastered both words and said them as she was instructed to the police receptionist, who relayed the call. Brooke was strolling through the designer racks in Manny's, flicking price tags, aimlessly circling the floor, when suddenly the fire alarm sounded. The salespeople rushed to the stairs, followed by the few customers who were on the floors or in the dressing rooms. Police were at the door, sirens wailed. The police gathered by an old handbag that Brooke had placed on the sunglasses counter. It looked fat, stuffed . . . a bomb? The bomb squad arrived, with masks, with oxygen tanks, with grim expressions on their leathery faces. Why wouldn't you be grim if your job was to defuse bombs and you hardly ever got to hone your skills, which on the one hand was a good thing and on the other was not?

Brooke was evacuated with everyone else, and like everyone else she stood on the street watching the action. Excited and afraid, like all the others, she watched as the police carried her old handbag out to the street and placed it in a steel box. Unlike all the other gawkers, she had on a remarkable silver jacket with feather trim that seemed a bit dressy for daytime but under the dramatic circumstances attracted no particular attention. This jacket had no store tag on it. Clothes of that elegance and delicacy did not have magnetic clips cutting into the fabulous fabric, worth as much per square foot as all the real estate in Gloria's hometown.

She wore her jacket to a reception for her father-in-law at the Hadleys' on Forest Avenue that very evening. The Hadleys were having a gathering to celebrate the completion of the new wing of Maple Hill Hospital, which had been donated, a tax-deductible gift, by the Hadley family. It would serve the community by offering alternative medicine techniques. It would treat the whole patient rather than just the illness. It would have on staff yoga teachers, meditation counselors, specialists in herbal medicine, acupuncturists, and even a voodoo practitioner from a tropical island for those whose confidence in their treatment would be enhanced by familiar rites. The new wing was painted in soothing pinks and creams. It would attract patients to the hospital, helping to ease certain budget deficits. It would contribute to the reputation of the city as the center of medical innovation. Of course Mel and Ruth and the entire family had been invited to the party, along with the press.

The Hadleys had given funds to the Museum of Contemporary Art, to the Native American Center (Hadley guilt because one of their ancestors had been part of a land trade that lost the local natives their real estate), the opera, Duncan Academy, and Thyme Hall, a girls' school so exclusive that only eighty years ago all its students had been related to the Hadley family. Their charitable gifts were prodigal and welcomed. Their women had been members of hospital boards and orchestra boards and clinics that served the poor for as long as such organizations had existed. No one could accuse the Hadleys of civic indifference. They had, however, been personally entertaining the likes of Mel and Ruth Rosenberg for a far shorter time. Mel knew he had to go to the party because he was mayor of all the citizens of his town, including the Hadleys, like it or not.

"They're going to talk about their polo games," said Mel gloomily to his wife in the car that was bringing them to the party. "Nobody plays polo anymore," said Ruth. "Well, those people would no more have let my father use their toilet than they would have gone naked to church." "Forget it," said Ruth, "don't hold a grudge." "I do," said Mel.

35

SERGEI CRASHES
THE HADLEY PARTY

The first thing to say about the Hadley reception for the new Alternative Healing Center was that the food was very spare—so spare, in fact, that Jacob snatched his wife's endive leaf stuffed with a thumbnail of crabmeat out of her hand without an apology. Mel shook Anston Hadley's hand but instead of looking him warmly in the eyes, as was his usual politician's habit, he kept his eyes on the tray of chestnuts wrapped in bacon that was passing by. "No, thanks," he said as the tray whisked past him and his stomach continued to growl.

The zinnias and carnations, the lilies and the irises bunched together in rainbow bends across the tables in the long living room, whose views took in the green of the park and the blue of the distant river. Jacob held Brooke by the elbow so that she would appear steadier on her feet than she actually was. Her jacket received compliments by the dozens. Ruth went into her purse and pulled out her wallet, showing pictures of her grandchildren to Audrey Hadley, photos of whose own grandchildren, sitting on the steps of an estate with what appeared to be a lawn the size of an early primary state, decorated the piano, each in a shining silver frame. The carpets were so valuable they were frayed with age, and the paintings on the walls were by Dutch masters, actually the students of Dutch masters, "Da Vinci drawings that had belonged to Poppy are on loan to the Louvre," so Anston Hadley explained to all who asked about them. The silverware at the table was monogrammed, the glasses were Steuben, the salt shakers were silver. There was nothing in the apartment that was brand-new; nothing shone one bit more than was decent. The couches were a discreet gray, the walls could have used a bit of paint. There was a brown stain on the windowsill. This was a window that had no need of vulgar preening.

"How did you meet your husband?" Ruth asked Audrey in an attempt to prop up the conversation between them. Audrey gave a quick, tight smile. "At my coming-out party," she said. "It sounds so Edith Wharton," said Ruth. "I don't believe I know her," said Audrey.

"Of course," said Dr. Morse, addressing the gathering from the front of the room, "we do use conventional medicine when it seems in order. All cancer cells do not respond to mood changes, but some do, many do. Of that there is no doubt." "Oh, isn't there," muttered Ina, who despite being young was very old-school. She did not like copper bracelets and weird positions that brought your toes up behind your ears. Sergei laughed. He too believed that if God was in the details, they were details that you could see under a microscope or one day would see when the technology improved. Which is why he emitted a loud noise used in his childhood in Moscow to indicate someone was filled with hot air when a woman stood up to tell the crowd that her rheumatoid arthritis had been cured by diet changes and a special technique of massaging that relaxed the deep muscles and involved being rocked in the masseuse's arms. "Look," she said, "my hands are now restored. I could play the piano."

Fortunately as Sergei emitted his rude sound the grandfather clock, six generations in the family and still going, sounded the hour with loud and solemn bongs. "This goes on all night?" Ruth whispered to Audrey. Audrey said she no longer heard the sound; as a bride it had bothered her, but in time she learned to ignore it. In fact, it was comforting; the ringing of the hour day after day, year after year, had become for her like a watchman walking on the streets, saying all's well, all's well, while swinging his lantern, whether or not all was well in fact.

When they went to their summer place or their Florida home, she confessed, she had trouble sleeping in the absence of the clock. "I would be awake forever without it," she said. "How lovely," said Ruth, thinking kindly of her own little alarm clock with a thumb-sized battery.

Mel was giving a speech about the wonders of philanthropy and how the city could not survive without it when Sergei, who had had a long day of injecting mice with a variety of viruses unknown in mice that lived in the field or behind the bookcases, leaned back against the wall. Just at that moment the woman with the cured arthritis who had made her way to the back of the room saw him, the maker of the scoffing noise. She moved toward him and in a subtle movement that no one else saw shoved him in his middle, not gently, not gently at all. He lost his footing. He fell into the clock. The clock tipped back and forth for a horrible second and then crashed, glass and works spilling on the rug, glass shards biting at nearby ankles. Fortunately, the heavy clock did not fall on anyone. The Imps of Darkness and the Imps of Mischief howled with joy at the ensuing chaos.

As the butlers were sweeping up pieces of glass and carrying out the remains of the clock, which seemed like a coffin in which the Hadley hopes had been buried, out of the Hadley kitchen the maids were bringing trays of bagels and lox and Hebrew National hot dogs with rolls and sauerkraut. "Where did this food come from?" Anston Hadley asked his wife. "I have no idea," she said. "There seems to be so much of it," she added.

Ruth was embarrassed. Mel whispered in her ear, "Never again invite Sergei anywhere." Standing before Ruth was a young woman in black leather pants, red boots, and a glare that was anything but demure. Audrey Anston appeared at Ruth's side. "This is my daughter, Buffy," she said. "Hi, Mom," said Buffy. "I brought Agatha and Tony." Agatha was plump and had short, spiky hair. Tony was four, their adopted son. Audrey leaned down and kissed Tony, who seemed to have come from Guatemala and arrived on Forest Avenue, which was good for him, probably. Ruth checked: Tony's photo was not in a silver frame on the piano. "I would never have imagined," Audrey said to Ruth, "that my daughter would bring me a daughter-in-law and that I would have a coffee-colored grandchild. But I do." She smiled at Ruth.

Ruth invited Audrey to have lunch with her. Ruth was certain Audrey would accept. This was the beginning of an important friendship. What would Edith Wharton have said?

36

THE TRUTH ABOUT
NEIL MAGUIRE

Brooke didn't know how to put it to her mother-in-law—nicely, that is. Ruth had been no Naomi to Brooke, which is an irony that Brooke of course did not appreciate but Ruth did. It is hard to know just what is wanted of a mother-in-law: nothing critical, of course, nothing cruel or condescending, never any expression at all of a wish for a different face at the family table.

Certainly it would be unkind to hold against Brooke the fact that she was born in a town in one of those states that always voted Republican, a town where the bagels were frozen and girls were proud to wave pompoms in the air. But conversation between the two women, even after Brooke had borne Ruth's grandchildren, had remained formal—cordial, of course, but lacking in banter, in tenderness—and had always proceeded cautiously, as if a yellow light blinked continuously above their sentences. It seemed to Ruth a slap in the face that her beloved son had selected for his life partner a woman as unlike herself as could be found in all the known universe.

Mel believed that his son's choice of wife was more of a jab at him, a father who had perhaps been too busy, didn't like throwing a ball in the park, had never liked the Rolling Stones, and had probably failed his child in mysterious ways that couldn't be known or even avoided. This, of course, was true of Abraham and Isaac and Jacob and Esau. Adam wouldn't have gotten the Father of the Year award from Cain, either. History just moved on. Mel wasn't so sorry to have Brooke at his table. She was a beauty. This of course he did not tell Ruth.

How hard it is to know, to really know, to deeply know, the adults your children marry. This, Ruth realized, was not necessarily a problem. A family should not be expected to satisfy every yearning of the heart. The ground was mined with memory, longing, inevitable disappointments. It was enough if things didn't explode. It was all right that Brooke was polite and Ruth was correct in all their conversations.

No, it wasn't all right.

If Ruth had been honest with herself, she would have admitted that spending a few hours with Brooke was enough to leave her depressed for a week. Which is why she sighed when Brooke asked her to lunch. "How lovely," she said to her daughter-in-law. "Spare me," she whispered into her mirror, which never revealed any of her secrets.

Ruth ordered a bowl of chili, and Brooke had a salad of field greens with beets. The restaurant Brooke had chosen had big glass windows that looked over the avenue. Ruth dipped her bread into the little bowl of olive oil placed in front of her. Brooke fiddled with the silverware. "I brought you a present," Brooke said. "It's not my birthday," said Ruth, who was nevertheless pleased. She opened the box placed in front of her. She unfolded the tissue paper. She pulled out a lavender sweater embroidered with beads, a bunch of flowers knitted into the pattern around the neck. Ruth gasped. This was an expensive sweater. This was not her style. She was trying to think of exactly the right words to thank Brooke when Brooke began to speak.

"I think," she said, "you have given up about clothes and things. I think," she added, "you could look more . . . exciting.

You could try. I could help you." Ruth was amazed. Here was an insult packaged in an offer of friendship, or was it an offer of friendship with an insult attached the way a label is sewn into a sweater? "You have a wonderful face," said Brooke. "It's really interesting. But . . . ," Brooke added, and here was the point of the lunch, "you really need to lose fifteen pounds, maybe twenty."

This Ruth knew was true. It had been a while since she had felt that power of hips swinging down the street, legs looking good as she passed by, men turning around for a second glance. It had been a long while since she considered herself a player in the game. She was now, biologically speaking, unnecessary. It grieved her.

"I'll help you," Brooke said. "I'll shop for you. I'll find a good diet for you. You can join my gym." Ruth looked in Brooke's eyes. There she saw what Brooke wanted, what Brooke was missing.

"I'll try," said Ruth. "If you help me, I can do it." In her mind's eye she saw herself young again, firm again, full of estrogen again. (A fantasy, but not a bad one.) It didn't matter, she understood, if she improved her closet's offerings. It only mattered that Brooke wanted to give something to her mother-in-law.

Ruth reached across the table and touched Brooke's face with her hand, gently, the way one might touch the petal of a flower. Brooke began to cry and then had to excuse herself to redo her makeup in the ladies' room.

"Damn," said the salesgirl in the boutique down the street. "Where is that lavender sweater we had out on the table this morning?"

Neil Maguire had been faithful to his wife, Bettina, for all his married life. Which didn't mean he had to be faithful forever. He loved her, of course, in the solid family way a man loves what is his, what he knows, what he has built. But the day after he figured out that the cash deposits to the city account for parking violations required his signature and his signature alone to be withdrawn, he invited the new clerk, Daquinne Johnson, in the Bureau of Records to lunch.

She had been soaking in the sun on the steps of city hall. He sat down next to her and breathed in her perfume and the smell of her herbal shampoo. She had just graduated from high school and lived in a one-room apartment with her mother and her aunt and her two younger sisters. The tops of her coppery breasts peeked out from under her blouse. She wore a gold ankle bracelet that sparkled in the light. She had, she assured him, learned Microsoft Word as well as data entry bookkeeping.

Daquinne had a gap between her two front teeth that Neil found beguiling. She adored the little presents he brought her. Her joy in simple things like a potted plant or a pair of silk pajamas made Neil happy. The rest he also enjoyed. The apartment he moved her into was paid for off the books, as were the courses in management at Agatha Murray's Business School that were meant to improve her job opportunities. All this was paid for in fact by violators of the parking laws. They were certainly not, it seemed to Neil, in a position to point fingers.

Maddie Miller opened a letter at her desk at the newspaper. It was written in a bold cursive hand. It was from the younger sister of a woman who had sold her soul to the devil who was in the parking commissioner's office, very high up. Something very crooked was going on, the letter indicated. "Nothing there," said Maddie's metro editor.

"I'll just check it out," said Maddie, who had a sixth sense that was close to uncanny. Which is why Maddie was in the parking commissioner's office, sitting in his old armchair while he looked her in the eye and expressed total surprise at such an accusation, promised to look into it immediately, and call Maddie if he found anything.

Neil was cool as a summer Popsicle. His hands didn't shake. He wasn't sweating. But he did pull the morning papers over the checkbook that was out on his desk as she entered, Maddie noticed.

37

A CITY
INFLAMED

A cow kicked over a lantern in Chicago and the whole town burned down," Mel muttered as the mayor's car, with its bubble blue police siren on top, roared uptown toward the fire. There had been no floods in the city, but fires were another matter. Fire leaped up staircases. Fire started in abandoned warehouses, smoldered in mattresses, and seared kitchen curtains. Fire started because a wire frayed or because grease spilled on the stove. Fire started because some human being was burned up, red with anger, out of control with grief, or maybe just needy for the insurance. Fire avoided the rich and followed the poor around like a numbers runner.

Fire, friend to those without a shredder, is the quickest way to unbuild, to wreak havoc, to let man pretend he is God. O Prometheus, perhaps you made a mistake. Flames rise from rooftops, searing walls, crumbling staircases, burning up photos of a child's third birthday, diplomas, divorce papers, deeds, wills, wallpaper. Fire seems so primitive, so out of place in a city, so raw and angry. Fire, after all, is unable to submit forms, pay taxes, line up, park on the alternate side of the street, throw litter in the trash can. Fire is for forests. Lightning is for forests. Pilot lights are for cities, radiators are for cities. In short, fire is the unexpected, the outlaw, the face of urban hell itself. It was high noon at 152nd Street and Pine. The siren roared, cars and taxis pulled to the side, the mayor's driver ran the lights, the mayor tilted from side to side as the car swerved and speeded forward.

When they reached the building, Mel saw immediately that the fire was not dying away gracefully. He saw that human faces were peering out of windows on the upper floors. He saw that black smoke curled ominously upward and broken glass lay on the ground. Many fire trucks had gathered. The dark helmets and the black jackets with a yellow stripe down the arm moved back and forth beneath the gray sooty sky, hoses spun their web and buildings cast their silhouettes down the narrow avenue.

Mel heard screams. He heard the firefighters talking over their pocket radios. He saw the slicker-covered figures rush forward into the building when all good sense would have told you to rush the other way. He heard the sound of gushing water. He stood flanked by the fire captain and the commissioner himself as well as an emergency-unit medic in need of oxygen. Mel had never considered himself a coward. On the other hand, he did not consider himself a brave man. These were categories that seemed old-fashioned, naive. But as he watched the firefighters dashing into the building and emerging with black on their faces and eyes wild with what they had seen inside, as he heard the sounds of pouring water, creaking ladders rising from truck beds, and saw the men touch each other on the shoulder, shout out warnings as their boots grew caked with mud and ash, he felt his heart grow heavy with love for them. He moved forward to go closer to the building's entrance. The fire captain smashed a hard hat down on his head.

He buckled the strap that had dangled beneath his chin. "Can I help you?" he asked the nearest firefighter. "No, sir, Mayor Rosenberg," came the answer. "Just stay out of the way." Mel moved forward right behind the man, feeling small, very small. What had he done with his life? There was a loud cracking sound, bricks crumbling, as a floor fell downward. There were shouts and screams and then quiet.

"God," said Mel. But God had no comment. There was a sulfur smell in the air. Someone had died, more than one. Mel thought he heard the playing of bagpipes. He didn't. He stood there, his feet turned to stone. He wished this were a television program or a movie. It wasn't. Mel had the worst thought in the world: orphans.

Hours later they were gingerly loading bodies into an ambulance, one that would head for the morgue for identification, to be claimed by mothers and wives and aunts and children in the days ahead. The press was there, cameras were on, reporters were combing their hair and looking bright-eyed into the lens. They were not at a loss for words. Mel, however, appeared to be unable to speak. The matter was unspeakable. "Mr. Mayor," said the green-eyed reporter from Channel 12, thrusting a mike in his face, "do you have anything to say to the citizens of the city right now?" Mel said nothing. She pursued him. The camera wheeled after him. "Mr. Mayor," she said, "do you think the firefighters deserve a raise? What about an increase in health care benefits, in death benefits? Shouldn't you remove the hiring freeze you imposed last year?"

Mel stopped. He found his voice. "Yes," he said, "the firefighters deserve more money, more money than corporate lawyers and plastic surgeons and investment managers, and yes, they should have more health care and pensions so large that they or their descendants could buy racehorses and mansions by the sea, but there is no more money to be had. You want to take it from the schools, from the clinics, from the prisons? You want to close the prisons?" Mel knew he was not behaving well. "These firefighters deserve the moon and the stars, but they'll get what they have. The budget is a stone. I cannot smite it and produce a well." The reporter gasped. "That's Mayor Rosenberg at 152nd Street and Pine," she said into the camera. When the camera light went out, the mayor hurried toward his car. The reporter followed him. "Mr. Mayor," she said, "your shoelace is undone. You're going to trip." Just as he was about to get into his car he saw Neil Maguire leaning against a lamppost. "What are you doing here?" he asked.

"Just passing by, saw the trucks," Neil said. "I couldn't resist stopping. I'm a fire buff, you know." Neil grinned. But there was something wrong with his smile. It didn't get as far as his eyes.

"Anything wrong?" the mayor asked. "I'm fine, I'm fine," Neil said. But he wasn't. Daquinne Johnson's sister, the envious one who may have written a letter to Maddie Miller's newspaper, lived at 152nd Street and Pine. He had been on his way to offer her a deal, a good deal, but someone seemed to have gotten to her first, or perhaps it was just a coincidence. Please, he thought, let it be a coincidence.

38

A FAMILY KILLED,
A MAN REPENTANT

There were eight victims of the fire: one firefighter and seven citizens. One was an old lady who had perhaps been dead long before the first flame cast its first shadow against its first wall— or so the smell in her apartment might indicate. Sent out into the night, evacuated residents had lost their belongings, destroyed by flame or water. Photos of high school graduations, nursing school diplomas, photos of Christmas trees and birthday cakes as well as green cards, blood pressure medicines, video games, television sets, heaters—they were all gone. Most of the dispossessed had relatives who took them in. A young boy took the opportunity to run off, perhaps to hop a train to a better life, perhaps to end up as a hustler in the park. His aunt would not look for him.

After the fire was out the trucks seemed to hang around, the firefighters slowly winding up hoses, ambulances riding out, each leaving a space on the street. The water ran down the grates in slowing streams. Ash fell from fire escapes. A coat of soot covered the parked cars down the block. A skinny cat ran across a backyard. A small white tow truck with the sign PRIX FIXE TOWING pulled out of an alley and made the light at the corner, disappearing down toward the hospital at the base of the hill.

Neighbors stared long after there was anything to stare at. The reporters were quiet, trying to form words into sentences as their bodies sagged from the letdown after the excitement. Soon they would snap at their editors and their significant others, regretting their choice of occupation. The hydrant at the corner was leaking.

The Johnson family, the aunt, the mother, the two sisters, had been wiped out. The family had been members of the small Baptist church on the next block. The pastor was praying in a fast, furious mumble in front of the twenty-four-hour convenience store, whose window was shattered for reasons that weren't clear. The fire had started in front of the Johnson family's door. It was not, definitely not, the fire inspector on his cell phone told the mayor as his car headed downtown, an accident. Not even possibly. The mayor sighed.

Arson was a crime that was not hard to solve. The arsonist was not often a clever person. Things could be traced, motive found. Sometimes the arsonist was a firebug with dreadful thoughts of hell. Sometimes the arsonist was a gang member or a punk hired by a business executive with a good insurance policy. Sometimes the arsonist was an entire government. Mel thought of the villages of Vietnam burning as one thatched hut after another sizzled beneath the stars.

Neil Maguire put his head on his wife's soft breasts and wrapped his arms around her. He had not meant to betray her with Daquinne Johnson. Gender was the only thing the two women had in common. Daquinne was almost as young as his daughters; at least, she belonged to their generation, not his. He did not love her. He had no history with her. If he never saw her again, it would be all right with him. A certain shiver in his body told him that he wasn't as indifferent to her as he had hoped. He had enjoyed himself enormously. There was something about the forbidden that made a man giddy with delight. He would confess this transgression. To his priest, of course, not his wife—why make her miserable with his misdeeds? Isn't a man entitled to stray once off the path? Isn't a man only a man?

He tried not to feel guilty, or not too guilty, or not so guilty that he would not be able to shake off the guilt and continue as he had. God had created sin when he created man. Daquinne, with her soft brown skin, she was temptation. She too was part of God's plan. But all through the night he stayed awake, clutching at his wife as she turned on her side, away from his hot breath. He did not feel well. His heart kept missing a beat.

Neil got up and went to the window and looked at the half moon. How many men had tasted another woman on the side? Must be in the billions, he reassured himself. He looked at his wife sleeping, trusting him, thinking that her body was the one he turned to for joy, for relief, for comfort, the only body.

Adultery was a big sin. He stood at the window. It was simply not possible that a man with as good a nature as his, as fond of his children (even the sick one) as he was, could be a big sinner. A man who had made a decent living all his life, who paid his bills, contributed to his church, sent his children to religious schools—could such a man be a sinner? The answer he saw in the face of the moon was yes, yes, yes. His stomach cramped. He had made a mistake with Daquinne. He would call it off. He would atone. He would not continue in this state. Dear God, he prayed, don't let anyone find out about my bank accounts. Protect me from my errors.

A wind blew down his block. It scattered the garbage cans. It rattled the windows next door, and it tipped over the bike left in the driveway two doors down. The dog across the street barked. The wind came off the water where Neil kept his boat and blew hard against his door. For a moment Neil was confused. Was he hearing the sound of wind or the sound of laughter? Was someone laughing at him? Neil stared at the roots of his wife's hair. She was late for her appointment at the beauty parlor. She was not as blond as she seemed. He was not as good as he seemed. They were perhaps equal?

The next morning he received a terse phone call. Meet me at our lunch place, said the familiar voice. It was his friend, his good friend, from Prix Fixe. There was something imperial in the tone. Something not quite polite. Neil didn't dare refuse. He had planned to find Daquinne at lunchtime and tell her it all was over. That would have to wait.

At lunch he ordered a scotch and soda. This lunch was a real drink lunch. That he already knew.

"Well," said his friend after they had ordered their steaks, both medium rare, "we do need to get a little more help from you. We want 15 percent return on every car we deliver to the pound. We think that is fair under the circumstances."

"What do you mean?" said Neil, feeling as if he had been punched in the chest. "It's time," said his friend, "that you help us out with a higher rate of return on our investment. Of course, if you don't, certain things can be slipped to certain reporters, and all will become known."

"You can't blackmail me," said Neil, rising to his feet. "I am an innocent man." His luncheon partner was embarrassed for his companion. He crumpled his napkin. Amateurs, he thought. Aloud he said nothing.

Neil sat down. His face had fallen. He looked like a man given a fatal diagnosis. He was.

39

THE MAYOR IS SPAT UPON AT
FIREFIGHTER BILLY FINNEGAN'S FUNERAL

Ruth had a meeting at her foundation with her board and was unable to go to the firefighter's funeral with Mel. She was not happy. She had been working at the Rothman Foundation since before Mel became mayor. She had invited Audrey Hadley to attend the meeting, and who knew what benefits might follow. Besides Jacob and Ina, the foundation was her justification for taking up space on the planet, but she knew that Mel would be missing her by his side. He liked to hold her hand when the coffin passed by. He liked to lean against her shoulder as the priest or minister comforted and exhorted and reminded all that God loved them.

In the hail of clichés, clichés that always accompanied such events, clichés that comforted precisely because they were so familiar they required no mental alertness, Ruth and Mel protected themselves by letting their legs touch, his ankle pressing against hers or her coat placed on his in the next seat. The trick with these funerals, they both had learned, was to stare at the windows and watch the patterns of sun fall through the colored glass, letting no expression cross one's face. And when they saw the widow and they saw the children, they knew they must shake hands and mumble words to ashen faces, allowing themselves only a moment or two of wild despair.

At a funeral despair is contagious, infectious, runs riot through the room. There is no vaccine for this. Ruth could feel her nose turn red as tears gathered behind her dark glasses. Mel would breathe deeply, concentrate on his rib cage, try not to think of his own father and mother, dig his fingers into his wife's arm as if she were his life raft and he was lost at sea. The trick was to push all that dark emotion away in time for the cameras, in time for the rest of the day to receive its due.

This time Mel would have to take his daughter, Ina, who had agreed to go in Ruth's place. Ina wore her black suit. She wore a gold circle pin on her lapel. She wore a yellow blouse with a diamond pattern. "Daddy," she said as they rode in the car to the distant neighborhood where Billy Finnegan had lived, "does anybody love anybody forever?" Mel heard her, a warning sound in his sky, a whisper of thunder that spoke of an approaching storm. "What are you talking about?" he said. "I don't know," said Ina. "You do know," said Mel. "Is it Sergei?" "No," said Ina. There was silence in the car. There is a way that a man knows his daughter that is quite beyond words; it has to do, perhaps, with animal smell, with the sharp regret a man feels when he realizes that his girlchild is not his alone, not forever.

Mel waited. Ina said, "I think he may find me dull." "Are you dull?" asked Mel. "Maybe," said Ina. They arrived at the Church of Perpetual Divinity. There were TV cameras at the steps. Ina blinked at the lights. She smiled because of the cameras. "Don't smile," whispered Mel. She had always smiled at cameras, a fake, stiff, hopeful, uneasy smile. The Rosenberg family albums were stuffed with that smile. Mel felt like crying already and he hadn't yet seen the widow and the two little boys at her side, one holding his father's helmet and the other what appeared to be a stuffed rabbit with one ear gone.

The service was not unusual. The coffin was covered with an American flag. Afterward bagpipes played on the church steps. Ina bent down and kissed one of the little boys on his cheek; the other dashed off behind his mother. Then one of the mourners came up to the mayor and spat in his face. "It's your fault, you son of a bitch. You cut the number of firemen down at our station. You didn't get us the new truck we were promised. You as good as killed Billy."

The words were heard all around. The mayor's personal staff reached out to grab the man, but the mayor moved faster than they did. He shoved the man in his chest, a hard shove that sent him reeling backward. "This isn't the place or the time for this," he said. There was a murmur in the crowd, the cameras gathered round like flies around the picnic table.

With his hand on the fellow's chest, Mel spoke. "The city does not have the money for more firefighters. We need firefighters. We gotta have people willing to give their lives for someone else in this town. Without that we become a city of piranhas. But I can't print dollars in the back of your firehouse. We have to make do. We have to go on together," he said, adding, "even if we are broke."

The young widow made her way up to the mayor and held out her hand. "Thank you for coming," she said. Mel reached out and gave her a hug. He held her in his arms, feeling her heart's quick beat, smelling the shampoo she had used that morning, the morning of her husband's funeral.

Someone threw a tomato at the mayor. It landed on Ina's face. Pulp ran down onto her yellow blouse. "Daddy," she whimpered. The police surrounded her and pushed through the crowd. The mayor, too, was surrounded by uniforms and cameras and a Secret Service agent, who appeared all of a sudden on the steps. The Imps of Misfortune howled with glee. One of them punctured the front tire of the mayor's car. *Crunch, crunch,* it went, and stopped. "Well," said the mayor when they were finally on their way, transferred into another car, "at least I wasn't shot."

Leonid walked down the deserted street to the corner in front of a dark warehouse where a single blue light flickered. There was a steel door and several large men guarding it. The hour was late. There were limos and bored drivers waiting. Leonid was let into the huge room where the music pounded and silhouetted figures danced wildly and strobe lights crisscrossed each other. The bar at the top of the stairs was crowded, and there was a smell in the room of striving id—of the limbic brain, of primal instincts seeking gratification, and flesh, vulnerable mortified flesh, sweating in clouds of smoke. Leonid had a drink and then another. He made his way to the bank of phones on a velvet wall. He dialed. A sleepy voice answered. It was Brooke. "It's me, Leonid. Want to come dance?"

40

BROOKE'S
SECONDHAND LIFE

Brooke hung up on Leonid. She put her head back down on her pillow, but she didn't fall asleep.

She stared at the rumpled hair of her husband, at the back of his neck, which was so white and somehow frail, a kind of stem that could easily be snapped. She stared at her closet thinking about what she would wear if she were going out dancing, which of course she wasn't. The phone rang again. It was Leonid. "Take a cab," he said. "434 Port Side. I'll meet you outside." "What time is it?" Brooke asked. "Time for change," said Leonid.

The doorman was sleeping on a bench when she slipped out. The cab driver said, "You look great, lady," as she opened her compact and checked her makeup for the fourth time. Inside the club the music drummed on. Her head spun. Her feet, too, as Leonid held her, swung her around, tipped her toward him, let his hands slide down her dress. "I'm married," she said to him. "I don't want to marry you," he answered, shouting above the noise. "Why not?" Brooke asked, offended despite herself. "I only marry a Jewish girl, Russian I prefer," he said. "Oh, that," said Brooke, and tossed her hair and let her white arms fly up toward the strobe lights. "Are you having fun?" Leonid asked. "Yes," said Brooke. She looked around at the waving limbs on the dance floor. She looked at Leonid, who moved like a wolf, sure on his feet. His eyes seemed to catch the light and hold it still, like a wild animal in the forest. She smoked what he offered. She drank what he put to her lips. She sat in the back of his car, which smelled of cheese and rubber. She allowed him to lie against her. Dawn was approaching. It was time for wolves to go back to their lairs. The new white light of tomorrow was seeping over the horizon's edge; soft and nonjudgmental, it inserted itself into her mind. Was she dreaming?

She arrived home just as the sky burst into pink and the street-lights extinguished themselves like souls that had overstayed their welcome. She went into her children's room. There they were, Kim asleep with her rabbit in her arms. Kelly with the covers off and her gym shorts on and a strange tattoo she had given herself with Magic Marker on her small chest. Brooke stared at her children as if she had never seen them before. If secondhand smoke could harm you, could inhaling a secondhand life, their mother's life, harm them? What was wrong with her? Why had she gone out of her house? Looking for what? And had she found it? Brooke was already in tears when Jacob, not finding her in bed next to him, woke and came into his children's room. "Why are you dressed like that? You can't take them to school in that outfit," he whispered, not wanting to wake the children. "I couldn't sleep. I had a bad dream. I was just trying on the dress to see if it still fit," Brooke said. "Well, get out of it," said Jacob. There was something unseemly about the way his wife smelled and looked. She did not seem ready for pancakes or Cheerios or soft-boiled eggs, and he doubted if she would read the *Daily World*'s op-ed page, the way he had asked her to do again and again.

Harold, the mayor's personal assistant, had a brilliant idea. "How about," he said to Mel, "we get ourselves some money by going after scofflaws?" "We do that," said Mel, "don't we?" "I mean," said Harold, "a huge campaign, a fleet of tow trucks, boots to put on very delinquent cars, and a pound for the most flagrant, thumb-your-nose-at-your-city types. We enforce thoroughly. We enforce without regard to ethnicity, gender, or title. Parking crimes are an ideal opportunity for a flat tax, falling equally oner-ously on all. We take the money and hire new firefighters and we have a press conference with the new guys in their perfectly creased uniforms, and the fire commissioner and the parking com-missioner can stand on either side of you and you can hug them both. The fire commissioner is a hunk—he probably works out."

"Never mind about the hugging," Mel said. "The idea is a good one. Do the figures, get Neil Maguire on the phone. Let's find out how much we're losing each year as we let some of those parking pirates escape our clutches. I bet we can squeeze millions out of these guys."

Harold was proud of his idea. He went to work immediately. By the end of the afternoon he had found out the Parking Violations Bureau was way down in income and way up in expenses. He had found out that there was no way to know how far down or what the exact figures were because Neil Maguire kept the books very close to his chest and no one was authorized to give out any information. Harold called the public relations office and told them to ready a campaign. He invited Neil to a meeting to help formulate the plans. He sent an intern down to the pound to see how many trucks could be put on duty.

The PR campaign was started by the end of the week. The announcement of the strict enforcement and the two-week amnesty program, amnesty as far as additional fines were con-cerned, was announced on the six, ten, and eleven o'clock news. Citizens were pulling out old tickets from their sock drawers, from filing cabinets, from spice cabinets, from shoe racks and sweater shelves where they had been hidden for months or years.

But of course many citizens didn't believe the city could actu-ally find them or had the personnel to go on a scofflaw hunt, and so they ignored the matter. The boots, big metal traps with steel jaws to be locked onto back tires, were loaded up into the trucks. Lists were printed of wanted license plates and the hunters were told the season was right, bring in the prey. Every neighborhood in the city was circled in red and in the early morning, before the owners of the cars had brushed their teeth or read their papers, or had their first cup of coffee, the hunt was on.

In the subways the placards had been plastered in the space usually reserved for advertising. There was a large picture of Neil Maguire, the parking commissioner, smiling down. DON'T BE A SCOFFLAW, the large print warned, OR WE'LL GET YOU. In his left hand the commissioner held a rat trap, and in the trap was a toy car. NEIL MAGUIRE, PARKING COMMISSIONER, WANTS YOU, said the ad. Every other subway car carried the sign as well as certain lampposts, fences at building sites, and the sides of litter baskets. Neil Maguire was not entirely happy at being stuck up all over the subway.

41

THE PRICE OF
SILENCE

Consider Daquinne Johnson, who had enjoyed the attentions she had received from the parking commissioner and certainly bore him no ill will. She liked to fix him his evening drink. She liked to walk past him in the shimmering Chinese robe he had brought her, which had slits at the side and if she tied it just right, allowed the fullness of her breasts to be seen rising and falling with her breath. She liked the small presents he almost never forgot: the pin in the shape of a penguin, the scarf with a design that showed the canals of Venice, in whose blue waters boats drifted and bridges floated. She was not concerned that there was no future for her as Mrs. Neil Maguire. She was not yet twenty and he was an old man, sweet enough but not her sweetheart. What she liked was showing her sister her bank card. What she liked was using his credit card at department stores near her place of work. What she liked was the way her heels clicked on the marble floor of the office building, tap, tap, tap, like an invitation to a party. What she liked was the way Neil wrapped his large arms around her and asked her to guess what was in the package he had brought with him. She liked her bragging rights. She saw no trouble ahead. She wasn't the worrying kind. She had no intention of ending up with three children and working the night shift at Benny's Burgers. She was not going to get the short end of the stick.

Daquinne had wept when her mother and her aunt and her two sisters had died in a fire. However, she was not surprised that she was the last member of the family to survive. She accepted condolences from all her co-workers, took a week off, wrote a letter of apology to her dead sister for every mean act that she could remember and then took a walk along the river promenade and dropped the letter into the swiftly moving waters. She prayed for the souls of her family. She prayed for her own soul. But these were prayers of custom, prayers that were expected. Daquinne Johnson was simply not given to religious fervor, although she did have a moment of prayer when Neil Maguire told her their relationship would have to end. She prayed that Neil would have a fatal heart attack there and then. She bought herself a new black suit on Neil's credit card and told him she needed to get away for a while to recover.

"Away?" he said. "I'll be back," she said. "Where are you going?" he asked. "Wouldn't you like to know," she said. She did accept a thousand dollars in cash and a luggage set in red leather. Neil thought of this as a good-bye present. Something about the glint in her eye as she opened the door for him made Neil wonder if he had really known her well. Had he just imagined that her soul matched her body in desirability? Neil realized that he should never have told her where all his funds were coming from. He should not have let her see his private books.

He had wanted someone to admire his genius and he thought he could trust her, but now with her gone he had second thoughts. She had asked questions. He had answered them. He liked to educate her. He felt puffed up with wisdom as he explained to her the ins and outs of a balance sheet, but perhaps he had told her more than was prudent.

He had. He considered going to confession. If he had trusted Daquinne, he could certainly trust Father Bertoli at St. Michael's.

But actually he didn't like Father Bertoli, who seemed to him sanctimonious, all too pleased with himself. He was probably one of those altar-boy-chasing priests. The more Neil thought about it, the less he was inclined to trust him.

After all, Neil consoled himself, Prix Fixe had towed the cars it was asked to tow, and if not all of the money found its way into the city's coffers, well, then, the city was large and indifferent, made of cement and glass, whereas he himself was a flesh-and-blood man struggling to make ends meet, a man with needs. Such a man God could forgive, surely. Surely? Maybe? Probably? Perhaps not?

Neil considered telling his wife about Daquinne. He rejected the idea. Sometimes the truth is merely hurtful. Sometimes a secret is better kept than revealed. Why should she know? Why should she be disappointed in him, she who trusted him in all matters of the world and had for so many years? And if the children found out? What a disaster. What kind of a role model would he be then?

The phone rang. It was Maddie Miller, calling to make a lunch date with him. What did that infernal reporter want now?

Daquinne went to the countryside, where her grandmother lived. She walked in the woods and considered her options. It was time to move on: onward and upward, as they say. "We will, we will," she sang. The song had become a commercial for tires and a cheer for football players, and its grinding, bumping sound comforted her. One minute her mother was standing in line in the supermarket holding a super-sized package of Wonder bread and the next the bread was soaking wet on the table and firefighters were carrying bodies out in black plastic bags.

She counted her assets again and again. Then it came to her, the same way religious visions come to some people, unexpectedly, brilliantly, in a flash of light, in a life-altering way. She possessed some information other people would find very valuable. Move slowly, she told herself, think this through. You have the winning lottery ticket in your hand. She was still enough of a child to leap

ANNE ROIPHE

up the three front steps of her grandmother's house and jump up and down on the porch. You gotta go—go, said her grandmother.

Mel Rosenberg and Ruth were having Friday night dinner at their home, and they had invited the Maguires. There were candles and a white tablecloth and bread that had been blessed. The two couples were talking about a movie they had all seen. Mel wondered why Neil looked so preoccupied. There were dark circles under his eyes. His heavy body seemed soft and deflated. Were they all just getting old?

Perhaps it was because the Sabbath Queen felt unappreciated or perhaps it was because the Imp of Imperfection felt a sudden need for attention—either explanation would do. Neil Maguire placed a large piece of chicken in his mouth and before he had swallowed the meat he added a huge portion of mashed potatoes, and suddenly he choked. Something went down the wrong way. Mel and Ruth stared. His wife pounded him on the back. In his anguish Neil tipped his chair backward and it went over. He was all right. The food came out and rested on the carpet. The Imp of Imperfection was vastly amused. The mood at the table was somber.

Later that night in bed, Mel asked Ruth, "Do you know how to do the Heimlich maneuver?" "Sure," said Ruth, but her voice betrayed her. "I wish you would learn," he said. "And it would be a good idea to take a CPR course." "All right," said Ruth. She sighed. "You too," she added. "I'm the mayor of a big city," he said. "I haven't the time." Ruth turned her back on him and went to sleep.

42

STRIKE
CENTRAL

Mel was alone in his office with the door closed, pacing up and down. He was confused. He had grown up hearing about the wonderful Franklin Delano Roosevelt. His uncle had been a socialist and his father had been a workingman and his mother had had a heart that bled for everyone. When he was a child it had been a simple matter. The boss was making money off the little guy, and the little guy had to organize and fight and march and hand out leaflets so that he could put food in his baby's mouth and have for himself, if he were lucky, a little piece of the American pie.

Mel remembered standing by his mother's side when they went to Ornstein's department store to buy him new shoes for the school year and there were men and women outside the store clapping hands to a chant, walking in a circle, and several were waving signs in the air. Mel's mother turned around. No shoes. "A decent person," she said, "never ever crosses a picket line." Mel remembered the sharp sting of regret about the shoes, and he remembered his amazement that by as simple an act as not shopping he had proved himself to be a decent person.

He had in his head pictures of miners with coal-stained faces shaking their fists at men in big black cars and police with red faces waving their clubs at women and children. His mother's cousin Delores had been an organizer for the garment workers, and she told him stories about fifteen-hour days seven days a week. He knew about workplaces without bathrooms and places where men and women lost their eyesight, their limbs, their lungs. However, he also knew that there were times in the recent past when the men in hard hats had turned into the red faces, when union bosses pocketed dues, when the difference between the union and the gangsters was blurred.

Mel thought about how important it was for a politician—and Mel was certainly a politican—to know where he stands with the fat cats in their long, shiny limousines and with the workers, immigrants, toiling in the belly of the beast.

But for Mel the matter had become complicated. The bus drivers wanted a 20 percent increase in pay, and he didn't know where it would come from. Should the city go into bankruptcy because the bus drivers wanted a bigger piece of the consumer pie? It turned out that the bus drivers had forged an alliance with the subway workers, the conductors and the repair people and the electricians and the track layers and the painters and the token booth operators who sat inside glass booths all day like sullen goldfish passing time in a place that time had abandoned. For reasons Mel wasn't clear about, the subway workers had an alliance, a sort of you-strike-we-strike pact, with the zookeepers, who were a branch of the sanitation workers union, and they had been rumbling themselves about striking if they weren't given an extra week's vacation. Mel knew he had no more money to give, never mind how fair the complaint, how needy the worker. But he didn't think they were needy; in fact, he thought they had too much as it was.

As Mel paced the floor in his office he knew that if a picket line were in front of him that very moment, he would cross it. He would cross it and wave; he would cross it and thumb his nose at the weary workers circling round. The budget would break if he granted the bus drivers' request and the requests of the other unions that would surely follow, the way day follows night. If the budget broke, there would be no glue that could bind the pieces together. There would be chaos, and he would be blamed for bad management, and his accusers would be right. He would say no to the bus drivers, his mother be damned.

"Harold," he screamed for his assistant, who came running in response to the panic in his boss's voice. "Harold, there's going to be a strike." Later at lunch with Moe Alter he said, "I'm sorry."

Two days later the buses were not running. The subways were not running. The zoo was closed, and volunteers from Fur Is Flesh, an organization whose members Mel had always thought were sexually disturbed misfits, were feeding the monkeys and the seals and the elephants. The teachers were talking about joining the strike. The city became giddy, the way it does in a great snowstorm. People were walking to work, throngs of people on all the main arteries. People were talking to each other, strangers; "I've come thirty blocks." "I waited three hours for a taxi." People with cars were picking up folks on street corners and driving out of their way to deposit these new friends at their destination. Some private schools closed. Duncan Academy stayed open, but the second-grade teacher and most of the students never made it to school. Enterprising youths from the projects "borrowed" cars and used them as group taxis. The hospital workers union was voting on whether to join the strike.

It was catastrophic. It was disastrous. It could get worse. The mayor was meeting in his office with his staff, and there was a huge chart propped up on a table showing that the city needed the bus drivers more than it needed the entire mayor's staff. "We close ourselves down," offered a young accountant, "and use the overhead to pay the drivers." No one listened. Mel's union negotiators, two lawyers and a prominent real estate figure, looked sorrowful. The talk shows were on high alert. Everyone blamed the mayor, especially after an interview with a bus driver's wife who was eight months pregnant and wasn't sure where she was going to get the money to pay the rent. "My family will be evicted," she told the camera, bursting into tears.

Mel went over it again and again. Would the federal government bring barrels of cash to the city to avert disaster? They would not. Would the head of the union, a fellow named Mike Derian, take pity on the city and back off? He would not. Would there be a divine intervention? Not likely. Where was the deus ex machina when you needed it.

There was a beautiful bridge at one end of the city. Built in 1874, its gleaming cables marked man's finest achievement. The bridge connected the city to the outer boroughs, and so it seemed an ideal place for the bus drivers and their buses to gather and like a great flock of urban buffalo they packed themselves in, nose to nose, rear to rear, honking their horns, strike signs on their windows. Cans of beer were passed from bus to bus. The scene was raucous, wild, hopeful, the way it always is when the order of things is undone. It is simply not true that real men don't cry. On the way to the bridge in the police car with a large police escort, the mayor felt his eyes reddening and his nose filling up. What was he going to do now? On his shoulder sat the Imp of Despair, picking at a scab on his scaly skin, running his scratchy cheek against the mayor's chin, pulling out one of the mayor's remaining hairs. It was a great day to be an Imp of Despair.

43

GREASING THE
BUSES' WHEELS

Mel was on the phone to his chief negotiator, who was back in the hotel suite with the leaders of the transit workers. The room wasn't as crowded as you might think. Smoking wasn't allowed, so the workers' representatives were constantly leaving the table to go stand outside in the cold and inhale whatever they wished.

The city's lead labor lawyer was a man named Vincent Impelleteri. He was a small man in his forties who was one of those rare people who had never lost his illusions about human nature because he had never had any. From the time he discovered who was taking money from the local parish's charity box he had always disbelieved the sanctimonious and decorative words that animate our language, the lovely structures we erect to convince ourselves that we are worthy and up to some good on this planet. He had always known that he lived in a jungle. Eat quickly and prepare to flee. Eat first and ask questions later. Push hard before you can be pushed. Nothing in his fine education disabused him of these truths, which he held to be self-evident. He was not charming. He was effective. He would give only the inch he had to and no more.

Mel trusted him and even liked him. He was hard but he was loyal. Loyalty was his only weakness.

"Vinnie," said Mel, "how's it going?" "Nothing," said Vinnie. "Are we going to have to cave?" said Mel. "I didn't hear that," said Vinnie, who knew that his boss was prone to doubt. Doubt in a mayor is a bad thing. So is irony. Vinnie, fortunately, had none of either. "Call me in an hour," he said.

The bus drivers were chanting, they were shouting, they were dropping coffee cups and french fry containers all over the bridge. They were sitting down in front of their big wheels playing poker, listening to the radio, using their cell phones. Meanwhile, the merchants on Walker Street called a press conference and told reporters that they expected the mayor to solve this problem. How could retailers retail if people couldn't get to them? It would be a catastrophe equivalent to a flood or a hurricane if the bus strike went on like this much longer.

The schoolteachers were meeting to decide whether or not to join the strike. Smelling blood, some of them were calling for brotherhood and unionhood and sisterhood, and their public relations officer was doodling slogans for the placards on her notepad. Others were urging restraint. *It's not our business* was the opposition cry. Action loomed, excitement caused heat in the room. Revolutions may begin because people enjoy being shoulder to shoulder with their fellows. Who needs Prozac when you can take to the streets and protest?

The mayor no longer felt like crying. The sight of the buses clogging up his bridge made him angry. Yes, he believed the working citizen was entitled to as good a life as he or she could win, in fact as good a life as the banker or the real estate tycoon. But this was America, and equality meant equality of opportunity, which itself was still something of a joke, because some were favored by genes and fortune and others were not, and some people got more of the spoils than others whether they deserved it or not, and so it was.

Mel asked for and received a megaphone. He was boosted up onto the hood of his car. He took his shoes off so he wouldn't make scuff marks or dent the metal. He felt somewhat unsteady up there. But he was mad, and so he yelled into his megaphone, "Grow up, guys. The city hasn't got the money. I don't care if you stay here all night, for forty nights and forty days or forty years. A bus driver gets what a bus driver gets, and if you want a better salary, go back to school, get a better job, become brain surgeons." There was a moment of silence. Then the bus drivers began to curse. They started to throw objects, pens and flashlights and coffee cups and beer bottles, at the mayor. He slid down from the hood of the car and took refuge within.

"Perhaps," said Harold, who was with him, "that wasn't the best tactic." "It wasn't a tactic," muttered the mayor as his car inched backward off the bridge, siren blaring. The TV cameras caught it all. They showed the mayor's head ducking as a metal object sailed by. They saw the redness in his face that reached up to the tip of his ears as he yelled as loudly as he could into his megaphone. They caught the buses themselves like a herd of restless beasts, rocking back and forth on their wheels as the drivers put them in gear and shouted to each other out the windows.

"Good going," said Vinnie to the mayor. In the hotel the fake palm trees sank in their brass pots and the grand chandelier blinked in the ballroom. The red-and-white-clothed waiters bustled back and forth with turkey sandwiches and beer, and coffee cups gathered in the hallway on silver carts faster than the waiters could remove them. The other guests in the hotel noticed the large number of police in the lobby. They saw all the TV paraphernalia leaning against the deep velvet couches by the elevators. An out-of-town family gathered around the TV reporter and asked for her autograph. She blushed. Would this improve her chances of getting a renewal on her contract? She had heard the office buzz that she would be dropped.

In the men's room of the hotel the mayor met with his lawyer. "What can we give so they can save face?" asked the mayor after checking that they were alone. "We give them bupkes," said Vinnie. "Where'd you learn that word?" asked Mel. "St. Ignatius," said Vinnie. "The priest that prepped us for the SATs. He used it all the time." "Vinnie," said Mel, "give them something." Vinnie shook his head. "Nothing. *Nada.*"

Mel called Mike Winston, owner of the city's baseball team, the Bears. "Mike," he said, "how would you like that extension to the stadium that you've been pushing me about granted and completed in a year's time?" "What do you want?" Mike asked. "I want you to give all the bus drivers and their families free tickets for two games during the season." "That's outrageous," said Mike. "Expensive," he added. "I know," said Mel. "Is it a deal?" Deal, it was. Vinnie made the proposal, an inflation adjustment of 2% a year in salary and tickets to the Bears for their opening game in the spring. The 2% had been agreed upon at the last contract. The tickets were the hard-won fruit of the strike. Mike Winston was on the evening news because he was clearly the savior of the city. No mention was made at that moment of the stadium's extension, and therefore no one interviewed the denizens of the five-block area that would be razed to make room for the enlargement. Someone's ox is always being gored. If you don't have an ox, you yourself can be gored.

But the wheels of the buses were going round and round once more. The mayor left his office late that night not unsatisfied with himself. It seemed that his performance at the bridge, his yelling at the strikers, had won him more friends than it had lost. I am, he thought as he waited for the elevator, two police officers at his side, something of a Jewish cowboy. He grinned at the reflection of himself in the polished brass of the elevator door. Not bad.

44

THE TRUTH BEHIND THE
SHOWER CURTAIN

Daquinne Johnson giggled. It was a shy, girlish giggle. She brought her napkin up to her mouth to cover it. Maddie Miller sighed. Daquinne had long lashes. She had soft black eyes and skinny arms that spoke of playgrounds and girls jumping rope as dusk falls. But she had worn a tight black T-shirt and a short leather skirt to lunch. She had on open-toed shoes with heels so high that the tendons in the legs were stretched to their limit. When Maddie came to the table she saw a copy of Terry McMillan's latest novel in her guest's hands. "It's the third time I've read it," said Daquinne. "She really gets it." "Does she?" said Maddie. "I'll have to read her sometime." God, this kid could be my daughter, Maddie thought. Daquinne had started giggling after Maddie told her that she didn't look like an accountant.

"I'm so sorry for your loss," said Maddie. "It must be hard to suddenly lose your family like that." Daquinne's eyes filled with tears. One dropped down her cheek and rested on the corner of her upper lip. "I'll be all right," said Daquinne, and Maddie did not doubt it. The conversation stopped. The older woman and the younger woman stared down at their menus. Maddie drank gulps of her water. Daquinne shifted from one small hip to another. "Well," said Maddie, "we're here to talk about Neil Maguire, so we might as well talk about him." She smiled reassuringly and looked Daquinne right in the eye. She promised nothing, but she hid nothing. "Do you mind?" she said, and took out a palm-sized black tape recorder from her bag. It was covered with powder; a compact had deconstructed while en route to the restaurant. Maddie brushed the tape recorder clean with her fingers and placed it next to the small vase in which one red rose trembled.

"So shoot," she said. "Tell me the whole story." "What do I get?" Daquinne asked. "Will your paper pay me?" Her eyes shone. "No," said Maddie, "but you will get justice. Also, someone may come and make a miniseries of the story. If it's sold to television, you will get money." "Oh," said Daquinne. "Do you think I need an agent?" "A lawyer," said Maddie, "might be a good idea." "Oh," said Daquinne. "You might even be interviewed on *48 Hours* or *Larry King Live* or be on the cover of *People* magazine," Maddie added. "Of course, no one can promise you that," said Maddie, "but one never knows. It depends on what you have to tell me." "A lot," said Daquinne, "a real lot."

Brooke and Jacob Rosenberg arrived at their first parent-teacher conference at the Duncan Academy. Jacob had talked into his cell phone the entire way to the school. Some client was threatening to leave the firm. "I promise you, I promise you," Jacob said over and over again. Brooke was pleased. She had clipped her hair into a tortoiseshell ring so that she would look serious, proper, and weighty. Neither parent had expected anything but pleasure from the meeting. Ms. Lublin had only fine words to say about Kelly, who was a joy to teach, but unfortunately Ms. Tarshis had serious concerns about Kim.

Ms. Tarshis said that Kim cried too easily. She annoyed other children while they were working. She seemed to have trouble concentrating. She got into fights. She had even bitten a child. She looked exhausted. "Is she sleeping well?" asked the teacher.

Brooke turned pale. Jacob felt nauseated. The teacher was young. She had a ponytail and wore no makeup. She sported a large pin in the shape of a rabbit on her sweater. Jacob glared at her.

In a small voice Brooke asked if the teacher didn't find Kim's artwork remarkable. Ms. Tarshis understood the mother's need and really wanted to please her, but she had a point to make, and so she said, "Her artwork might be fine if she were able to finish anything." "I don't notice that at home," Brooke said stiffly. But of course she wasn't paying attention at home to the artwork. It had never occurred to her that Kim was not perfect in every way. "She might be better off in a class with her twin," said Ms. Tarshis. "We'd like you to consider that and make an appointment with a psychologist and have her tested. The school has several fine doctors it can recommend." "Oh, for God's sake," said Jacob, "she's only in first grade." "Yes," said Ms. Tarshis, "that's good, you know. To catch problems early is good." Brooke didn't want to cry in front of the teacher. She knew that would irritate Jacob, who was already irritated. She stared at the bookshelf in the empty classroom. Through the glass panel of the door she could see the next set of parents waiting.

Brooke felt a great weight on her chest. Had she been a bad mother? What kind of a mother went dancing in the small hours of the morning with a man who was not her husband? Was it her fault? It was her fault—of that she had no doubt. What kind of a woman has a child who bites other children? Shame overcame her, along with pity and fear for her child. Love for Kim flowed through her thoughts, and sorrow followed.

Daquinne leaned forward, leaving the coffee in her cup to get cold. The tape recorder whirred on, no longer noticed, like the hum of an air conditioner. "He bought his wife a new shower curtain." "Uh-huh," said Maddie. "No, you don't understand," said Daquinne. "There was an article about this designer in the paper and there were these shower curtains with gold and silver woven into the plastic in the shape of little coins and he thought it was great and he bought it for me but I thought it was an ugly thing. I told him I'd rather have the cash. So he took it home to his wife. It cost thirteen thousand dollars." "A shower curtain?" asked Maddie, who had thought nothing could shock her anymore. "Yes, a shower curtain," Daquinne said.

That very night Bettina Maguire, who had been to the dentist to have her teeth cleaned that day and taken Kevin to his outpatient appointment and had the tires on the car rotated and tried to buy herself a dress for the All Souls Benefit at the Marriott in two weeks and noticed her double chin in the mirror and the way the silk material pulled across her abdomen and realized she could no longer wear a size fourteen, was in the shower letting the hot water run over her body, wakening cells, pounding and cleansing away sins of thought, sins of pride, sins of self-loathing. Neil, a naked Neil whom she had left watching football in the den on the sports channel, came abruptly into the shower and began soaping her back. "The curtain is really great," she said to her husband, watching the glitter of the coins under the rain of water. "I can't believe they gave these things out as party favors at the Civic Luncheon," which was what she had been told and should not in fact have believed. Neil said nothing. She turned around to him and realized he was crying, crying like a big baby.

45

GIMPEL STOPS
DON GIOVANNI

Everything was saturated with gold paint. The seats were red velvet, and a red carpet led the way from row Z to the orchestra pit. The mayor looked up toward the rings of balconies above. He could see the opera lovers with their binoculars hung about their necks in the highest tier. He could hear the rustle of silk dresses and programs being opened and closed.

He put his hand on his wife's hand and whispered in her ear, "Do we have to stay to the end?" "Yes," she whispered back. The mayor's stomach ached. "I think I'm getting sick," he said. "Don't be ridiculous," his wife said. Brooke had lent Ruth a silver sequined jacket with white feather trim. It was small, but Ruth had squeezed into it. It didn't close across the chest, but Brooke said that didn't matter. Ruth was pleased. She didn't know much about the opera, but that didn't bother her. She was open to new pleasures.

They had come to the opera as the guests of the Hadleys. They had come because the night was a benefit for the Society of the Palms, which had raised money in the city for the last two hundred years and gave it away for the terminal care and burial of the indigent. This particular philanthropy had been Audrey Hadley's mother's favorite, and sustaining the organization was a family priority. Audrey had explained it all to Ruth, as well as the very complicated plot of *Don Giovanni*.

The mayor was tired and rubbed his eyes. The conductor stood up, and a light shone on his head. The music began. The curtain was raised. The cad Don Giovanni and his servant came rushing out of Donna Anna's house. Despite himself, the mayor was transported as the music came over him in a tumble of exhilarating sound. Don Giovanni deserved to go to the Devil because of his indifference to the feelings of others, for the degradation clearly exposed in his endless sexual urges, for his lies, for his corruption of love, for his disregard for all but passing satisfaction, like a brute animal. As the mayor listened he felt anger at the arrogant Don, and then as the two young lovers sang "La ci darem la mano," he felt a ballooning of tenderness, a gentleness that seemed as if it would shatter him. His tie felt tight about his throat. Something in the music made the mayor sad, sad for his daughter and his grandchildren, sad for Brooke and Jacob and for the way that love was always either too wild or too tame and hearts seemed made to break. He himself suddenly longed for someone, not anyone he knew. Not that he would betray anyone, not that the Devil would have him in the end, but he longed nevertheless. His body suddenly floated up out of itself and dropped tears of disappointment on his own head. *I understand you, I understand you,* he wanted to shout at Don Giovanni.

Audrey leaned toward him in the intermission. She had to bend down. "How are you enjoying it?" she asked. The mayor sighed. "Don Giovanni is a man without a soul." "Yes," said Audrey, "that's the point." "On the other hand," said the mayor, "Don Giovanni is not a sheep or a dog or one to suffer indignity. He dares to reach for what he wants. In his way he is a hero. I don't despise him." "You don't?" said Ruth, genuinely surprised. Audrey smiled at her guests. "You don't have to take it so seriously," she said.

"Just enjoy the Mozart." "But it *is* serious," said the mayor. "What kind of a world would it be if every man were a Don Giovanni, and what kind of a world would it be if no one were a Don Giovanni?"

Audrey stared at the mayor. What was the matter with that man? Everything was so earnest, so unnecessarily earnest. Perhaps, she thought, that is what is meant by Jewish charm. Was it charming or was it irritating? She would consider that matter at another time.

They returned at the end of intermission to their seats. Three balconies above them a young man sat alone at the end of his aisle. Nothing is true, everything is a deceit, he thought. There is no God, and if there is no God, then nothing matters; all is empty, untrue, and without purpose.

The young man's thoughts were large and very philosophical, but actually his problems were smaller and more particular. He had run out of funds and seemed unable to complete his novel. He was writing a novel that would be great if he finished it, but he was unable to finish it. He worked in the library in the stacks replacing books. He worked as a waiter in a restaurant that served low-tipping college students. He had no girlfriend. His television had broken. His mother had moved to Florida with her boyfriend. His sister invited him to dinner at least once a month, but even she did not seem glad to see him.

From high above he saw the shining head of the mayor and leaned down over the rail to spit on him. The spit floated downward but dispersed in the long distance it had to travel, and by the time it reached the orchestra it had no chance to dampen the mayor in his seat in the fourth row. The young man was furious. He reached into a satchel by his side and threw into the air the pages of his book, into which all his hope and all his gift had been poured. He watched for a second as the pages floated down onto the heads of the audience below, catching the eye of the violinist and the flautist as like daisy petals they sank—*he loves me, he loves me not*—and then the would-be famous author leaned even further forward and, placing his stomach on the gold rail, he lifted up his feet. He intended to follow his manuscript down to the floor, an act of bravado, an act of desperation, perhaps a final act. A fury filled his soul, aggravated by the antics of Don Giovanni, who knew no bounds, aggravated by his sense that he was himself Icarus, who would fall into the sea unnoticed by the toiling peasants on the shore. He spread out his arms just as the conductor signaled the orchestra and the drums rolled and the ghost of the murdered father appeared on the stage arriving in time for dinner, and the mayor's heart was beating with some kind of unholy regret, and Ruth was wondering if Mel loved her as he had when he was a young man. There was a terrible crash in the seats in the middle of the orchestra. Behind the mayor a woman screamed; there was the sound of people jumping up, and a howling of some sort, like that of an animal in pain. The conductor had his back to the audience, so he kept on conducting and his orchestra kept on playing, but the singers were uncertain and stepped forward toward the footlights so they could see what had happened.

The young man, Gimpel Bernstein, who had purchased his ticket with money he had better saved for his rent, was lying now across two seats, his head back and his neck broken and his legs dangling uselessly, and beneath him was an old lady; she was bruised and her arm was broken and blood dripped from her mouth and her escort, who was a paid escort and very handsome at that, was pushing at the body. The mayor's police bodyguards, who had been standing in the back of the orchestra, came down the aisle and began giving instructions; there were calls for a doctor, a doctor in the house, and two dozen doctors stood up and tried to make their way to the accident. The closest doctor happened to be a psychoanalyst, who had forgotten all he had once learned about anatomy. He was relieved when a cardiologist appeared at his side.

"I'm so sorry," said Audrey to Ruth. "It's not your fault," said Ruth, who very badly wanted the opera to continue but was ashamed of the thought.

That night in bed the mayor said to Ruth, "No one ever threw themselves into the orchestra at the Yiddish theater, I'll bet you that." "What makes you so sure?" said Ruth. "At least not before the end of the play," said the mayor. "My father loved Luther Adler; he saw him in Hamlet," he added. "Well, I love the opera," Ruth said, and turned her back on the philistine who shared her bed.

46

LILITH'S SPAWN
ON THE LOOSE

t was all over the papers. His driver's license photo was right there on the front page, high forehead, long nose, shifty eyes, curly hair a touch too long. Gimpel Bernstein, unpublished writer, would-be winner of the Pulitzer prize, would-be object of literary adoration and, in a fantasy that had replayed in his head night after night, recipient of vast royalties and owner of an apartment with sufficient closet space, had fallen, more likely jumped, out of the third-tier box in which he had been sitting, watching a performance of *Don Giovanni*. He had crushed a woman below, who was in critical condition at MetroCity Hospital.

The paper ran an interview with a prominent editor at Fine, Starling, and Stribling. The editor, Matthew Korn, said, "While Gimpel's death was a tragedy, of course, the fact remains that the city is home to thousands, if not hundreds of thousands, of unpublished writers seeking fame and fortune through their manuscripts, most of which belong quite rightly in the shredder. Many are called, few are chosen. The others should get real jobs and contribute to the GNP." "Maybe," said the reporter, "Gimpel Bernstein had real talent." "Ha," said Matthew, "and maybe I'll grow elephant tusks out of my cheeks." "Don't you like writers?" the reporter asked. "No," said Matthew. "If they are good, I envy them. If they are bad, I despise them." "May I quote you?" she had asked. "Quote me and I'll sue your paper for libel," he responded, and so he wasn't quoted.

Gimpel had been depressed. But who wouldn't be depressed with the large collection he held of rejection slips. Gimpel had suffered from insomnia and stomach ulcers, which followed quite reasonably on his fear of failure. He no longer approached his computer with energy or hope but rather dragged himself to it, cradling his coffee, keeping an eye on his Advil, feeling dead inside. He would call his sister, who was a trial lawyer and had no time for him. She had loved him, of course, but the way most of us love our siblings: at a respectable distance. She had kept their conversations short. Gimpel had been lonely.

Women who had flocked to his side in college when he was an aspiring writer now seemed to avoid him as if he had a contagious disease. They had been right. It was poverty. His former roommates were making fortunes in the real world, buying apartments and houses in Malibu and having children, talking about IRAs. He had lost count of how many weddings he had been to. The bridesmaids had often looked him over, noticing his sensitive eyes, but they had turned away as soon as they found out that he was working on a book.

The window of opportunity opens only briefly. We are romantic and desired one day and then discarded and pitied the next. If the window slams down on one's fingers, alas, there is nothing to be done for it. This was how Gimpel had seen it.

"Should we have a memorial service for him?" Gimpel's sister asked her boyfriend. "Who would come?" he responded, and that was that. His sister scattered his ashes on the steps outside the public library, where the pigeons gathered about her feet, hoping that crumbs were falling. The wind carried Gimpel off.

Mel suggested to Ruth on reading about Gimpel in the papers, that perhaps her foundation should set up a fund for struggling artists, to reward their effort to create something worthy. "Not in our mission statement," she said. "You can't grieve for every writer that falls from the sky," she said. "Think of the actors waiting on tables and the musicians working at video stores and the whole army of unsuccessful wanna-be Picassos and Martha Grahams. It's easier to become a Martha Stewart than to become a Martha Graham. It's a tough world out there. Don't go getting soppy on me now."

"All right," said Mel. "I just want to say," he added, "that it is possible that Gimpel Bernstein would have written a great book, one that would have joined our list of masterpieces or at least been made into a movie if he had lived another year." "You are a soft-boiled man," said Ruth.

Brooke saw Leonid pacing up and down in front of her apartment building as she approached. The doorman was looking at him with suspicion. He was wearing a black leather jacket and smoking. He had on bright yellow shoes and his hair was slicked back and he wore a gold chain around his neck and a gold earring dangled from his left ear. "Good afternoon, Mrs. Rosenberg," said the doorman. Brooke could smell some hair tonic on Leonid that was not unpleasant. "I'm just going around the block for some air," she told the doorman, and disappeared around the corner. Leonid followed her. "You ashamed of me?" he asked. "Of course not," Brooke replied, and blushed. "But," she said, "after all . . ." "After all what?" he asked. "I'm not good enough for your house?" "I'm married," said Brooke. Leonid laughed. "Come for a walk with me in the park. I will buy you a balloon." Brooke giggled. "Two balloons," she said. "Two if you are good," he said. "I'm always good," said Brooke, who believed that with all her heart. It was the world that was wicked. Leonid was wicked. He had a tattoo on his upper arm. Jacob would never have a tattoo.

Brooke needed to get home. She had in her pocketbook the telephone number of the psychologist that Duncan Academy had recommended for Kim. She needed to call, but she also needed to escape the harsh words of Kim's teacher, the grip of fear on her heart that something had harmed her child, so she took Leonid's arm and they went into the park. The air was cold, and this was no day for admiring nature's work. Instead Leonid admired Brooke, and Brooke admired Leonid. They walked quickly, with the wind biting at their necks and their faces turned pink with cold, but some heat passed back and forth between them that kept them walking. Brooke in fact felt beautiful, the way a woman does with a man who wants her, and Leonid felt that America was after all a refuge from the dark continent on which he had first sharpened his survival skills.

The Spawn of Lilith flew through the air, invisible but present on earth. They held no love for the citizens of Mel Rosenberg's city. They held no love for any human, but they enjoyed the passing scene. How rich it was in plot and subplot and disasters that could be counted on to undo whatever order remained. In the zoo one of the elephants banged his head against the bars of his cage and one of his tusks dropped to the floor. In his office Matthew Korn felt a terrible pain in his mouth. One of his teeth had exploded in size and seemed to be piercing his face. It felt to him as if he were grow-ing a tusk. The Spawn of Lilith were highly amused when he called for an emergency dental appointment.

The pages of Gimpel Bernstein's novel had fallen all over the audience, been trampled in the ensuing melee, and been gathered up by the cleaning crew and tossed into the large plastic bags that were destined for the dump, where rain and bugs, decay and weather would reduce the words to dust more or less in tandem with the flesh of their author. However, Gimpel had not been work-ing on an old typewriter, though he would have liked to think of himself as that kind of man. He had been working on a Dell In-spiron laptop, and he had two backup disks in his desk drawer. And so when his sister, Leora, was cleaning out his apartment she took, along with a photograph of their parents on their honeymoon in Venice with a gaggle of pigeons at their feet, his computer, his disks, and also his old green sweater, which had become soft with age and would emphasize by contrast her delicate collarbone. For some weeks she didn't open his computer, but then she wondered if he had written anything about her. It was worth a look.

What she read was a sorrowful story of a young writer who was addicted to peering into other people's windows and then imagining their lives, envying their lives. In chapter 1 she read about the hero, an alter ego for Gimpel himself, musing on his childhood and remembering the day his dog died. It hadn't been his dog. It had been Leora's dog. Reading about the final scene at the vet and the dog's limp, matted fur irritated Leora. That had been her very own memory. In it she had forgotten her little brother, whose chin hardly reached the vet's examining table. The hero of the novel traced his literary beginnings to the death of this dog, which forced him to consider his own mortality—which the author himself had obviously spent far too much time contemplating ever after, when he should have gone for antidepressants and a vacation in a warm clime.

Leora was no judge of literary quality. She assumed her brother's manuscript had none.

Gimpel's hero, Leora found as she read on, in passage after passage, spoke of the inadequacies of other writers whose names Leora recognized, who had won prizes, who were reading in this or that bookstore around town. Gimpel's hero, Walter, knew they were frauds, incompetents, and that only accident had brought them the success he had so dearly wanted. Leora felt sad for her brother, her ambitious, once so promising brother, editor of his school paper, writer of poems and essays for his college literary magazine, who looked at you with dark and brooding eyes as his black hair fell across his forehead but ended up splayed across the seats of the opera house with only his manuscript to show that he had lived in this place and in this time.

Leora read on. She came to the passage about the hero's sister, an ordinary woman, with hips that were too wide for her upper torso, with a whining voice, with a way of driving men away by expecting them to leave before they had even thought of it. Leora read this description of herself and remembered why she hated her brother.

Writers are users of the people they are related to, innocents who are marked for mockery or pity or a role in someone else's fantasy only because they have been born in the wrong family or stumbled across the writer himself, masquerading as an ordinary person who would not betray or stab or humiliate a friend in public. Writing for many authors is an act of revenge. It is an act of aggression by those who dislike aggression. We can find writers who sign peace petitions, who protest the death penalty, who lead fundraising efforts for starving populations, yet who when faced with a blank page rush to fill it with significant revelations about thinly veiled ex-girlfriends, unashamed ridicule of parents and siblings and teachers and friends. Writers do not respect privacy. They do not seek it for themselves. They don't care about yours. They ignore NO TRESPASSING signs and have no interest in the dignity of others. Beware the writer; pray that the ones you may be close to will never be published. Writers are most often soul murderers (recidivists again and again committing the sin of *l'shon hara*) even as they amuse us by holding up a mirror to our lives.

After Gimpel's funeral, at his sister Leora's apartment, Leora told her boyfriend that she had heard from a friend who worked at the metropolitan desk of the paper that a nasty scandal about city hall that would ruin the mayor was about to break. The boyfriend told his dentist, who told his wife, who was a friend of the interior decorator who was redesigning Ruth's foundation's offices, which had gotten shabby over the years. The interior decorator told Ruth's assistant, Martin, who was worried that Ruth might shoot the messenger but decided that it was all too exciting not to repeat. Ruth said nothing to her assistant, changed the subject immediately, so that Martin was not even certain she had heard him, but she told Mel as soon as she could reach him by phone. "Don't worry," he said, "just a rumor." He worried.

47

IS THE MAYOR IN
ON THE TAKE?

Ruth knew, knew the way she knew the slope of her own thighs, that Mel was incapable of stealing a dime of public money. She knew that he had an almost infuriating disinterest in the fancy things of the world. He would still be clipping coupons and walking ten blocks to the store to purchase a cheaper orange juice if she hadn't laughed at him. He had a distinct love of power, no lack of ambition, but he was tone-deaf when it came to objects. He liked good coffee made from French-roasted beans. He liked soul food and Mexican food, and he would eat sushi if necessary. He liked Chinese food from Emperor Lu's Palace, which was so upscale that Audrey Hadley's book club met there for lunch once a month. But he just wasn't taken with cars. He had no interest in furniture, and art, he believed, belonged in the museum, where he hoped his wife would forget to drag him. He liked a soft napkin and he liked a sheet that didn't scratch. He liked his wine under ten dollars a bottle and claimed it tasted better that way. He did not long for a power machine to drive him up a cliff so he could see the view.

Mel couldn't understand why people wanted to own mansions or apartments with terraces and views of the river. He was happy to admire these places but he had no desire to live there. He knew that in this he was an oddball. But what could he do? The real estate section of the paper did not excite his envy or warm his blood. He had never wanted a country estate. He liked a fall trip to see the leaves in their red and yellow finery. He liked to go swimming in the summer in the ocean, but he was uninterested in dominion over the land. He had come from people so long denied the right to own land that his genes had lost all interest in personal possession of the earth. A walk in the park served him nicely. He wanted everyone else to have what they wanted, and he understood that his way was a drag on the economy. He just did not want wealth. It was not on his radar. Ruth had known that when she married him, and he had proved consistent—at least in this, which was all right with her.

She knew they had adequate health care and that Ina and Jacob and their children could live well enough, in Jacob's case perhaps too well. She knew, knew that Mel had not, *had not,* dipped into the public bank account. But she was alarmed nevertheless. She had heard Martin—freckled, anxious Martin, who liked having a woman boss, or said he did. She had seen the look of sympathy tinged with excitement that had crossed his face. She did not dismiss the communication as rank falsehood. Ruth had been around the block enough times to believe that even a good mayor could harbor a criminal in the midst of his administration. So she worried the matter back and forth. *Where there's smoke there's fire* is a stupid cliché, she thought; that's what anti-Semites say when they want to justify the unjustifiable, saying the Jews must have done something to deserve it, but where there's a city government with all those millions floating about from department to department . . . rot could so easily set in and honor go awry. It's just too tempting, all those dollars allocated here and there, moving back and forth like so many nasty insects buzzing above the garbage dump. It was Mel's responsibility to pick good men to guard the funds. Of course he had, she thought, or had he?

"Stop obsessing about it, we've been over it and over it," Jacob said to Brooke that night as they got ready for bed. "So what if some damn teacher doesn't think our daughter is the best child in the world? We'll fix it if it needs fixing. Nobody insulted you. She's simply intense, restless, unusual in her energy, an imaginative child—like me." "You?" said Brooke. "What are you talking about?" There he was, his pajamas hanging straight from his limbs, his clean hair glistening, his laptop packed up in its case by his bedside, resting there the way a dog might if they had a dog, loyally, quietly. "But," said Brooke, "maybe I—" "Maybe you nothing," said Jacob. "You're beautiful and so are our daughters." He reached out to comfort his wife, who was twisting her hands together and cracking her knuckles in a way that particularly annoyed him, but he thought it best not to mention it. "I don't know," said Brooke. "I think I am not the mother I wanted to be." "Oh, for God's sake," said Jacob. "No one is the mother they wanted to be, or the father," he added. "Grow up," he said, and tried to ruffle her hair. She had just brushed it and didn't want it to be ruffled, or perhaps she was ruffled enough. She got into bed and turned her back on her husband. She didn't want him to see the tears that she couldn't stop from falling down her cheeks. How could he understand the pain in her heart?

Jacob walked down the hall to the children's room. The nightlight was on. He could see that the girls were sleeping. Light came in from the windows across the side street, scattering shadows across the floor. Kim's pajamas were red and white, and Kelly's were yellow and white. They were not identical twins. Kelly had a sweet face reminding him of his mother, a certain crinkling around the eyes, a less than perfect nose, but her light hair was thick, she smelled of soap and powder. Kim was darker and perhaps more perfectly formed, but she had an anxious expression on her face and tossed and turned under the covers. Was she having a bad dream? He sat down on the floor by her bed and put his hand on her chest. She stopped thrashing about. He looked at her small body, at the pile of dolls on the chair in the corner. His mind was racing. Was it his fault? What could he do? Love for both his children filled his soul, battered his brain, sent chemicals across his blinking synapses. "Oh, God," he whispered, "protect my children." From what? his mind asked. From me, he answered, from my life.

He returned to his bedroom. He curled up next to his wife. He wanted to comfort her. He wanted to seek comfort from her. "Brooke," he said, "we'll do better. You'll see," he said. "Everything will be all right." But Brooke was playing dead; she did not move. She kept her breathing steady. She waited for him to fall asleep.

In the morning. Jacob brushed his teeth so hard that the toothbrush broke in his hand. At breakfast he told his girls jokes, old jokes from his childhood: *Knock-knock. Who's there? Knock-knock. Who's not there?*

"Hey, Dad," he said, talking on his cell phone as he walked to his office. "Want a little free legal advice?" "Sure," said Mel, who heard his son say he wanted a little advice.

48

ON THE TRAIL OF A
SUGAR DADDY'S SUGAR

I t was not true that the *Daily World* was about to expose a scandal
within the Mayor's administration. They were close but not ready
to print. They needed one more piece of evidence. They lacked
the clincher, the nail in the coffin, the irrefutable fact that would
hold up in court in case anyone sued for libel, and sue someone
would. Four seconds after the paper hit the stands lawyers would
descend from the skies to munch on the road kill, as they always
did, and Maddie's editor, a man known for his eye for detail, wanted
more details, more proof before the presses rolled. They had
Daquinne's statements on tape. They had a copy of the letter from
Daquinne's sister, who, being dead, could not verify anything.
They had the fire marshal's report of suspected arson. They had,
through electronic stealth, obtained records of Neil Maguire's boat
purchase, the increase in his standard of living. A friend of Neil's
older daughter told an inquiring reporter who was talking to neighbors that she had seen a most extraordinary shower curtain in the
Maguire bathroom, one with gold and silver threads in it. But what
the newspaper needed before the DA could arrest and arraign and

they could publish without fear of a libel suit was a look at the cooked books themselves.

Honorable journalists don't break into the offices of public servants in the middle of the night. They leave that sort of thing to Nixon's plumbers. Unlike the FBI, they do not listen in on suspects' telephone calls or go searching under mattresses. Members in good standing in the fourth estate would never sink so low, but they are not beyond some carefully crafted deception in the name of justice. They obtained the names of all the companies that had submitted bids for the parking violations towing, and visited each one. Daquinne had told them the name of the company she thought was providing the sugar her sugar daddy fed her. She had found a batch of swizzle sticks in his briefcase with the name of the company embossed in the plastic. She had found a key chain with the monogram *PF* in Neil's pants pocket. She had asked him about the company, and he had laid a finger on her lips and grinned sheepishly.

In the Atlantis Boulevard offices of Prix Fixe, Maddie found a sweet young thing answering the phones. The phones were not ringing. "So who is your boss?" Maddie asked. "The real boss," asked the young thing, "or the one we're supposed to say?" "Both," said Maddie. When Maddie heard who was really running things, she thanked God she had no children who needed her and no lover whose heart might break if she wound up in the river with cement shoes. She handed her card and a note to the sweet young thing and asked the girl to give them to her boss, the fake one. The note carried a promise to leave his name out of the story when they ran it if he helped her in any way. She went back to her office and sat by the phone waiting for the call. It wasn't the same as waiting for a guy to call after a date. It was more like waiting for the doctor to ring with results of a biopsy: *good news, bad news, God loves me, he doesn't.* This was the kind of thing that made the heart race, the spine ache, the muscles in the back cramp. This was an addictive pleasure . . . not entirely healthy but exciting, very exciting.

At last the phone rang. No polite exchange, no name given, just an offer to take a boat ride in the bay that afternoon. It was arranged. Cement boots, cement boots, she thought. She told her editor she had a meeting, and she placed a key to her apartment on his desk. If she didn't return, she wanted him to rescue her cat. He offered to come with her. She gave him her withering is-this-sexual-harassment look and took off.

When the message from Maddie found its way to the man in charge of such matters, he wasn't surprised. He knew Neil Maguire, a man with a conscience, a man unused to deception and accustomed to having nothing much to say in confession besides the usual lusts that make any experienced priest fight off sleep in the darkened box where guilt is often dumped like toxic waste. There would be other Neil Maguires, useful for a while and finally a liability, capable of causing grave disruption to comfortable transactions. He read Maddie Miller in the *Daily World.* She was a regular pig when it came to finding the buried truffles in the forest floor. He didn't want trouble. He didn't want publicity. When it all came out Prix Fixe would be gone, vanished in the wind, and Neil Maguire would be left holding a very dirty bag.

"Maddie Miller, I assume." He introduced himself. "My name is Michael Jordan." "Not really," said Maddie. "Not really," he agreed. He then nodded to the three men who had accompanied him to the dock. "Let's go for a ride. You don't get seasick, do you?" he asked with what might have been genuine concern for either Maddie or the cushions on his boat. "A short ride," said Maddie. "Very short," he said, and the entire party boarded the midsized boat with fishing gear that waited at the end of the pier. The motor purred; the boat tipped and bobbed in the not entirely calm waters. The sky was gray. "Storm expected," said the man behind the boat's wheel. "There's always some goddamn storm," said Michael Jordan. Maddie said nothing.

The boat stopped abruptly. Maddie could see the shoreline, little houses, miniature trees in the distance. Gulls flew by, cawing into the wind. The bay did not smell fresh. "Have you ever seen an albatross?" Maddie asked, just to make conversation. "No," said Michael Jordan. "What is it?" "A big bird," said Maddie, "that you're not supposed to kill." "Yeah, yeah," said Michael Jordan, "somebody's always ready to ruin your fun." Maddie nodded in agreement. She crossed and uncrossed her legs. She thought a little steam might help matters along.

"We got Neil Maguire," she said. "It's going to be a great story. I may get a Pulitzer for it." (This, Maddie believed in her heart of hearts, was a sure thing.) "If you want to get caught in this net, fine, but if you get me his real books, not the ones he opens when it's time for show-and-tell, off you go—a catch-and-release sort of thing."

Michael Jordan leaned back in his swivel chair. "Great blues running now," he said. "You want to fish a while?" Maddie did. She baited her own hook; she later hit the ten-pounder she caught over the head with the stick provided for her. She was having a ball. "My guess is," said Michael Jordan, "you're a lady that gets everything she wants. Am I right?" "Uh-huh," Maddie said, but certain shadows swept across her mind. There were some things she didn't think she would ever get.

49

FISTICUFFS ON
THE BOARDWALK

D o you think you were a good father?" Jacob said to Mel as they drank coffee in the cafeteria. Mel caught his breath. This was not going to be a conversation any sane man would look forward to. Mel shrugged, a shrug that meant yes. It also meant no; it also meant *what the hell kind of question is that?* "What I mean is, were you ever worried about me when I was a kid?" "Worry?" said Mel. "I kind of left that up to your mother. You seemed all right to me. What's wrong?" Mel asked, but he wasn't sure he wanted to hear the answer. Was his son having some weird early-middle-age identity problem? "Nothing's wrong with me," said Jacob. "Good," said Mel. "But," added Jacob, "Kim's teacher thinks she isn't adjusting to school well. They think she may not be a happy child." As he said the words, Jacob bit at his lip. "Yeah," said Mel, resisting the anxious impulse to look at his watch, said, "she's a beautiful little girl." "I know," said Jacob. They sat in silence for a moment. Mel said, "Kids have problems all the time." "Not my kids," said Jacob. Mel sighed, deeply, forlornly, hopelessly. "Can't you fix this?" Mel asked. "I hope so," said Jacob. "Well, you have my support," said Mel. "Whatever I can do." "Come and visit the kids more," said Jacob. "You can't be an absent grandfather." "You think Kim's problems are my fault?" Mel asked. "No," said Jacob. He blushed. "Brooke's fault?" Mel asked. Jacob said, "Maybe . . . maybe not just Brooke's." "Don't worry," Mel said. "Kids grow up whatever you do." "Yeah," said Jacob, "but—" He searched his mind for the exact words. "She may grow up and take drugs." Mel looked at his son as if he were a Stepford son, an alien in his son's body. "She's not even in second grade," he said. "That's not the point, Dad," said Jacob. Mel wanted to hug his son, who looked like a whipped puppy, fine suit and all, so he punched him lightly on the shoulder. "It'll be okay." Was I a good father? Mel wanted to ask. But he didn't.

Brooke was having her hair highlighted. The soft halogen lights above the high black chairs were sending up a strange mist. White cream covered the bunches of hair that were tied in aluminum papers. Brooke tried to read the article in her magazine on vitamin needs for the chronic dieter, but her mind wandered. Her nails had been done, and she hoped they would dry before she had to put her fingers into her purse to extract her ringing cell phone. Leonid was going to call her and they were going to have lunch downtown, so far downtown that no one who knew her or Jacob would appear in the restaurant. After lunch? Well, she was ready for any possibility.

She was rinsed. A strange smell of pine and lily lifted off from her head.

She walked out into the street, her cell phone on, waiting for the ring. She window-shopped along the avenue: boots, leather gloves, a reclining chair. The brisk air made her cheeks glow. She felt happy until she looked at her watch. He had said he would call before noon. It was nearly one o'clock. He had said he would devote the afternoon to her. She liked the word *devote,* the way he said it with his Russian accent. She walked around the block. She found a coffee shop and sat down, ordering herself a diet Coke. She stared out the window. The faces of the passersby blurred one into the other. No one stopped and looked at her. Was she invisible? She jig-gled her leg under the table and couldn't seem to stop. No phone call. By two o'clock she had consumed three more sodas, reapplied her lipstick twice, and considered how fickle men were, how unreli-able, how treacherously she had been treated.

Brooke gave up and went into Portnoy's jewelry store to look around. There was nothing there she wanted. Nothing there she would take if the clerk turned his back which he didn't seem about to do. She felt flat, like sparkling water left on the table too long. She went home and with all her clothes on fell on her bed in what she suspected was terminal exhaustion.

Leonid had not tried to call Brooke. He had one phone call, and he certainly wasn't going to waste it to cancel lunch. He was being held in the basement of some gray building. His brother, Sergei, would come to fetch him. It was a little altercation, a small banging of fists, and he had meant only to teach the man who had approached him a good lesson, but perhaps he had let his temper get the better of him; perhaps he should have shrugged and walked away.

He had been stopped on the boardwalk by two young men in black suits with big black hats and scraggly fuzzy beards and glasses on crooked wire frames. He had not liked the way they looked at him as if he were dinner for a falcon. "Excuse me," one said, "are you Jewish?" "Yes," said Leonid, and tried to walk on. They blocked his way. "Would you come with us and say the morning prayers?" "No," said Leonid. "Do you know how?" asked the other. "No," said Leonid, "and I don't want to." "You would like it, I'm sure," said the one with a toothy smile. "I wouldn't," said Leonid. "I don't want to talk to God. Thank you." The two men did not step aside. One pulled on Leonid's elbow. "Come with us for your father's sake." Leonid did not like his father, who had left home before his sons could open the door for themselves. "No," said Leonid. "You need us, I can tell," one said. "I don't," said Leonid, and shoved the man, who was not quite a man as much as a boy with acne. A small lady who was standing at the corner waiting for the light to change yelled at Leonid. "What way is that to treat a fellow Jew? What are you anyway, a Cossack?"

Leonid did not consider smashing the little lady in the mouth, but he wheeled around and punched the young man with the fringes dripping out of his jacket, hidden under his very white shirt. Before he knew it there was a fight and there was a police car and everyone said it was his fault. There was blood all over those white shirts and hats had fallen off heads and glasses were smashed. He didn't have a mark on him. So the other guys were taken off to the hospital. Big deal. In America everything is a big deal.

If he didn't want to say prayers, he wouldn't. What he really wanted to say to God would break God's heart if ever he could find the right words. Sitting in the holding pen, waiting for whatever was going to happen next, Leonid felt godforsaken, which is an odd thing in a man who doesn't believe in God.

One thing he knew: His bad temper was going to cost him what was called in this country a bundle.

50

MEL COMES UNDER FIRE

(AND THE EYES OF APOLLO)

M el had a long day in front of him. He had breakfast with Shirley
Fine, the newly elected president of the teachers union. She
showed him pictures of her children, which was her way of
befriending him. What Mel really wanted, however, was some hint
of concessions to come. That he did not get. He had a conference
call with the chief of police and the head of the EMS, each of whom
blamed the other for a nasty incident in which a patrol officer
seemed to have been run over by an ambulance, or an ambulance
had been prevented from doing its job by an overeager and now
flattened police officer. Mel made peace but was left with the belief that his police chief should take a course in anger management
and the EMS needed a leadership transfusion, but he left that for
another time. Then he had to go over the Sanitation Department's
urgent request for at least four new trucks and a new dump, somewhere in someone's neighborhood. Whose? Could he build a new
incinerator? Where and with what money? Through the afternoon
he worked on all the unglamorous details of city life: the traffic
lights that didn't work and the homeless shelters that some organization was suing the city to close and the parents group that

objected to a second-grade reader that apparently insulted children with unruly hair. So when Maddie came into his office just before he was about to leave for home, where he would change for the opening at the museum of the Indonesian sculpture show, at which he had promised his aides he would make an appearance as well as a short welcoming speech to the Indonesian diplomat who had accompanied the show and was a relative of the prime minister, he looked at her tense face and sighed. "I haven't the time, whatever it is."

"You do," she said. "You'd better sit down." He did.

"You can prove this?" he asked. She nodded. "I don't believe you," he said.

She pulled out a folder and opened it to a random page. There was Neil Maguire's secret bank account; there was the submitted bid with Prix Fixe's letterhead. There were the competitive bids that were clearly under Prix Fixe's. There was Daquinne's statement, notarized. There in the file was a copy of the letter sent to Maddie from Daquinne's sister, now dead. A report on the fire in the Johnson family apartment, and there was a copy of the purchase slips for earrings and bracelets, a yacht, a slip in the marina, a shower curtain, and dozens of other items that showed up on a credit card printout Maddie had obtained through less-than-aboveboard methods. "How could a shower curtain cost this much?" said Mel. "I don't believe it," Mel said and then groaned.

Maddie watched him carefully, wondering if he was acting. "So the question is," said Maddie, "did you know about this?" "You know goddamn well I didn't," said Mel, turning pink. "Ah, but it's your administration. It's your job to know what's going on. That's what our editorial is going to say." Mel said nothing. "You want to tell me anything?" she said. "You can still get your side into the story. It's all going to be in the papers tomorrow morning." "I have to talk to Neil," he said, "before I say anything." "You don't have time," said Maddie. "If I were you, I'd jump on this early, before everyone points out what a good friend you have in a crook like Neil Maguire."

"You could have framed him. All this"—and Mel waved his hand over her files—"could be faked. I don't turn on my friends without at least a conversation. I want my lawyers to look at this. I want my accountant in here. I want to see the books myself." He was yelling.

Was he acting? Or was he just loyal to an old buddy? Didn't he see the danger to himself in all this? "Perhaps," said Maddie, "there are others in your administration who are skimming cream from the public's milk?" Mel said nothing. First he had to go to the museum. Perhaps he should have moved to Israel when he was a young man. Perhaps he should have gone to Australia and become an importer of exotic spices. There was a time when he could have had any life he chose, and he, the idiot, had chosen this one. But here he was. Neil and Kevin—he thought of the night Neil had called him in a panic and he had gone with Neil to take Kevin to the hospital, the son glaring at the father, a dark and irrational hatred beaming from his unmedicated eyes, and the father with his hand on his son's arm, guiding him up the steps, his arm around his child as they sat in the emergency room waiting for attention, and Mel watching his friend, loving his friend, in that odd choked-up sort of way that is communicated in the clumsy gestures of antelopes meeting on the veld. When Ruth had asked him about the admission, how it went, he had said, "All right," although he had meant much more than that, was filled in fact with the fear that hospitals always engender in those who are not yet afflicted.

Audrey Hadley and her husband were at the rotunda in the museum's hall. Those invited to the opening were the sponsors of the show, members of the museum board, and "special friends" who had donated large amounts to the public institution. The marble floors gleamed. There were flowers the size of a child's head in large vases on the coat check table. A bar had been set up under a

Greek statue that had lost its arms in another metropolis in another time but still with its blank eyes and muscled pose endured. In the corner a trio of musicians played Vivaldi. The curator of the Indonesian show was telling guests a fascinating story of obtaining a mural from a wall by cutting down the wall, shipping it in pieces that had been reassembled in the museum gallery. The Indonesian diplomat was enjoying his wine, that much was instantly clear. The crowd was pleased with itself, the place, the clothes, the occasion, the hint of the exotic, the multicultural swirl of a truly metropolitan event. The champagne was not the best, as Audrey Hadley knew, but the crowd was A-list all the way.

Mel was making his way toward Ruth, who was wearing a very attractive red dress, when he saw her breast rise ever so slightly with her breath, and he needed her right then. "Excuse me," he said to the cluster of people in his way, and then he looked up at the statue that loomed above her. He saw the blank right eye of the statue suddenly open as if it were a real eye. It had a pupil that was blue as the blue of the Mediterranean Sea, the white of the eye swam with red threads, as if the statue had endured a late night or perhaps had been weeping. Mel stood still and stared. The eye closed; the lid was stone gray. Mel stared. The lid opened again and closed quickly. Had Apollo winked?

51

THE MAYOR AND THE
LIONS OF JUDAH

Neil hadn't shaved for over a week. This had nothing to do with religious custom; he just didn't have the energy. He had spent the last few days in bed. He kept the shades drawn, and if Bettina came into the room and let in the sunlight, he jumped from his bed and returned the room to darkness. It was inevitable, he felt, that the truth would come out. Prix Fixe Towing had closed its office. The management had disappeared. So had the assistants and the files. Contracts were being drawn up for a new tenant, the Singh Travel Agency.

Neil considered a long and perhaps permanent trip abroad. He pictured himself in a white panama hat, like Humphrey Bogart, sitting in a Venezuelan hotel while the fan circulated air above his head and a servant in slippers brought him scotch and sodas. But he didn't rise from the bed. He hated the tropics. He was afraid of lizards, at least the one that had entered their room on their four-day, three-night trip to Aruba on which he had received the worst sunburn of his life. His ears had peeled and peeled for months afterward. In fact, he was a city man, a person who knew his way around the corridors of civic affairs.

He could take vows and become a priest and the Church would protect him, of that he was sure, but he could never, would never—his mother would spin in her grave—take vows to escape from the law. Neil fought off the waves of self-pity that washed over him hourly. He blamed no one else for his trouble. He was ashamed. He knew Bettina would be ashamed even if she didn't say so. And the children—what a role model he'd been. Of course he had provided for them very well, and perhaps as they played their stereos and DVDs and DTL televisions and drove their new Lexus around town they might spare a moment to think kindly of him, but then again they might not.

The shame of being Neil Maguire made him dive right under the covers. That's where he would be when the cops came to arrest him. He closed his eyes and dreamed of Daquinne and her soft young legs wrapping themselves around his neck, tighter and tighter, until he realized it wasn't Daquinne at all but rather a slimy-skinned boa constrictor with bad breath and designs on his flesh.

When he woke he considered going to confession. Let them find him there, absolution granted, soul as new as a baby, money from bank accounts they may not have found turned over to the priest for the fund for the elderly. But to go to church required that he get out of bed and shave and go downstairs, and this he was unwilling or unable do.

Bettina Maguire had talked to her sister. She had talked to her oldest friend, Milly Keats. She had told the children Daddy had a bad flu, and they went about their lives, not even knocking at his door or asking about him at the dinner table. Bettina walked the dog, an old dog who had tremors in his legs and whose eyes were milky beneath their long dog lashes. She knew that her husband was having the worse of better or worse, and she had no intention of giving him the third degree. She brought him dinner on a tray. He left it untouched. She brought him a scotch and he drained the glass clean. She called on Mary, Mother of God, to give her guidance. She felt as if her husband had left for a long trip, not telling her where he was going, leaving no instructions behind, just going without her. But he had gone nowhere, was in bed upstairs right there. She felt ridiculous and scolded herself for her weakness. Whatever it was, together they would overcome it. Of this she was determined. Bettina Maguire had character; all the nuns had said so. Everyone who knew her knew it. She was no will-o'-the wisp that Fate could make short shrift of; no, she was a rock. Even if at the moment it seemed as if she were wearing a boulder around her neck.

Harold made phone calls one after another. Where was Neil Maguire? Not in his office, not at the marina. No one knew. Bettina said he wasn't at home, but Harold picked up on something in her voice, the tickle of a lie. "I think he's there," he said. So Mel started out and he needed to get there quickly and he had a siren on the roof of his car and it wailed like a coyote in a trap or at least the way a city man might think a coyote wails.

The gossip columns were aflame. The mayor was in bed with a guy who had fleeced the city of millions—or was it billions? The mayor had appointed him knowing his tastes were above his station and his honesty dubious. What kind of mayor had the city got itself? Was the corruption as deep as a channel that served the barges that floated upriver, or was it like the dump, a hill of manure that would stink until the Messiah's arrival?

A rather large group of skeptical journalists were hot on the trail. One rotten apple was unlikely. Did the police commissioner pay for his vacation at a golf resort or had the city picked up the tab? Had the schools chancellor bought his daughter a laptop out of office funds? Had the city's largesse paid for the mayor's aide, Harold, to attend a $600-per-head gay benefit wearing an Armani gown? How would a mere aide come up with the money for both dress and ticket? Hackers hired by the opposition party as well as certain private citizens who had their own reasons for seeking the map to Neil's fortune were trying to sneak into the bank accounts of other city employees; journalists were interviewing upstairs neighbors and dentists for signs of unseemly wealth. The administration—which, according to the polls shortly before the news about Neil Maguire's troubles with the law had become the talk of the town, had been held in high estimation—was now a wounded lame duck of an administration. Who would trust it? Who would reelect the mayor, who had at the very least such bad friends? There was a rumor going around the better clubs in the city that the mayor was a member of a Jewish mafia called Lions of Judah. It was said they wore gold lion pins that had diamonds for eyes. No one could locate the headquarters of the Lions of Judah because they had learned from their Arab enemies, their fellow Semites, how to fold their tents and slip away in the middle of the night.

The mayor headed out to Neil's house, his heart in his mouth. He was as angry as he had ever been. He had been betrayed by a friend. He felt naked and stupid and ready to scream. He was not a violent man, but in his imagination he saw his hands on Neil Maguire's throat squeezing away. This unlikely vision (Neil was the larger man by 100 pounds and five inches), which he repeated over and over in his head, gave some comfort to his troubled mind.

52

THE PARKING COMMISSIONER'S
MOVING
VIOLATION

The district attorney's office was ready with its warrant, ready to
go before a grand jury, ready to stand on the courthouse steps
and announce the indictment. The printers had hummed, the
staples had clicked, all was ready. The district attorney was ready
for the perp walk. No, it would be more accurate to say that he was
looking forward to seeing Neil Maguire's perp walk past the cameras, up the courthouse steps.

The young deputy DAs had been up for nights on end preparing
papers, drinking coffee, joking with investigators. They were
groggy but triumphant. They were not interested in the political
implications for the mayor or his party. They were not, at least not
most of them, overly eager to have their own pictures in the paper;
what they wanted was primal and true and now within their grasp—
justice. They wanted the lady with the scales to rule the city with a
strong hand.

They knew, these deputy DAs and their better-known, more
experienced superiors, that a blow for justice was in fact a glancing
blow, a poke, a prick, a nick on the dragon's neck. The dragon blew
his flames, ate up little children, siphoned off money from health

clinics and schools and construction sites. The dragon was eternal. District attorneys come and go, and their assistants age and go to work for the defendants and the dragon huffs on, era after era, administration after administration, sinking his teeth into the soup kitchens and affordable housing and the dental plans and the renovations of hospitals and the shoring up of bridges. Bribery, slime, ooze are as much a part of metropolitan life as the jugglers on the museum steps, the merry-go-round in the park, the taxis with lights on their roofs, the pigeons on the statues in the park, dripping waste on famous generals whose battles have been long forgotten.

This was going to be a good day for the law. The police sirens roared. The DA was in touch with the drivers of the convoy of four police cars by cell phone. They headed out to Neil's quiet neighborhood with as much noise as possible. Why did it take four cars full of armed police to capture a noodle like Neil Maguire, whose most violent crime to date had been the frequently rued moment he had caught the cat's tail in a slam of a refrigerator door? Perhaps because form matters, and if Neil was brought in head bowed, hands cuffed behind his back, and the police were surrounding him as if he were an al-Qaeda operative, the citizens of the city would feel reassured and sleep the sleep of innocents in their beds. It should have been just as easy as that.

But the mayor wanted to see Neil before he was arrested. He urged his driver to ever greater feats of passing cars that blocked his way. He urged his driver over curbs and through red lights, and he kept dialing ahead, although there was no answer at the Maguire home. As the driver pulled up to the Maguires, the mayor leaped out of the car, rang the bell, and banged at the door. Bettina let him in. She looked stunned. There were circles under her eyes. "What is it?" she said. "What's happening?" Mel wanted to tell her but didn't have time, not now. "Where is he?" he said.

In the bedroom in his pajamas, although it was after noon, Neil was curled up under the comforter, his eyes open but unfocused.

Mel pulled off the covers. "For God's sake, what have you done? Is it true? Do you have a defense? What the hell happened? You were my friend," Mel added. "Were?" said Neil. "Oh, God," mumbled Mel, sitting down on the edge of the bed. "A boat, what did you want with a boat?" "I like fishing," said Neil. Mel looked at his friend, pale and puffed, his belly sticking out of his striped pajama bottom. "You need a lawyer," he said. "Call a lawyer now. You need a criminal lawyer. They're on the way from the DAs office. They say they have all the evidence they need. You better tell Bettina and the kids now."

"Do you hate me?" Neil asked as he looked for his slippers. "Oh, Neil," said Mel. "You haven't helped my reputation. You may have ruined me forever. Would I hate you for a thing like that?" Mel tried to smile. Neil said, "Wait here—I'll be right back. I'm going downstairs to get Bettina."

Mel sank into the chair. There was a smell in the bedroom of soiled sheets and perspiration. Mel wanted to open a window. He walked to the window, stopping to look at the sports section of the paper, which was lying on the floor. He knew better than to think that because his team had lost a game that Fate was against him, but each time his team came up short a small voice within clamored at him, "If they lost, you can lose." Mel shook away the thought and looked out the window as he pulled at the sill. He saw Neil, in his pajamas, open his car door and jump in. Mel heard the car motor start and saw Neil head out the driveway into the street. "Neil!" he shouted out of the partially opened window, but of course it was too late. The culprit had escaped. What Mel didn't know was that Neil had stopped in the kitchen, kissed his wife briskly, and grabbed something from a kitchen drawer. That's what Bettina said when Mel went down to talk to her.

Moments later the convoy of police cars arrived; along with them two vans of television news crews pulled up on the lawn. Maddie Miller jumped out of her red Saturn, which she'd parked across the street. The police knocked on the door. "He's gone," said Mel, standing in the doorway. "Where?" shouted the officer in charge. Mel shrugged. Bettina wept. Photographers snapped away as Mel put his arm around Bettina and led her back into the house followed by the crowd.

Neil drove to the highway. Where he was going and what he was going to do he did not know. His pajama bottoms were not tied as tightly as they should have been, and they slipped down his hips. His hands were wet with sweat. He headed toward the marina. He wanted to go to his boat, his ill-begotten boat, his beloved boat. He wanted to go down to the sea. He wanted to understand what had happened. How had he come to this place. He wanted to know whether it was the girl or the money or both that had tempted him. He didn't believe in the Devil but he didn't believe that he would have done this all on his own. How could he? He, after all, was a good man, had always been a good man. What would his children think?

As Neil slowed the car down for a red light shame came over him. Unbearable shame. He had seen it in Mel's eyes: the look of contempt, as if he were no longer a man but some kind of other creature, condemned and corrupt, forevermore outside the circle of respectable souls, sucked down to hell, where he would burn— never mind that he didn't really believe in hell, or did he?

The Imps of Misfortune assured each other that this was not their fault. Neil had made his own choices and would lie in the bed he had made. Fact: The Imps of Misfortune do not have as much say in the world as we are prone to think.

53

HATE HIM
IF YOU CAN

You are welcome to hate Neil Maguire, whose fondness for shiny toys and a young girl led him to keep a double set of books, to break his trust with the public, to betray his old friend Mel Rosenberg, to cheat on his wife, who had borne his children, suffered the pain of his child with a mind that broke in a thousand pieces, who held his head in the night when he wept about his child, when he cursed God on behalf of his sick child. This is the wife who laid her body against his so that the cold air of an empty, indifferent universe wouldn't give him goose bumps. He broke his wedding vow. He broke his own code of decency. He was greedy like a child, undisciplined like a puppy that chews the furniture and spoils the rugs. But who among us doesn't feel a twinge of pity? *There but for the grace of God go I.* Who among us doesn't know that Neil is a man who could use a back rub, a kindness addressed to his personal parts? He is no monster, no murderer, no callous, unfeeling CEO polluting the forests or lakes or pushing cigarettes on innocent lungs. Which is why Neil Maguire, revving up the motor of his yacht, driving in his shiny car, hand on Daquinne's pretty leg, is more to be pitied than censored. Forgive him if you can. Cast the first stone if there is no larceny in your heart. But remember about glass houses. There are many glass houses in this city.

He drove along the slate-gray inlet where the boats were sailing in the slight wind that blew from the north. He drove under the bridge whose steel cables formed lines like a spider's web against the sky. He saw the clouds, small white puffs blowing out to sea. He felt a weight on his chest; perhaps he would have a heart attack. He listened to his breath and waited. It wasn't a heart attack at all; it was just the enormity of his shame sitting on his chest, hoping to crush him. He drove further along the road. It was afternoon; a school bus was blocking his way. He could see the children jumping and heads bobbing in windows. He had been a child. He remembered being a child. A gas truck passed him on the inside lane. He was driving too slowly. He considered the gas truck. He could catch up with it and smash into its rear and there would be fire, but Neil did not want to harm the driver. He slowed down and pulled over on the grass. He could see the ducks at the shoreline, a family of seven, webbed feet paddling, feathers of green and white and black and eyes on either side of their heads. How did the images from each eye turn into one image in the brain? So many facts he didn't know. Where was the Internet exactly? What was a microchip? What was an amino acid? What was currency called in Tokyo? Was this trivial, or was this failure of his central to the other failures? He was uncertain. He was confused. Was he a fat man or just a stout man? Did he have kind eyes, or was he more like a snake whose eyes held secrets no sane person would want to know? As he sat there by the bay he felt himself growing soft at the edges, fuzzy just like the TV picture as it was about to fade into darkness.

Mel went back to his office. He called Ruth. "What can I do?" said Ruth. "Should I go to Bettina and the children?" "Maybe not," said Mel. "Why not?" said Ruth. Mel paused. "Are you worried that it will look bad, that the press will get a picture of me at the door of an archcriminal?" Ruth asked, a certain dryness in her tone alerting Mel to the moral issue at hand. "I don't know," said Mel. "We don't have to make this any worse than it is." Ruth said, "I'm going to Bettina. You should too. He's your friend." "But," said Mel, "he let me down." "I don't think it was about you," said Ruth. "I know," said Mel. "So go," said Ruth, "now. You can pick me up in ten minutes. The hell with the press." "The hell with my career," said Mel. "I'll support you," said Ruth. "Thanks," said Mel. "That's why I married you," he added, "in case I wrecked my career."

The word was out over the radio. It was on the TV news channels. Neil Maguire had run away from the arresting officers. There was a chase on. Helicopters were circling the metropolitan skies. One newspaper went to press with the headline "Fire Maguire the Liar." A cartoon on the editorial page showed Mel in bed with Neil, the covers pulled up to their chins. The vans from the TV stations were following the cop cars, listening in on their calls to each other. Maddie was headed out to the marina. She knew where Neil kept his boat. She thought he might try to escape to South America by sea. His boat might make it. The police had alerted the airlines. All flights were being held up. Leonid called Sergei in his lab. "I can't believe," he said. "So much excitement for one little thief doing what is common like the cold. What is it with this country? Bad news for your father-in-law, yes?" "Yes," said Sergei.

Neil knew the police were after him. His car plates had been broadcast to every cop car across the city. He didn't have much time. God, the ducks were swimming along the bank toward him. He could see the ripples in the water as they moved. He picked up the kitchen knife, the one he used for carving the turkey at Thanksgiving, the ham at Christmas, the lamb at Easter, and with a quick, determined motion slit his wrists. As he saw it, he had no choice. As he saw it, he deserved to die. As he saw it, the blood that flowed onto his lap and seeped onto the car seat was sacrificial, a plea to God to understand. It would also allow him to avoid all that would come if he had not had the courage to pierce his own skin. Let no one say he was a man without courage. Of course, some would; he knew that. His body sagged behind the wheel. His hands fluttered and stilled. The knife rested near the brake where it had fallen.

The ducks swam by and went on past the shining black Lexus parked on the grass. A big paper container from a KFC lay empty under a row of cattails at the shore. A package of condoms, unused, floated by in the water. It was several hours before a police cruiser saw the parked car and pulled over next to it.

Do we feel Justice was done or Justice was cheated? Perhaps both.

54

A CRITIQUE OF ROBIN HOOD
AS AN ECONOMIST

The papers were dripping with schadenfreude. The fall of Neil Maguire was the lead editorial, even in the local Arabic-language paper, which a translator had kindly placed in the pile that spread across the conference table. There was a picture of the widow at the funeral holding her daughters' hands. There was the car photographed again and again with Neil's arm hanging oddly at his side. There was Daquinne's statement that she had been sexually harassed by Neil Maguire and forced into acts she found abhorrent. Her lawyer was threatening to sue the city. There was a protest in front of the parking commissioner's office by scofflaws who wanted a general amnesty. There was a cartoon of Mel, his sad eyes sadder than ever, saying "Good night, sweet prince," over Neil Maguire's yacht, which was sinking in the water.

"I could," said Mel to Moe, who was nervously taking big bites out of a pastrami sandwich that was spilling onto his shirt, "issue a statement: 'I am not a crook.' That's a joke," he said when Moe stared at him stony-faced. His aides were sitting around the conference table. *Morose* was the right word for the mood in the room. Moe said, "One rotten apple turned up. So what? We stay cool.

What we need now is a political move, a popular political move, to divert attention." Moe raised his coffee to his lips; it went down the wrong pipe, and he choked and spat coffee across the table. "Nice," said Mel. "Sorry," Moe said.

"What would you suggest?" Mel asked Harold, who had entered bearing paper towels and had begun to wipe the table. "How about you hold a gay ball in city hall, a municipal costume ball, come as you dream you are? That would be daring and diverting." "I'll think about it," said Mel, who wondered if he came as Napoleon, would the Press catch the irony or think he was delusional. In a flash of a synapse he nixed the Napoleon costume, and before the next neuron could spark, he canceled the gay ball.

"You could," said the young assistant to the head of the Department of Finance, "declare a tax amnesty for a year." "Sure," said Mel, "and the entire administration could take to riding the subways with a paper cup in hand and a sign worn about our necks: CITY NEEDS HELP, HAS HIV, HOMELESS, HUNGRY, AND IN DEBT. "Maybe not," the young assistant blushed. "Let's have a massive firing," said the press officer, "a clean sweep of the ranks, a sign to the public that we won't put up with any wrongdoing." "But who's done wrong?" said Mel. "Only tyrants fire people for no reason." "It would look good," said the press officer. "But it wouldn't *be* good," said Mel. It crossed his mind that perhaps he should fire the press officer, but he held that thought for another time.

Mel stood up. He had had enough advice. "Moe, stay. Everyone else, leave. I am going to talk to the people of the city on the radio this afternoon. Arrange it. Now." The crowd left. Moe, who had a fondness for ties with animals on them and regretted the mustard stain on his, said, "Let's sit down and do it."

"This better be good," said Ruth. Jacob called: "Break a leg." "I'm not an actor," his father grumbled at him. "You'd better be," said Jacob. "Don't worry, Daddy," Ina called. "I know you're a great mayor." "Thank you, sweetheart," said Mel. Of course, Hitler's daughter, if he had had one, would have cooed at her daddy, too. A daughter's love is hardly proof of more than paternity.

He walked into the studio, Moe at his side, Harold holding his coat, four police officers at the door. He put on the headphones, heard Daisy Bartlett, who ordinarily led the popular four o'clock call-in show about gripes and grievances, announce that her program would be interrupted by words from the mayor, words of importance to all the citizens of the city.

He began. "I want to tell you about Neil Maguire. He was my friend. My good friend. He knew how to make me laugh. He knew how to stand at my side. He was a caring man who loved his family. I remember how he brought me a pot of his mother's meatballs when I was studying to pass the bar, and I know that whatever he did and whatever happened in recent years to his sense of honor and decency, it was once the envy of everyone who knew him. He was a good man who let himself down and let me down. I'm angry at him about that. But I will miss him, and so will his family, and so will this city, in which his presence was an addition, his unique human soul a source of light like all our souls. Let the ghouls who are dancing on his grave slink back into the shadows. In this world there is so much to tempt a man, which is not meant to excuse but to explain why I grieve for Neil Maguire. He was my friend, and I will never take my friendship back.

"Now let me talk about this city, our city. These are tight times, when money is scarce. We cannot build new parks or open public theaters or even furnish our hospitals with the newest machines or find enough nurses to answer a call. I can barely fix the potholes that will appear as the snow melts. I can barely get the rust off the steel cables on our bridges. We could raise taxes on the rich, but the rich bring us income. If they leave, they leave us deeper in debt. I am not Robin Hood. He was a sweet fellow but no economist.

"My friends, what I can do is to look for opportunities in the cracks. What I can do is to hold high our spirits and remind everyone that this city is made up of so many refugees and immigrants—our taxi drivers wear turbans or pray at mosques, and our grocers speak Korean, and our Chinatown has the best dumplings in America. Our city remains the hope of the future, a metaphor for the world as it could be. We don't kill each other, not in large numbers. We work together side by side, we ride the subways and buses side by side. In the end we will care for our sick and our elderly and our poor, and maybe we will have more jobs and more resources in the coming years. We will believe in ourselves, our imperfect but inventive selves. We rush to catch the train. We rush to work. We rush to go to the movies, to the theater. We go to museums, we picnic in the park, we ride the carousel, we bear children, we bury our dead, we are brave in the face of our own frailty. Some of us are too sad, sadder than anyone should have to be, and some of us are too greedy and selfish and cruel. So we have always been. What a wonderful noise we make each day. We live in a great city that is great because we live in it."

With that Mel Rosenberg said thank you to his listeners and went home.

55

A LIGHTBULB GOES ON OVER
LEONID'S HEAD

Moe Alter was staring at the e-mail on his computer. It was from the polling firm he had hired with funds from the mayor's last campaign. The mayor's radio speech had been corny, but the mayor was corny. The people of the city loved corn. It had worked—the poll numbers were fantastic, incredible, very, very good. Moe Alter was not a man to believe in miracles, but as he looked at the figures from across the neighborhoods, he saw that his mayor, who recently had been a long shot for reelection, had become a first-class commodity, a real celebrity. The president of a small African country had sent a magnificent multicolored coat made of wool so that the mayor could stay warm. The mayor wanted to wear the coat: river blue, mud brown, grass green, red as blood, a stripe of black, like the night sky. The coat had orange pockets, in one of which the mayor found a good-luck charm, a tooth from a lion or a panther hanging from a gold silk rope, or of course it might have been the president's own canine tooth. Ruth laughed when he tried the coat on for her the night after it arrived. "You look like an ancient hippie, a cast member of a *Hair* revival," she said. "I do not," Mel glared. "I look like Joseph." Ruth sighed. "You could get arrested in that coat," she said. "For what?" said Mel, trying to see his back in the full-length mirror that hung on their closet door. "For possession," said Ruth, "or for walking around under the influence of hubris," and closed her eyes. The next morning, when Mel wore the coat to the office, Harold gasped and clapped his hands. He, at least, thought his boss looked splendid. Moe said the coat could hang on a hook on the coatrack in the outer office but must never leave the building. He had an intern compose a long thank-you letter to the African president. Mel slipped the tooth into the top drawer of his desk.

Leonid had sent Brooke a bouquet of orchids he had gotten from a friend who worked in the flower district with the truckers who brought the day's posies flown in from Venezuela or Ghana or places where the sun burns hot and seeds burst into flame year-round to the stores in the neighborhoods where they would sit in green buckets of water, wrapped in cellophane, guarded by workers who were not as legally imported as their fragile charges. He had tried to explain why he had stood her up without going into all the gory details like his actual incarceration. Fortunately, all charges had been dropped (Sergei was out several thousand dollars), and he was back on top of his game. Brooke hung up on him twice, but the third time she listened to his story, which had something to do with a friend who was run over and the need to stay by the friend's side for the ambulance ride to the hospital and the loss of his cell phone in the process and the friend's out-of-body experience in the emergency room. As he spun his tale, Leonid's accent grew thicker, and Brooke missed some of his words; in the end she heard only his intense desire to have her forgive him, and so she did. She was taking Kim to her therapy appointment. The doctor's office was near Kim's school. She would have about forty-five minutes to meet Leonid while Kim and the doctor did whatever they did.

Leonid was waiting for Brooke a few doors down from the doctor's building. He was smoking, as usual. His skin was yellow from smoke. His teeth were not what they had been when he was younger. His eyes, however, still had the dark, troubled look that spoke of suffering and battle and long nights in bad places. It was a look that made Brooke's heart beat fast. Leonid, however, was not the denizen of the night that he pretended to be. He was not as tough and leathery as he looked. What he wanted was a way to make a legitimate living. What he wanted was to have a fine profession in the world like his brother, Sergei. He wanted to know the names of the painters whose work hung in the museum, and he wanted a beach house, a dacha of his own. He wanted to wake up each morning and know that whatever he would do that day, it would not be illegal. He envied everyone he saw on the subway who had a briefcase, who was carrying a paper with the financial news. He wanted it to matter to him, too, whether the economy was in good shape or bad. He had made it to America with Sergei's help, but he had not yet made it in America, and he was getting older and more alarmed; when he looked at himself in the mirror he got the shakes. It really was time he pulled himself together. Brooke saw none of this. She saw the swagger and the Russian hint of hard drink and rough times.

They sat in a hamburger place, a very upscale hamburger place with glass tables and hanging plants. They sat in the back. Leonid tapped the tabletop with his fingers. Brooke was making conversation. "Were you in the army?" she asked. Leonid looked at her as though she were crazy. "You take me for a fool," he said. Brooke paused. Her father had been in the army in the Korean War. He was very proud of it. "I did nearly join the navy," said Leonid. "Why didn't you?" asked Brooke. The truth was that he had been down at the docks hanging around thinking there might be something worthy of being pinched, and a battleship came in. He saw a cluster of what seemed like hundreds of pretty girls waving and babies in strollers and women with their best finery, and when the men came down the plank the women surged forward and he heard little cries and sounds of kissing and the buzzing of words and the pressing of bodies. As he watched from the side of the dock, he felt a desire to join the navy. The sailors had uniforms that seemed to him to enhance their appeal, to explain why the women had been so patient while the men rode the waves around the globe.

Leonid suddenly laughed. "You would look so fine in a Russian sailor's beret," he said. "It has a pompom on the top. It is made of soft blue wool. You would be so beautiful in that hat." As he leaned across the table to touch Brooke's fingers he realized he meant what he said. A Russian sailor's hat would look wonderful on an American girl. "I will make you this hat and you will see," he said. Perhaps, he thought, I can make a dozen and sell them to the stores. He was restless and said his good-bye even before Brooke had to pick up Kim.

An Imp of Misfortune fell into Brooke's diet Coke and drowned.

56

A SNOWSTORM
HITS HARD

arly in the morning the weather reports said a small snowstorm—an inch and a half, perhaps, by the following dawn—was
approaching over the mountains. "Wear your boots," said the
weather girl, waving cheerfully at the camera. By noon the Weather
Channel was purring about possible ice patches as the snow turned
to rain around midnight. But by the evening rush hour the first
flakes had in fact begun to swirl around the lampposts, thick and
fast. The ice skaters in the park circled the rink with snow gathering in their eyelashes, sticking to the ice in clumps, shining under
the lights of the office buildings beyond, dusting the trees with
white and the railings and benches in the park where each-with-its-
own lace crystals that had once been mere moisture were now
floating in the westward wind promising renewal, glory. The
evening news, repeated again and again in the crawl under the
talking heads on TV, contained a report of a real storm, the kind
that closed schools and clogged roads, paralyzed neighborhoods,
caused babies to be born at bus stops. "It's coming," said the
weather forecaster, dressed in a parka and wearing waterproof
mittens.

In the subway there was a smell of wet wool and a certain hilarity among the crowds that pushed through the waiting doors. The trombonist who every afternoon serenaded the downtown riders at the midtown stop, his fedora on the ground like an open hand waiting to clasp good fortune, was throwing his head back and blowing his horn as if he were an angel announcing a truce between Lucifer and God, which would have been good news for the citizens of the city, certainly. There were rivers of water in the center aisle of the buses. The trash cans at the corners were filling up with snow, so too the parked cars sprouted white roofs, and with each passing hour they sank further into the snow like ships going down. The traffic lights were blurry as the snow passed their lenses, and the brake lights of the still-moving cars dotted the streets with red smears.

All through the night the snow fell, and on into the next morning. When Mel woke it was still coming down strong. When Ruth saw the snow out her window she smiled and went back to bed. When Ina saw the snow she snuggled her little girl and promised her son a snowman as large as he was, which wasn't very large, but he didn't know that. Kim would not make her doctor's appointment, which did not please her. Brooke considered how to pass the day with her children. Her boots all had high heels and were not well suited for sledding in the park. Leonid had made an appointment with a hat manufacturer to discuss his design, his original design for a woman's hat, but that appointment would have to wait. Leonid in his small apartment at the far end of the city was impatient. He drank three cups of coffee but didn't have a cigarette. He had quit at his brother's urging.

The great behemoth snow removers and salt scatterers moved out from the city garages and began their stately parade down the streets, pushing the snow to the sides, creating tunnels in the center. The salt was flying in the air and settling on the curbs, and the dogs on leashes burned their feet in the innocent-appearing snow and whimpered and limped in the cold. Minutes after the snow removers passed, the snowpiles had piled up again. This was a blizzard, a blizzard perhaps of record depth. Was the city prepared?

Mel made his way to his office with the help of three police cars, all moving at two miles an hour through the blizzard. His staff was not in, but the phones were ringing. Where were the snow removers? Had they slighted the African American neighborhoods? Had they forgotten the Caribbean immigrants? Didn't they know that Pakistanis and refugees from Bangladesh needed their paychecks? Why weren't their streets cleared? Ministers sent e-mails, and pastors of storefront churches who couldn't open their doors because of the high snow called the emergency hot line, and there was an angry conference call from a minister who headed a large uptown congregation that included the Hadleys among its parishioners, many of whom had made a significant contribution to the mayor's campaign fund and at least expected their streets to be cleared promptly. The mayor soothed and sweet-talked. He suggested to the minister that his congregation send their servants out into the streets to shovel. He hummed anxiously to himself. He called Hernando Ruiz, his parks commissioner, who was in his command center. "We don't have enough trucks," said Ruiz. "I told you that last summer." In the summer snow removers had not seemed high on the list of necessities. Mel felt a cold coming on. The financial district was closed. The market did not go up or down; it hovered where it was, a ghostly voice over the white city. And still the snow fell.

Commerce may have been stilled but inspiration was undaunted. Leonid with a paper and a pen redesigned his hat. He took a piece of felt from the arm of his couch and cut it with scissors. He took glue from his neighbor and made a red pompom from wool torn from a pocket of his cardigan. He tried again and again until he got it just right.

The bridges were uncrossable, the docks were unreachable, the universities had neither students nor professors. The entire city was holding its breath, waiting for the snow to stop. Soot was falling from chimneys but not fast enough to stain the city, which for the moment seemed to be an innocent place made for children. One almost expected candy to be hanging from the branches of the trees in the park.

Then a snow remover, a large yellow truck with big wheels and a plow, pushed down the avenue and turned up the snow. An arm appeared, an arm in a black jacket, and a head followed. They were attached, but just barely. "For God's sake," yelled the driver as he pulled over to the side of the street and saw behind several other hands and heads and half-buried bodies sticking out of the snow. "What the hell?" he yelled into his phone. He got out of his truck and wrung his hands. "I didn't see them," he said to the police, who came forty minutes later. But he hadn't run them over with his plow. They were all Jews from the neighborhood, black-coated Jews with their black hats and beards and curls and tallit frozen to their skins. What had happened? Who had done this? The news trucks were so slow in arriving that by the time they got there the bodies had been stacked up and covered with blankets borrowed from homes down the street. The neighbors were gathered at the curb, many of them with tears in their eyes. "A pogrom," said one. "A pogrom," said another. Who had done it? The gathering crowd, snow on their hats, snow on their tongues, knew who had done it.

57

INA TELLS SERGEI
HER SECRET

The snow was grand indeed, also relentless. It weighed down on the yellow crime-scene tape, causing it to fall and disappear in the rising drifts. The police cars left tracks in the snow that were soon covered up, and the red lights on the roof of the cars appeared as blunt horns on a prehistoric Arctic beast. Four bodies were found. Perhaps there were more. Shovels were borrowed from homeowners and volunteers from the crowd began to clear the street, but the more they shoveled the faster fell the snow. A snowplow turned up a body and then dumped it in the middle of the street; the plow right behind it ran it over, and the crowd gasped. The little children were not playing in the white wonderland. They were holding tight to their mother's hands or huddled down deep into their strollers. The phone was ringing in the Pointshrub Yeshiva, the large brick building that dominated the Pointshrub section of the city. All the parents wanted to talk to their children. Who was missing? What had happened? The head of the local chapter of the Anti-Defamation League, a man named Sam Linxman with a small tank of a body designed for front-line warfare, was trying to find a subway connection to Pointshrub. He had a fur hat he had bought in the tourist shop in the airport during his many visits to Soviet Jews some years back, and he was now struggling to get it on his head, which seemed to have swollen in the intervening years. The bodies needed to be identified and buried before the day was over, according to religious law. Civic law wanted autopsies. Religious law, in the person of the four rabbis who had gathered at the site, was adamantly opposed. Were they shot, were they poisoned, what had happened? The police commissioner tried to explain his need to find means and motive. "There doesn't have to be a motive for a pogrom," said Rabbi Mendelsohn. "But there has to be a means," said the police commissioner. It was hard to undress bodies with heavy gloves on, but if the police took off their gloves, their hands soon turned stiff and red and useless. They pulled one of the bodies into a car and turned on the heat and pulled off his black coat, which had a hole in it near where its owner's heart would have been. They took off the boy's torn, blood-stained white shirt, his tallit. His small bare unbreathing chest was that of a young boy—a man, almost, but despite having had his bar mitzvah, not yet a man in a full hormonal sense. His glasses had fallen off. But you could tell that he had worn them recently by the red pinch lines about his nose. His acne was still florid on his forehead, and his hands were soft and his nails bitten down to the quick. He also had a bullet hole in his chest, and all the signs of blood and tear and splinters of bone that followed. "Is it a gang war?" asked the Hispanic cop who had undressed the boy. "These people don't have gangs," said the other cop, "they have enemies." "It sure appears that way," said the first.

Mel couldn't find his rubber boots. He had worn them to his office, but now they had disappeared. "The hell with them, I'm going in my sneakers," he said. Harold offered Mel his but Harold's boots had frog eyes on the toes and Mel, weighing his dignity against wet feet, chose wet feet. Moe Alter said he was too old to go chasing murderers in the storm. He'd stay by the phones. The police commissioner called to say it was still snowing in Pointshrub.

They couldn't get the ambulances through to take the bodies to the morgue. "There are many women in the street," he said. "They are staring at us. This is not a friendly crowd. You'd better come down." "I'm coming," said Mel, "as fast as I can."

"Sergei," said Ina, "you look like Bigfoot." "Is that good?" he asked. Ina laughed. His eyebrows were thick with white flakes, his black curly hair had turned white, and his eyes seemed blacker than ever in his pale face. They were pulling their children on a sled in the park. Their son held the baby tight in his arms, taking his responsibility with the full gravity it deserved. Ina had the hood of her parka with its fake fur trim pulled tight around her face. Around them other parents trudged with plastic sleds of bright blue and green, children ran and fell into the soft drifts on purpose, and there was above it all a strange silence, the hum of traffic stilled. "Did you have a sled," Ina asked her husband, "when you were a boy?" He shook his head. "We used our bottoms. We had snowball wars. I was always killed quickly." "Did you have hot chocolate when you came home?" Ina asked. "We had coffee in big mugs." "Coffee," Ina sniffed. "Not good for you." "I survived," said Sergei.

"I have a secret to tell you," Ina said. They reached the top of the small hill, and Ina took the baby from her son. Noah took the sled and waited at the top for his courage to push him forward. "What?" said Sergei, who was not expecting anything in particular. "I had an idea while I was floating in the bathtub a few weeks ago. It's about cell reproduction," and she told him the rest in one breathless swoop. "I had a picture come into my mind," she said. Her eyes focused on his face as if they were spotlights and he the lead singer on a bare stage. He paused. He had to think. This was something new. He considered. He moved his hands inside his gloves; the cold was getting through. He looked at his wife as if she were an apparition from another world. "Have you tested?" he asked. "Yes," she said, and smiled. "But much more testing is needed. We could do it together." "It's your idea," he said. "But I need you," Ina said. "There is so much work before we could publish." Sergei was silent. It was a gift she was offering him. For a moment he was humiliated. Then he was grateful. There was something else. She did in fact, this woman who concentrated like a hawk on her slides, want him—need him. She had chosen him and intended to keep him. Sergei for the first time believed he was an American to whom dreams come true and who can live out their lives at home.

And then he felt his mind racing. The things they would have to do to prove, to double-check, to answer the critics before they could publish. He was more methodical and patient than she. Or so she allowed him to believe. They would do it together.

In the park as the afternoon passed and the snow gathered higher and the city seemed ever more a candy replica of itself, Ina held Sergei's hand. To be in love with your husband and for him to be in love with you is a matter easily taken for granted, easily absorbed into the day, but when on occasion that love becomes apparent it can cover your life with something akin to joy, or as near as most human beings come to that elusive and always temporary state.

58

LEONID BECOMES
A CAPITALIST

Brooke called Leonid. He had no time to talk. He had to appear in court. He had to pay a fine. He had to discuss his immigration status with a lawyer. He made a million excuses. He was busy. He was working. This was true. He was really working. He designed a jacket to go with his hat. He met with a friend of a friend whose friend had a dress company, a small dress company with a loft in the garment district. Leonid had not been to the garment district before. The snow was pushed against the sides of the still-buried cars. Soot had colored it gray. The tramp of boots had created black lines and puddles at the crosswalks. The sky was still heavy and swollen with threatening clouds. Though he could see his frosty breath as he made his way to his appointment, Leonid was warm with a new eagerness. Sergei had told him to wear a shirt that didn't stink of nicotine, and he had bought himself a proper tie with little dots to wear with the suit that Sergei had given him, which was a little long in the arms and needed to be hitched up with a belt but otherwise was fine. In the streets he saw three men pushing a rack filled with spring dresses, pink silk covered with berries and irises. Leonid stared. It was as if April had walked past him in the snow, sending out beckoning colors, promises made just to him. Big trucks were parked at strange angles in the snow waiting for boxes that were being shipped to stores all around the country. God, how Leonid loved women and their need to be dressed. More men passed him by, pushing women's blouses with bows and flowers pinned to the neck. A great round container was waiting on a cart, and when Leonid stood on tiptoe to peer into the barrel he saw straw hats with wide brims and ribbons, pressed one into another. Everyone on the street hurried, worried, moved with determination. This was not a street for bluff, for dreaming, for pretending. The racks of clothing heading toward trucks were real, as real as anything Leonid had ever known. Steam was rising from paper coffee cups carried in gloved hands as heavyset men with wool headbands over their ears and open parkas carried and pulled at merchandise that seemed to be late, late for what, Leonid did not know. They looked months early to Leonid. He made a discovery: The scent of commerce was every bit as overwhelming as the scent of women who might be willing. Under his arm Leonid carried a black portfolio he had shoplifted from Staples downtown. In the portfolio he had placed his sketches. His mother had admired his drawings when he was a child, which was probably not enough to give him confidence today, but Leonid hung on to the image of her approving face that floated in and out of his mind as he made his way up one snowdrift and across a street to the old building with an outside fire escape and huge windows that loomed in front of him. He took a breath mint and entered the building.

School had opened again. Brooke was alone in her apartment. The maid had called in to say the trains were still not running from her part of the city and she couldn't get in. This may or may not have been true. Brooke took out her photo album. There were her mother and father—boring people, she knew, but somehow she missed them. Could a grown woman be homesick? It was not possible. Tears ran down her cheeks. She licked them with her tongue.

Kim's therapist had said she wasn't a bad mother at all. She just needed to focus on the children, listen to them more carefully, or perhaps get a job. This seemed like contradictory advice. Brooke didn't want a job. She had almost explained to the therapist that she had been the star quarterback's girlfriend at her high school but then remembered that in this city that fact seemed to embarrass people or make them stare at her with pity, as if she were a lost child found in the streets. Was she a lost child? She considered the possibility. Did she love Jacob at all? What was love, anyway? Had she ever known it, received it, given it? Perhaps she should take up charity work.

In the back room of Synagogue Beth El a group of young men all in black jackets and white shirts, some with heavy beards and others with beards that had just begun, and some with curls on the sides of their heads and some without, had gathered. Many of them wore glasses; a few of them had braces still from Moishe Mendel, the local orthodontist, who was responsible for most of the flashes of silver on the smiles of the neighborhood boys. Their faces were grim, their bodies were tense. "We are not going to be murdered again," one said. "We are here to make a plan, to turn ourselves into protectors of our people. They will pay for this." "But who is they?" said one young man. "We will find out. We will take pre-emptive action. We will not wait for them to strike again." But the young man said, "Who is it who did this?" The speaker stopped. He decided to stand on a chair to answer this question. He needed to be both closer to God and above his fellows. "We know who did this. It is the enemy of the Jews, those who have hated us and spread libels about us through the centuries. The Poles who chased our ancestors in the streets. The Russians who hunted them on horseback. The Italians who converted our children and stole them away. The French who turned their backs when little children were herded into train stations and sent away right before their indifferent eyes. We know who did this." "Yes," said the young man who had already spoken, "but who did *this*?"

"It doesn't matter," said the speaker. "What we must do is send our message out to the world clear and sure. Don't harm us or we will harm you. We must take revenge." "Yes," said the young man who had already spoken, "but on whom?" "Bernard Fine, get out of here," yelled the leader, almost toppling from his chair. "You are not one of us. Throw him out, that Bontche Schweig," he trumpeted in the deep and awe-inspiring voice that destined him for great things. The others pushed against Bernard, who was in fact willing to leave on his own. One pulled Bernard's hat off his head, and when Bernard went to retrieve it, someone pushed him down and stepped on his chest. "We are strong," said Dan Krugel, "if we stay together." Bernard was allowed to leave the room. The others sat down in their seats and clapped each other on the back and shook hands. It was certain now that something would be done.

Up in heaven Bontche Schweig, hero or fool, the well-known ancestor of Charlie Brown, created by Isaac Loeb Peretz, was awakened from his sleep by a group of angels who rang bells in his ears. "Look down," they said. "Listen." Bontche Schweig did, as he always did, as he was told. "What do you think of that?" asked one of the angels.

59

KIBITZING FROM
A FRONT-ROW SEAT
IN HEAVEN

Bontche Schweig looked down from the heavens on the group of yeshiva students in Pointshrub making plans to protect their neighborhood, themselves, their families from the course of history, whose tides could always be counted on to wash Jewish bodies up on the shore. Bontche Schweig's eyes widened; his shoulders hunched. He took a bite of his warm roll and felt the sweet taste of butter as it went down his throat. Was this the way it should be? Had he been a fool to accept without complaint all the cruelties of his life—the way his wife left him with their child, the way his child had thrown him out of the house, the way he died because the doctor wouldn't come because he had no money? He remembered now with a bitterness he had not felt at the time the sorrows of his life lined with poverty and loneliness. Should he, like these brave young yeshiva students wearing clothes he recognized, but wearing them with a swagger he did not, have fought back, pushed hard against his sad fate, done something, anything to better his days? Bontche Schweig stared down from the heavens where, yes, he was a favorite, but he couldn't help knowing that some smiled at him with pity in their eyes, a pity that bordered on contempt. Some of heaven's citizens smiled at him as if he were a pet, a bird from some exotic place with pretty feathers. No one asked his opinion. No one seemed to notice if he slept all the time or followed the conversations that swirled about him. He may have been offered the crown jewels of heaven on his arrival because he was such a modest, pure, God-loving man, but as the centuries turned he realized that he could and should have asked for more than a warm roll, and that God himself seemed to find him boring.

Bontche Schweig listened to the young men as they made their plans. He could hardly believe his ears. These Jews in Pointshrub sounded like Cossacks. They spoke of getting bats and hammers and knives, and one spoke of an Uzi his cousin had brought home from a trip to Israel and stashed in the family cellar. Bontche Schweig felt faint. These were not nice Jewish boys.

"Ah," said one of the angels, the one Bontche asked for an explanation. "Humankind learns from experience, you know." "What?" asked Bontche. The angel went on: "Lining up when you are told, suffering without response, getting on trains for trips you hadn't planned—these things did not end well. Now Jews do not wait for the winds of time to blow good fortune on their heads. They take matters into their own hands. How else can 'Never again' be never again?" "Oh," said Bontche, considering the matter. "I feel," he said, "old-fashioned, out of date." "You're dead," said another one of the angels. "What should I have done?" asked Bontche. "I was poor, I barely knew my letters, everyone took advantage of me." "Now you whine," said one of the angels. "You should have shaken your fist at God and some of your contemporaries as well." "Oh," said Bontche. "Look at that," he pointed down. The yeshiva students put on their black coats and moved in a group out the door, headed toward Muttonneck, walking across the now gray soot-covered snow that lined the streets to the next neighborhood over, where the families, new to America, from Yemen and Bangladesh and Pakistan, had opened grocery stores, candy stores, cleaners, and flower shops. "Oy vey," said Bontche, but his heart filled with excitement and something akin to joy. Revenge would be like sugar on the tongue; stand up and fight, he thought, don't take it lying down. I was wrong, he wanted to call out from the sky. Kill them, he wanted to add, and then was ashamed of the thought.

The police had canvassed all the houses on the street on which the bodies had been found. No one had noticed anything. No one had heard a shot. The snow had been falling all night. The mothers of the murdered boys were weeping in their homes. The rabbis and the teachers at the yeshiva were praying. The boys had been buried immediately, and the families were sitting shiva. Some of the murdered had come to the yeshiva from other cities. The little children in the neighborhood knew they could not go out into the snow and throw snowballs at one another; they stayed indoors, staring out the window. When a man went to the store he looked over his shoulder to see who was following him. Everyone was afraid to answer the bell, even when they were expecting a visitor. The phones buzzed constantly. The police asked all the merchants in the area, the wig merchant and the silver merchant, if they had noticed any strangers lurking in the last weeks. No one had seen anything. At the pizza store the police asked the delivery boy if he knew anything, if he had heard anything. No information turned up. All they had was the cluster of corpses stuck in the snow, the youngest fourteen, the oldest seventeen.

The police investigators went to the yeshiva. The rabbis knew nothing, could imagine nothing. "Beasts, beasts did it," an old man leaning over an open book said to the officer.

And now a word about the mothers of the murdered boys. All of them except for Ruthie Kleinschmidt had other children, other boys. Nevertheless, there was in Pointshrub enough anguish for all the trees on 35th, 34th, and 32nd Streets, now in winter hibernation, to snap their branches and uproot themselves, and they were now lying at strange angles across the streets and in the backyards, reproaches to nature itself. The Parks Department sent out a special truck to pick up the dead trees, which had keeled over due to the tears of too many mothers in too close proximity. In the wig shop on 35th Street all the wigs, the beautiful expensive wigs, blond and brunette, shining black and copper-toned, red wigs and auburn wigs, turned gray, every last one of them, the day after the discovery of the bodies, a washed-out, empty-color gray. A shop full of suddenly gray wigs was something no insurance could cover.

Mel, in his office, spoke to the police commissioner's assistant. "It's probably the Arabs in Muttonhead." "Maybe," said the assistant, "but no one saw a single Arab in the neighborhood. This seems more like a Mafia thing. A sort of Valentine Day's shooting." "Oh, please," said Mel, "You've been watching too much television. These were innocent yeshiva boys, not members of Tony Soprano's family." "You got something against Italians?" asked the assistant commissioner. Mel sighed. "I didn't mean that. Sorry."

That evening the newspapers carried the report that the mayor suspected mob involvement in the yeshiva murders.

60

LEONID ASKS FOR
A LOAN

The funerals in Pointshrub had brought throngs to the street following the coffins for blocks and blocks. The police had put up barriers along the streets on which the procession would move. The mourners walked slowly, their booted feet leaving prints in the snow. The women and girls stood on the sidewalks, bunched together, shadows moving slowly with the procession. Women and girls holding each other's hands, adjusting each other's wool scarves, staring ahead, served like the quotation marks around dialogue on a page, observers of the conversation. Sounds of sobbing cut into the icy air. The puffs of white breath that came from the mouths of the mourners was visible proof that life went on.

Rabbi Gedali, his old eyes red with weeping, his lapel torn in the traditional sign of mourning, had gathered the young men of his yeshiva and spoke to them of the tragedy, the ways in which Jews bore their pain from the time that Abraham obediently offered Isaac on the mountaintop. He spoke of other destructions — temple walls falling, sanctuaries invaded, simple people fleeing from those who would harm them — and he spoke of God's covenant with the Jewish people and the return of the Messiah, who would surely come to the aid of his suffering people when all was ready for him. His listeners had heard all this before, but the way the rabbi leaned forward into his words like a man walking against a great wind made them catch each thought anew, as if for the first time, as if now swaddled in blankets against the cold of the eons, as if they could together with the strength of their love for God, their gratitude for life, and their willingness to suffer his commands redeem the world, as if they were not a bunch of largely nearsighted boys with the usual pushing and pulling among them like so many bear cubs waking from a long winter in a dark cave but rather oarsmen pulling together toward a distant shore, oarsmen pulling the communal boat toward its sacred destination.

The murders of the young men of the yeshiva might seem to others an interesting story, a singular event, a terrible crime that caught the heart of the curious before the eye moved on to other disasters reported in the papers: a volcano erupting, a glass window falling off a construction site and breaking the back of a woman on her way to work, a child abandoned by persons unknown in a welfare office. But for the students of the yeshiva it was clear that whatever had happened, the death of their companions was attached to a long line of catastrophes. It was folded into and became inseparable from the harsh movement of history toward its final destination.

Rabbi Gedali was driven in a police car down to the mayor's office. Moe Alter was well aware of how many votes Pointshrub could deliver in the next election. The mayor was well aware of how politically disastrous it would be if the rabbis of the neighborhood denounced him. He also wanted to be sure that no one would try to take justice into his own hands. "Give the police a chance," he said to Rabbi Gedali, offering him a doughnut, which the rabbi would not touch. "Water?" asked Mel. The rabbi would take water in a paper cup. "Rabbi," said Mel, "we will not let you down." The rabbi liked the mayor's office with its view of the city out the window. "Such a view," he said, "a God's-eye view."

Leonid was watching the seamstress work at the bench in front of him. She had taken his design and was holding it up to the light. She was from the Chinese mainland and her English was not clear, at least not to Leonid. She smiled at him, a smile that contained one gold tooth and a few odd spaces. She was neither young nor old, just a woman who knew how to work the machines, but Leonid stared at her hands. To him they seemed miraculous—look how fast she could move her fingers, look how steady the line of her stitches, look at the way she rocked slightly as she pulled the blue wool material toward her bobbing needle. She was making him a Russian sailor's hat with a soft beret shape and a red pompom on the top. In half an hour she made five of them. The boss, Vladi Schransky, came over and tried one on his head. He smiled at himself in the mirror. "For girls," he said. He tried one on the seamstress. "Good," he said. He tried one on his assistant, whose bleached blond curls stuck out from the sides of the hat. "Good," he said. "Let me keep it," said his assistant. "Goddamn it," Vladi said, "you can buy one like everyone else. You think I'm running the Salvation Army here?" The seamstress tucked one of the hats into her lap and tried to stuff it into the large pockets of her apron. The boss grabbed it out of her pocket. "These are samples," he said. "Make your own on your own time and pay me for the material." The Chinese seamstress nodded her head, but when he went to lunch she made another hat for her daughter and stashed it under her Chinese newspaper, to be smuggled out at closing time.

Leonid did not take time for lunch. He needed a lawyer right away. A man had a good idea only so often. He did not intend to give it away. How in America did a man with an idea, a design, make sure no one stole it from him? He called his brother in his lab. When Sergei heard Leonid's voice his stomach knotted. What now? Will I always be my brother's keeper? He was tired of police stations, bail forms. He was tired of carrying his brother. The cash he slipped him out of the joint account he and Ina shared was making it hard for him to pay the rent on their apartment each month. The kindergarten bill for his son was enough to buy a Russian family a dacha, at least it had been when he was last in Moscow. He heard the tension in his own voice as he greeted Leonid. But then he heard an extraordinary request. A lawyer to make sure his hat would not be stolen. A business lawyer, who could incorporate. A small request for funds that would be returned, that were a start-up loan. This was not so bad. His brother had not knifed or punched anyone. He had not made a deal with gamblers or thieves, at least not yet. Sergei agreed to the loan, even though it would mean selling the bonds he had bought for his son's college fund. He turned back to the experiment he was conducting, the thing that had been Ina's idea but was promising, still promising. He forgot about his brother as he calculated and measured and stared into space all afternoon.

Brooke took a long bath, poured body oil into every crevice she could find. Dried herself with a fluffy towel. Brushed her hair, put perfume on her shoulders, and lay down naked in her bed. She was considering her life. The Imp of Divorce danced on her nose and laid himself down in her ear. Was divorce from Jacob what she wanted, really wanted?

61

A JOURNEY IN
SEARCH OF JUSTICE

The distance from the yeshiva on River Parkway to the main thoroughfare of Muttonneck was only a matter of minutes on the subway, but it was a walk of an hour or so. The group was slowed down by the snowdrifts piled up at the curbs, by the fact that Shimmel had not been able to find his boots, which meant that his black shoes were soaking wet and stains were sinking into the leather and he complained and asked that they stop every few blocks. The wind was still blowing, and their black hats were lifted from time to time from their heads and then they had to chase them, backward, across the street. The buses were running, but the cars were few. The buses bore down on the group as they chased their hats into the center of the street. Eli had lost his gloves and kept his hands balled up in his pockets, which made it hard for him to balance when he climbed the snowdrifts; he fell down more than once, and the ice had cut his cheek, so he left blood drops on the corners of 22nd and 44th Streets. Nathaniel was the fastest and the most eager of the young men, and he urged the others on: *hurry, stand up, keep moving, we are not going to die like dogs, are we?* Nathaniel, unlike most of the other young men, was not pale or thin. He was broad-shouldered and olive-skinned and when he had been born his mother had said, "Let the other mothers have lambs. I have a lion in my family," and she told him that often as he grew. It was a wonder he didn't grow a tail.

Four of the young men had baseball bats they had borrowed from their younger brothers. Two had razors. Three had knives from their mothers' kitchens: the meat knife used for roast beef, the cheese knife from the dairy cupboard, and one had taken the bread knife, which wasn't very sharp but had a good handle for him to grasp. "We buried our dead," said Nathaniel, "now we show them." "We won't know exactly who did it," pointed out Eli. "That doesn't matter," said Nathaniel. "They are all guilty of wishing us dead." Moishe, who was the youngest, the one with the bread knife wrapped in a towel and tucked into his shirt, said, "The Babylonian Tractate says," and he began to quote, but Nathaniel interrupted him. "If we are not for ourselves, who will be? One Hillel trumps a hundred others." The group moved on. "I'm hungry," said Shimmel, "let's stop." They had passed out of their own neighborhood. No place near to eat or drink was kosher. "Eat some snow," said Eli. "What, you think I'm a deer?" said Shimmel.

Bontche Schweig looked down from heaven. With the outsized fervor of the former communist, the new convert, the former smoker, the revolutionary from a monarchist family, "Go, go, go," he shouted in his high voice. But of course he couldn't be heard down at the edge of Pointshrub, just at the border of the Mutton-neck district.

Maddie Miller bumped into the mayor as he was seeing Rabbi Gedali out to the elevator. The rabbi averted his eyes. Mel steadied Maddie, who seemed a little rocky on her high-heeled boots. He smelled her shampoo—something pine and strawberry, he thought. "What's the word?" she said to him. "Any suspects?" "Not yet," he told her. "Arabs, right?" she said. "I don't know," said Mel. "You'll hear as soon as I hear," and he touched her on the shoulder. She seemed to shiver a little. "Are you cold?" said Mel.

She looked at him, and there was something sweet, something yearning in her face, something lonely, something extremely inviting about her smile, something new, a softness in the tilt of her head. Perhaps it was a new hairstyle. It was hard to tell with women, Mel thought, just what it was that had changed; they changed themselves so often. The elevator door opened, and the rabbi, with his eyes still on the floor, entered and disappeared. Maddie was left alone with Mel, or perhaps it should be stated the other way around: Mel was left alone with Maddie. "Do you want to have coffee?" asked Mel in his most proper mayoral voice. "That would be good," said Maddie, as if she hadn't caught the tremor in his hand as he held it on her back, as if she had no idea why he might ask her at this moment for coffee.

"Let's not talk about the city or the news or the murders in Pointshrub," said the mayor as he sipped his café latte, leaving a small milky mustache on his upper lip, which seemed to Maddie a sign of something good-tasting to come. "Where did you grow up? Where did you go to school, and do you have a boyfriend—a man friend?" Mel hoped this wasn't sexual harassment. He hoped she wouldn't jump up and report to all the world that he had made a pass at her in the local coffee shop. He held his breath, stared at her face for a sign of her response. It was a while coming. Then she leaned forward on the table and gave him all the answers to his questions. The important one, the one that made his heart both sink and soar, was the last one: no boyfriend at the moment. She seemed, she said, "to get involved with unavailable men." That, thank God, he thought, included him. Of course, he wasn't that kind of man. He believed in fidelity with all his heart and had never betrayed Ruth and would not start now, or would he? He felt a yearning for the woman opposite him at the small table, her nose in her coffee, her hand on the table, her eyes searching his face for a sign of welcome. "It must be hard to be a career woman," he said, "taking care of yourself." "Yes," sighed Maddie, "it is hard, especially late at night, in bed alone. I never planned on being alone, when I thought how my life might be." Her eyes seemed wet. Did Ruth know someone she could introduce to Maddie? Did he truly want to introduce someone, some unworthy person, to Maddie? He felt conflicted. "I have to go back to work," he said. "Of course," said Maddie, "but you could come Saturday at lunchtime to my apartment and I could fix you my special shrimp salad." "I don't really eat shrimp," said the mayor, "out of deference to my parents." "I'll make you a chicken salad," said Maddie, "if you come." "I don't know," said the mayor, but he put his hand on her sleeve and kept it there a moment longer than was entirely proper.

The flesh is weak. Maddie had reminded him that he had flesh that might still experience something new, something wondrous, something unknown. But Mel Rosenberg was not that kind of man. He was a grandfather, a mayor of a city with budget problems, and now there was a massacre of young men that might turn into something worse. He steadied himself in the elevator. He straightened his tie as if he had been tumbling about in the backseat of a car with his high school date. He called Ruth as soon as he got back to his desk. "What is it?" she asked. "Nothing in particular," he said, "just thinking of you." "I'm really busy," she said. He hung up. Of course she was busy.

62

PUSH ME AND I'LL
PUSH YOU BACK

T his thing," said Moe Alter, "with the dead Jewish boys found in
the snow, it could explode on us. We better react now. A statement from the mayor filled with sympathy for the loss of promising life, et cetera, et cetera, and expressing horror, et cetera, et
cetera, would be good. Also include a pro forma respect for all the
people from so many countries, of so many religions, et cetera, et
cetera." Sam Linxman, representing the Anti-Defamation League,
was demanding the mayor condemn anti-Semitism wherever it
appeared, in the international councils or on the local streets. He
wanted his picture taken with the mayor when he issued his statement. "We should do that," said Moe. "How about the other Jewish organizations? You better get them in on it, too," Mel sighed.
Worse than offending every Jew in the city would be a snub to one
Jewish leader in favor of another. As the old saying goes, there is no
fury like a Jewish leader scorned. However, when Moe called Rabbi
Arnold Gluck of the major Reform temple, with its congregation of
prominent and wealthy families, Rabbi Gluck explained that he
had an important meeting with his board and would be tied up all

afternoon. He extended his sympathy to the mothers and fathers of Pointshrub. A man, after all, is known by the company he keeps.

Moe crafted the statement. Harold vetted it and complained that it did not include a rejection of hate crimes against gays and transgender people. Mel promised Harold that at his next meeting with the governor he would press the state's chief executive to sign a bill permitting gay marriage. The phone rang. It was Maddie. "Would you like to meet me in an hour at my place?" she asked. Mel felt sweat break out across his forehead. "I can't do that," he whispered into the phone. He felt guilt oozing out of his pores. "All right," said Maddie, "I'll join you instead." Mel meant to say, "No, no, you can't, I don't want to see you." What he said was, "See you later." The tongue and the brain, like the left hand and the right hand, sometimes do not know what the other is doing.

Crossing into a street where the signs seemed to be in Arabic, where many of the women wearing boots in the snow were also wearing head scarves, the crew from the yeshiva bunched tighter together and stopped talking. The man unpacking a crate of apples in front of his store turned to stare at them. The newspaper kiosk at the corner appeared empty. Its owner had ducked down. It was not that the Jewish boys looked so threatening, but rather that they were so out of place, so odd, so different, bumping against each other like puppies in the pet store window. It was like sighting a flock of canaries riding the tram at a ski resort in the mountains.

"What are we looking for?" said Eli. "Where is their school?" said Shimmel. "They don't go to school," said Nathaniel. They walked on. "Listen," said Eli, "I don't think this is such a good idea. We don't know they did it—I mean, not for certain." "Who else?" said Shimmel. "We got to show them." "I don't think—" began Eli, but he was interrupted. "Who cares what you think? Go home if you want." This Eli didn't have the courage to do. Rounding the corner, they saw a video store. There were no video stores in their own neighborhood. They walked through the door. It was a small, narrow store. There were about five young men, high school

ANNE ROIPHE

246

age, standing about the counter. "What you want?" said the man at the cash register. Nathaniel knocked over a rack of games. The man behind the cash register let out a yell. From the back of the store a woman came running. "I call police," she said. "I call police, get out of here." Nathaniel took a step toward one of the scared-looking boys, a boy with soft down fuzz on his cheeks, and punched him in the stomach. The other boys jumped on Nathaniel. Shimmel took out his mother's knife. Eli was screaming, more from fear than anything else. The other two yeshiva boys were pushing and shoving and punching and kicking, and the videos were falling like fruit from a tree. Nathaniel put his hands on a boy's neck. He had never harmed a living creature before this. He squeezed. He squeezed with all his strength. He was shouting, "You can't kill us and get away with it." "Who killed you?" said one of the Arab boys as blood streamed from his nostrils. The woman called the police. The woman called her brother. Soon the little store was filled with flailing arms and kicking legs, and Arab and Jew tore at each other's faces and at each other's clothing and Shimmel plunged in his knife and blood flowed on the floor.

Eli had tears in his eyes as he joined the yeshiva boys, who ran out the door, around the back side of a mosque, through a playground, around the yard of a Little Sisters of Mercy day care center, past St. Michael's, past the newsstand that sold papers in Arabic and Polish down the street, ducked behind a truck, went down an alley and tossed their knives and bats in a Dumpster, and moved quicker than lightning until they reached their own neighborhood, where—somewhat disheveled, without their hats, which had fallen along the way, looking like men who had been fighting, but familiar men, men whose mothers were shopping on 35th Street, whose little sisters were in the Yeshiva Bet Jacob—they cleaned up and went back to school. They did not look at each other—not in the eye, that is.

The police medic reported three dead, two wounded. An unprovoked attack. Witnesses were eager to come forward. The attackers had worn black hats, black coats, white shirts. They were young men. They had knives and bats, and they asked no questions. Jewish, yes, Jews. Where were they? The witnesses shrugged and pointed in a general direction. Ambulances and police cars blocked the road. Everyone in the Muttonneck neighborhood knew within a half hour that the Jews had come and boys had died in the video store, someone's son, someone's brother, someone's hope, someone with an admission in his pocket to college, someone with a bill of sale for a carpet for his teenage wife, dead.

The police radio broadcast its alert. Police cars by the dozens entered Pointshrub. They cruised down the shopping streets. They stopped in the silver store. They examined the faces of the boys eating pizza in the corner pizza shop. They went into the music store, klezmer and sacred CDs in racks. Every male they looked at looked back at them, startled. What had happened?

Bontche Schweig clapped his hands and jumped up and down on his little feet. "You did it," he called out. "That'll stop them next time," he added. But will it? Will it really? Mel, on hearing the news, put his head in his hands and moaned. He knew. The police commissioner knew the answer to that one, Moe knew, Harold knew, Maddie—who had just arrived for lunch, cucumber and Brie sandwiches in her bag—knew. Some cats should never be let out of the bag. Some cans of worms should be buried in the dirt. Revenge is sweet, but sweet is not so good for a diabetic world.

63

ARE YOU
CAIN OR ABEL?

Jews do not take lives, do not use their fists. Are you Cain or Abel? Are you repairing the world or pulling it apart? Who are you?" Rabbi Gedali addressed his students, who had gathered in the study hall, all of them, some sitting on the floor, some standing against the walls. "What have our sages taught us? *Justice, justice thou shalt pursue.* Where is the justice when boys in a store are attacked? Did you do this? If it is you, you will have broken an old man's heart. How could you study and study and let the words die before they enter your brains? If any of you did this, you have behaved like brutes—men without Torah, men without respect for the creation itself that each morning you pretend to praise. You praise but do not respect. To take a life, to harm the flesh of another being, yes, equally a non-Jewish being, separates you from God, not now, today, but forevermore. I am ashamed of you if you did this." In the study room there was silence. Each young man felt a pressure on his chest, a shame for himself and his brothers. Most, of course, had no knowledge, no sense of what had happened, but they felt contaminated nevertheless. Rabbi Gedali, wise and gentle, who had always a kind word, an encouraging pat, who had friends all over the world who wrote him long e-mails and asked him questions on the law and called him up in his private study on the fifth floor when an elderly parent could no longer take care of himself or a child needed a hearing test or a family could not afford the tuition—Rabbi Gedali, who never raised his voice, had now raised his voice. It was a moment every man present would remember for the rest of his life and tell his wife how strange and terrible it was. Rabbi Gedali went on to cite texts, one after the other. Then he stopped reciting texts and paused. "Think," he said to his students. "Close your eyes and think of the beauty of the baby, how it needs our care, how fragile is life, without a parent how it would cry and wilt and turn back into dust, how the flame of life flickers in the newborn and how it is that love and hate and knowledge will grow in the baby as the baby grows into a man. What a vile thing it is to kill a man with a mind and a heart and an intestine and a will of his own, who will feel the sun on his face, the rain on his neck, do his deeds good and not so good, struggle with his needs, bring his soul as close as he can to do the bidding of his God."

This speech was delivered in a flow of multiple languages, as if all the syntax and grammar and vocabulary the rabbi had ever learned were rising in a boil in his mind. He gasped for breath. A rancid smell of something unspeakable hung in the air. Rabbi Gedali walked out the door, his back bent with disappointment, just as the police entered to question the students, to get one to turn on another. They were doing this in several yeshivas. They were also considering the possibility that the murders were retaliation by a radical group with a tie to a Jewish gang in Cincinnati. They had not ruled out the possiblity that some other Middle Eastern group had disguised themselves as yeshiva students in order to place the blame on the Jews and stir up hatreds in the city. This was Mel's theory. "Your hope," said Ruth when he mentioned it to her. Mel had a book he had read a thousand times as a child, *Famous Jewish Sports Heroes.* He had long since taken a more universalist view of the human condition, but he still, the child in him, still could not believe that the dead boys in Muttonneck had been done in by Jewish hands. "I guess I'm stuck in the past," said Mel. "Uh-huh," said Ruth. "But," Mel went on, "Rabbi Gedali is practically a saint. How could anyone who knew him, who studied with him, do such a thing?" "Sainthood," said Ruth, "is not a communicable disease." But Mel wasn't quite ready to let it go. "Remember the Boston Tea Party?" he said to Ruth. "Those were not real Indians." "Native Americans," she corrected him.

Kim and Kelly sat on the floor of their room surrounded by their favorite stuffed animals. They were playing a game of house, or at least that was how it might have seemed to the casual observer. Actually they were deciding which of their stuffed animals—the old cat whose whiskers had gone, or the giraffe whose neck was bent and whose spots had faded away, or the frog who had lost his eye—should be exiled from the family, thrown out on the street for misdeeds that were hinted at but never explicitly named. The game was exciting. There was a lot at stake if you were a frog or a giraffe or an old cat. Brooke passed by in the hall and then stood in the doorway and watched, which caused the children to lower their voices, so she could not hear their exact words.

She thought of the girls as females, of what they would have to endure as they grew. Their bodies would change, and they would be frightened, and men would touch them, and they would want it and not want it, and they would be guilty. Brooke had been guilty. They would have children of their own, and they would love and be abandoned, and love would scar them and leave them bitter, and perhaps they wouldn't recover. There was a terrible lump in her throat as she considered all the terrible things that might happen to hurt her children. Her love for them grew sharp like a needle and pierced her to the bone.

How could she save her children? Was there a God who could help her? She was not a believer. She had never been one to pray. There was something wooden in the God she had been given as a child, something distant and unreal, and she had never felt she had his ear or his heart or his full attention. She watched as the girls put their heads together and the whispering grew in intensity. Then Kelly picked up the old cat by the tail. She walked into the bathroom, and placed the cat gently into the bowl, and flushed. Of course the cat did not go down the toilet; of course water backed up onto the bathroom floor. "Why were you trying to drown the cat?" asked Brooke. "He was bad," said Kelly. Brooke called the super to come with the plunger. "We'll rescue him," she said to her daughters, who had lost interest in the game and were now dressing their Barbie dolls for a date with a rich banker. Brooke, on the other hand, wanted to get the cat out of the toilet not simply so her plumbing would work but because the old cat, with its mangy fur, seemed to her a precious possession, a needed object, a household god that might indeed keep them all safe.

64

COLD COMFORT IN
COLD TIMES

et's talk turkey, not the Thanksgiving kind. Was the outrage at
the young men's bodily harm equally spread among the two
afflicted populations? Was a Jewish death as calamitous as an
Arab or Moslem death? Was a Bangladeshi's death as much a cause
for mourning as a Jewish death? It depended on who your parents
were, on whether you secretly felt one or the other group deserved
to bleed a little. At least that was true of most of the city. Those
African Americans whose sympathies were with the third world
and the darker peoples of the subcontinents were not for the most
part truly equally sorry for the tragedy that had befallen so many
families. The Jews who lived on Forest Avenue, some of them, were
most eager not to appear overly sympathetic to the ones who lived
in Pointshrub and stubbornly persisted in wearing the clothes of
another century as well as following laws that many sensible Jews,
forward-thinking modern Jews, had abandoned two or three generations before. The leftist liberals in the city—the ones who attended
glamorous dinners at which movie stars urged on grape pickers or
expressed solidarity with hospital workers or pledged themselves
to preserve the separation between church and state—those liberals

while deploring the violence on both sides did not see the matter so much as a pogrom as a question of gang warfare spurred on by insular attitudes and too much religion, which worked as it always worked: like a match on kerosene poured on old rags in the attic. Audrey Hadley and her husband, Anston, looking at the terrible pictures of the Jewish students lying in the snowdrifts and the Arab boys' legs and arms flung outward in the video store, were momentarily saddened.

Audrey Hadley thought that the problem was a result of the waves of recent immigration that had created a cheek-by-jowl living situation for peoples not yet truly American. This she announced over her morning eggs. Anston Hadley agreed. "That's always the way it has been," he said. "The Irish and the Italians, the Jews and the Poles—from the moment they first stepped off the boats, they split up the streets, drew invisible markers on the sidewalks, and killed each other from time to time. So now it's the Pakistanis and the Jews, the Lebanese and the Jews, the Syrians and the Jews." Anston paused and blew his nose. "You know there isn't a drop of anti-Semitism in my veins," he said to his wife, "you know I am the most unprejudiced man in America, but it is true that wherever there is trouble, there are Jews. Remarkable, isn't it? I don't say it's their fault, but they sure do attract calamity." Audrey shook her head, perhaps in agreement or perhaps not; her pearls bounced against her collarbone. "The entire Middle East may explode," said Anston. We may have to eat dinner by candlelight every night, and ride a horse and carriage to get to our house in Oyster Bay, and bombs may fly about and American boys will die, and exactly who is at the center of that storm? I ask you, can history consist entirely of coincidences?" Audrey reached for the echinacea that sat in the middle of their breakfast table. She thought she must be catching Anston's cold, which he thought he had caught from the doorman at his club. The doorman's name, Anston reported with some satisfaction, was Bruno Levy, a recent arrival, a Jew with germs from the Ukraine.

Sam Linxman was on television at least three times a day, claiming that the voices of intolerance had spoken and must be met with a firm hand. He deplored the killings in Muttonneck but repeated over and over again that this would not have happened had the massacre in Pointshrub not started the trouble. He wore perhaps a little bit too much pancake makeup, which made his complexion seem like stale bread. He had combed his hair carefully over his bald spot, and he thanked each talk show host warmly, calling him or her by name and implying an old and wonderful friendship. He loved appearing on television and ordered tapes of each show for his private library, where they would rest for posterity, for the biographer he most certainly believed he would have.

Mel went on the six o'clock news. He promised a swift investigation. He called for hands across the neighborhoods. He refused to blame the anti-Semites in the Moslem world. He looked unhappy. He had shadows under his eyes. Maddie still found him interesting; perhaps this was because of his features, or perhaps it was because he was the mayor and the office made any occupant of it appealing, or at least more appealing than he would have been without it. He called the school's chancellor. "Let's get the public schoolchildren to bring flowers to the sites, both of them," he suggested. The chancellor pointed out that the Jewish children were at religious schools not under his control. "Get the rabbis in Pointshrub to bring their children to Muttonneck, and I'll get the principal of P.S. 245 to bring the kids to any school you like in Pointshrub for a milk-and-cookies sit-down." "Forget it," said Mel, who realized he would need all of Fort Dix to protect all the children from the rage of the very riled up, the mad—both the angry and the other kind.

On the steps of the yeshiva of Pointshrub the mayor turned toward the photographers and reporters waiting there, ready to report any breaking news. "I have nothing to say," he said. "We don't understand this yet." The mayor was about to go on when a reporter interrupted. "Any evidence of foreign influence here on our streets? Was this a a terrorist attack? Do we allow the Mossad to operate in our city?" "No," said the mayor. "No, we don't invite the Mossad in to do our work. No foreign group has claimed credit for the original killings. It seems as if this tragedy is homegrown, but we're open to anything, we're investigating everything."

The weather had turned colder. The snow had changed to ice. Icicles hung off the branches of the trees of the city, tiny shimmering daggers pointing downward at the heads of passersby. The sun glanced off the ice ponds and made the eye blink with its stabbing light. Cars skidded across intersections. Buses crawled. People wore mufflers over their mouths. They pulled hats down over their ears. They were afraid of each other. The social contract, the Hobbesian contract that prevented chaos if citizens relinquished their rights to murder their neighbors, had not been broken, of course, but it was definitely the worse for wear.

"We have to wait for the inspectors to do their job," said Maddie, putting her hand on the mayor's knee while they drove in the police car back to the mayor's office. He didn't notice. Or he was too preoccupied to notice.

65

A CONVERSATION ABOUT
UNCIVIL THINGS AT
THE CIVICS CLUB

Ruth was having lunch with Audrey at the Civics Club, a women-only club, where the walls were painted pink and the staircase railing was white and the ladies' room had fresh roses in Ming vases and the luncheon buffet table held six kinds of salad and there was a great silver samovar that served hot chocolate. A small dish of miniature marshmallows sat on each table, and the room was surrounded by portraits of women who had served as president of the club in past years. They all had worn their pearls and low-cut ball gowns for their portraits.

"A drink?" asked Audrey. Ruth shook her head. "I'm going to have a whiskey sour," said Audrey. "I need it today." "What's wrong?" said Ruth. "Everything's fine," said Audrey. Ruth commented, "You're lucky—everything is never fine in my house." Audrey looked at her friend—a new friend to be sure, a strange friend, who seemed to see through her, right into her heart, the way none of her friends, not even her old roommate from Vassar, could. Her eyes filled with tears, which she tried to hide behind a napkin. "Audrey," said Ruth in a no-nonsense voice, "tell me the truth." The word *truth* made Audrey weep some more. "It's my daughter," said Audrey. "She says I was never there for her. I hired too many nannies. Everyone did in those days; it was expected." Ruth nodded. "She says," Audrey went on, "that I failed her. I never let her experience her anger, her therapist says; I was controlling and repressive and would not allow her to express her genuine feelings. My daughter says I don't know how to love." Audrey whispered these terrible accusations even though the women at the next table were deeply engrossed in their own conversation. Audrey was pale as a ghost. She looked old, older than usual. Her skin seemed to sag around her mouth. She was the portrait of defeat itself, female-style defeat. Ruth wanted to eat her chicken salad, which sat on the table before her, all tempting greens and cucumber, but she felt it rude to chew in the middle of this particular conversation.

Ruth said, "Did you expect to be given a medal for good parenting?" She smiled to show that this was a joke, sort of a joke. Audrey sighed and gulped her whiskey sour. "Look," said Ruth, "our children have many complaints, mine too. Of course they do. We are imperfect, mortal mothers who had our own aches and pains and our own bad memories, and we are jealous and competitive and weak at least some of the time. If we are waiting for a therapist's stamp of approval, we might as well die right now. That is not news." "But," said Audrey. "I tried. I really tried so hard." "We all did," said Ruth, "but it was in the cards that we would step on their delicate, fragile heads at some point or other. They remember the stepping on but not all the other things. They forget about how we got up at night and held them when they were sick." Audrey sobbed so audibly that the women at the next table did turn around to stare. "I think I hired a nanny to do that." "Well," said Ruth, "you did many other things, didn't you?" "I did," said Audrey. "I watched my daughter ride week after week, and I hate horses." "I know," said Ruth. "You loved your daughter, and if she can't see it right now, she will someday. Anyhow," Ruth added with her own deep sigh, "we are not in the business of child rearing to be praised or rewarded with appreciation and affection. This is a job we do out of blind obedience to the dictates of biology. We do it because we convince ourselves we must. Our only repayment is the knowledge that we lived our lives, placed our mark on someone. Why do you think that they declared a Mother's Day?" Audrey looked startled. "For commercial reasons?" she guessed. "No," said Ruth. "It's so children would remember for one day of the year that they were not raised by crocodiles." "Shouldn't we tell young women this, before they begin their families? We could start an organization to reveal the truth about the ingratitude of children." Audrey was back to her normal color, thinking of a way to serve society. "I'm sure we could have the Civics Club for a benefit dinner. I know a lot of women who would like to be on our board," she added. "No," said Ruth. "If our offspring knew what we know, they might not bear children, and think what that might do to the social security system, to the economy. Besides, I like having grandchildren." "What can we do?" Audrey asked, noticing her salad and picking up her fork. "Nothing," said Ruth. "Of course," she added, "you could cut down on the whiskey sours."

Ruth called Mel on her cell phone from the cab on her way back to her office. "Any news?" she asked. "No," said Mel. "I'm sorry," Ruth said. "I'm sorry, too," said Mel. "What if they never solve this? It sticks in the craw of the city. We could have imitation massacres, an epidemic of tribal warfare—the African Americans decide to off a group of Koreans, and the Chinese decide to get the Irish, and the Protestants get the Catholics, and we have to take over a Wal-Mart to accommodate all the corpses." "Get a grip," said Ruth.

She called her daughter in her lab. "I'm very busy, Mother," Ina said. "I know," said Ruth. "I just had to ask you something." "What?" said Ina, trying but not succeeding in keeping the irritation out of her voice. "I just was thinking," Ruth said, "we haven't had much time to talk recently. I miss you." Ina sighed audibly. "It's all right," said Ruth, "I gotta go now." Ina heard something in her mother's voice, a catch, a rasp, a whisper of a plea, an unsaid word that left an echo in the phone line. "Mother," said Ina, "do you remember how we used to play gin when we rented that beach house the summer I was eight and how you always let me win?" "I do," said Ruth thinking of the rain on the roof and the wet towels growing mildew on the porch. "Well, thanks," said Ina. "See you soon." "Sure," said Ruth, who if she had been a cat would have purred, so content was she.

"Yeeew," said the Imp of Misfortune. "How sentimental, how icky these mortals be." "Yeah," said the Imp of Itches-in-Hard-to-Reach-Places, "they'll get what's coming to them." The imps laughed their smart-aleck laughs, which sound to human ears like the drill of the dentist.

66

BROOKE CROSSES
A BRIDGE

rooke had made an appointment with a divorce lawyer, an old
law school classmate of Jacob's, and she wanted a new serious
outfit, perhaps a gray suit with a white satin blouse, for their
first meeting. She had not yet discussed her intentions with Jacob.
She wanted to understand the bottom line before she began a
process she might not wish to finish. Brooke decided to go to the
outlet mall across the bridge, which not only took her out of the
city but as soon as you exited off the ramp you were right in another
state, one that actually had no sales tax. She decided to take Kim
and Kelly with her. That way she would be certain to purchase her
selections, which seemed a good idea on the whole, because a
record of arrests could be held against her in the divorce process.
On Saturday morning she packed her children into a bright blue
Mini Cooper she had borrowed from her friend Norma, who was a
food stylist and would have been using her car but was staying in
bed waiting for her Zoloft to kick in. When you really noticed your
children, Brooke had discovered, their joys may be infinite and
their laughter spontaneous at the worst jokes ever invented, but
they spend a large portion of their time jockeying for advantage,

feeling hurt by remarks someone carelessly made, or suffering physical pain from a jab in the ribs or a poke in the eye. Truly observing your offspring leaves you again and again stabbed in your pincushion heart.

The visit to the mall went well. She bought Kim and Kelly each a new Beanie Baby from the rack of animals in the toy store. They stopped and had hot chocolate and cookies and they watched the skaters at the indoor rink. Brooke bought nothing for herself because she remembered that Jacob really liked her in dresses better than suits, which was irrelevant under the circumstances, but nevertheless . . . She bought the girls new wool hats with rabbit ears that they both found enchanting.

As they left the mall the sky was turning gray-blue; the sun was already winter white on the horizon. Traffic was heavy pulling up to the bridge, and the wait at the toll booth was long. The heat in the car was too high, and Brooke opened the window for a breath of fresh air. Her head felt heavy. She was fighting sleep. It had been a long day.

Halfway across the river, in the middle of the bridge, there was a sudden thump against the Mini Cooper's hood. A moaning sound came from the front of the car. Years ago, home from college, she had driven a back road and hit a deer. She remembered that sound. But of course there were no deer on the bridge. Brooke hit the brake. She was hardly moving; she couldn't have harmed anything. There was no stopped car in front of her. She told the children to wait and not to unbuckle their seat belts, and she walked to the front of her car. Other cars were moving around her as if she were a rock in a river whose waters were in a hurry to reach the sea. There on the ground in front of her car she saw him, an old man, or was he an old man? A drunk perhaps, a beggar, but perhaps not—his hair was long, yellow curls framed his white face, but he was wrinkled, he was old, older than any living person Brooke had ever seen. He was wearing sandals, and he seemed to have a cane that lay now at his side. He had no coat. He did not smell of whiskey or urine. Brooke bent over him. "Don't move," she said. "We'll get an ambulance." She went back to her car to get her cell phone. She dialed, but there was no ring. Perhaps her cell phone didn't work suspended over water.

She tried to flag down a car, but no one stopped. Kim had undone her seat belt. She came to Brooke's side. "Oh," the child said. "His fingers are so long." "Shh," said Brooke, "it's rude," she whispered to her daughter, "to make personal comments like that." But it was true—the man she had hit had hands like a conductor, a musician, long fingers meant to reach across keys or strings. Kim leaned down and did the only thing she could think of doing to rectify her rudeness: She kissed his cheek, very gently. The man stirred. Brooke smelled his breath. He had not been drinking. What are you doing here, in the middle of the bridge? she almost yelled at him, but then she didn't.

The man slowly got to his feet, pulled his garments around him, and stood up. He was very tall, maybe seven feet. His back was straight, and his skin seemed paper thin; beneath it Brooke could see the pulsing of veins. "Please," said Brooke, "you shouldn't stand, you might have broken something inside, you might be bleeding. I should take you to a hospital. Get in my car and we'll go." "It's all right," said the man. "I was just stunned." "Why were you walking here?" Brooke asked. "In traffic," she added, a touch of exasperation in her voice. "I was waiting for you," the man said. "Sure," said Brooke.

"I'm not going to the hospital," said the man. "It is not necessary, but it is kind of you to offer to take me." He had an accent, a strange accent, Israeli but not exactly, one Brooke had never heard before. "I want you to know that you are not as alone as you think you are," the man said. "What?" said Brooke, who was beginning to think the man had escaped from the Metro Psychiatric Institute, which was just on the city side of the bridge. "No," said the man, as if he could read her thoughts. "I'm not out of my mind. Last year, at your in-laws' seder, I touched your shoulder. Do you remember me?" Brooke shook her head. There were a few people at the seder she had not known, but not this man, this enormously tall man with the yellow curls and the beard and the very white fingernails at the end of his long fingers. "No," said Brooke, "I don't remember you." "The door was opened and a wind blew and I was there." The man was so tall that Brooke had to tip her head back to look in his face. "If you were Jewish," said the man, "you would know who I am, and you would be glad that I am your friend." Brooke felt dizzy. She closed her eyes for a moment. When she opened them he was gone. She looked at the side of the bridge and ahead of her, then walked to the back of the car. He was gone. Kim and Kelly were waiting for her in the car. Brooke got back in the driver's seat. The traffic moved in its usual flow. The girls were quiet. "What a strange man," said Brooke. "What man?" said Kim. "What man, where?" asked Kelly. "Back there, the man I hit with the car." "When?" asked Kim. "Are you sure?" said Kelly. Brooke had a headache.

67

MADDIE MAKES
HER MOVE

The mayor and Moe Alter were at the hospital once again. This hospital was in Nancy Beach, where the Greeks and the Italians had settled many generations ago. It seems that a young black man and his girlfriend had come to Nancy Beach in answer to an advertisement for baby equipment, secondhand and cheap: a car seat, a stroller, a bassinet. The girl was expecting. The boy was trying to stay in college and get a degree in accounting. When they got out of the subway a crowd of white kids followed them along the street, and there was some kind of confrontation. The boy had been hit on the head with a bat and was now unconscious in Nancy Beach Hospital. Racism and riot were in the air. The black ministers were calling on police officials to make arrests, but mothers were not opening their doors to the police, and no witnesses had been found. There was talk of a group of black boys storming Nancy Beach to get revenge. Riot police were out in their scary gear, helmets pulled down over their faces, horses leaving dung in the gutters, guns at hips, ready for what might come. The boy who was hit with a bat might recover fully or he might remain a vegetable. His mother sat by his bedside dry-eyed. Her minister stood behind her, and in the waiting area her lawyer paced up and down. Mel wanted to touch the mother, to place his arm around her shoulders. But he saw the way she was looking at him, and so he retreated. God, how he hated hospitals and tubes and having to comfort mothers who might or might not get their children returned to them. The press photographers wanted a picture of him next to the bedside with the heart monitor bleeping behind him. Mel refused. He ducked his head just as if he were a perp on a walk to jail. "You're just the mayor," Maddie said to him on their way back to city hall. "You're no archangel or anything like that."

Rabbi Gedali sat in his office and considered the situation. Why, he wondered, had he not been able to find anyone—not a vendor of pretzels, not a mother with a child on the way to a friend's, not a man coming or going from prayer or work—who had seen the Arab boys coming through the streets? No insomniac had noticed them out his window. No woman had been tossing and turning, fearing whatever she feared in the dark. The night watchman at the store that sold olive oil and spices had not heard any footsteps, and the store was just around the corner from where the boys had been found. Yes, it was snowing and had snowed all night, which was why there were no footsteps to trace, no signs of trespass on the ground, but was it possible in a neighborhood as crowded as this one that no one had seen or heard anything? What were his boys doing out in the snow? Playing games, perhaps, but they should have been studying or sleeping in their beds. What were they doing in harm's way, and who had put them there? Rabbi Gedali had not honed his reasoning on the Talmud for nothing. He knew when something was odd and the easy answers too easy. He also knew that the *yetzer hara* was everywhere, his own community not excepted, and that something worse than what everyone now believed might have happened in Pointshrub. But how to find out what, how to settle the matter? His heart was prone to skipping a beat or two when he got excited. His doctor had given him medicine so this wouldn't happen. It was happening anyway.

Rabbi Gedali knew what he had to do next. The police were all over the yeshiva, interviewing everyone they could find, but the boys kept their eyes down, their hands in the pockets of their black coats, and excused themselves as fast as they could. The police wrote down each boy's name but then had trouble telling them apart, remembering their faces. They seemed to blur into one boy, with *payeus,* with a black hat, with pants perhaps a little too big for his hips. The police would never get any information out of these boys, who had been raised with a distrust of uniforms, of officials, nursed on suspicions of officials, a suspicion that had served their grandparents well and increased survival rates. This distrust was not so much passed on in whispers, father to son, as mutated into the genetic code. Rabbi Gedali would have to conduct his own investigation, and fast.

Back in the mayor's office Maddie sat down across from Mel and crossed and uncrossed her long legs. Mel felt a lump rise in his throat. "Aren't you cold?" he said to Maddie. "Maybe you want to wear your coat." "I'm fine," she answered. "I think," she said, "it is time you came to my apartment and we enjoyed ourselves. What the hell are we waiting for? I could make you happy," said Maddie. "I know you would like to come. All you have to do is say so." What an offer, what a thing for a man who has not been approached like that in years, who was shy when he courted his wife and afraid she might find him too ambitious, too pushy, too full of words to want him in her life ever after. Mel was flattered. He was pleased. He was tempted. He was aroused—that he knew for sure. "Maddie," he said, "excuse me," and he walked out the door. In his outer office, where Harold was bringing his computer up to date and working the antivirus thing for all it was worth, he took a deep breath. He put his head against the windowpane in hopes of cooling himself off. Was he a coward? Would another man jump at the chance he was trying to avoid? "Want something?" asked Harold. Moe burst in through the door. The boy in the Nancy Beach hospital had come out of his coma. He would be all right. Mel let out a war yell, the kind he had emitted as a child when they played cowboys and Indians (Native Americans, he corrected himself) on the steps of the brownstones that lined his old block.

Maddie heard his war yell and came out of the office. She smiled a big smile when she heard the news. "Send flowers to the hospital," said Mel to the young lady who worked at a nearby desk. "Poor lawyers," said Maddie, "this case will settle." "Nothing poor about the lawyers," said Moe.

Maddie knew that her moment had passed. She knew that Mel was a married man she couldn't have. That fact was stored in a part of her mind that held other rejections, older ones. It would not interfere with her job or her plans to win a Pulitzer before she was forty, but it did make her consider—not for the first time, of course—why she didn't have a man of her own.

68

A CONFESSION THAT CHANGES EVERYTHING

That night Brooke slept as she hadn't slept since she was a girl. Jacob came home late from the office and saw that his children were in their beds, where they belonged, and then he poured himself a glass of good pinot grigio so his muscles would relax and the back of his neck once again sink down on his shoulders. When he walked into the bedroom he hung up his suit very carefully so that it would appear perfectly pressed the next time he wore it. He set out a clean, ironed shirt, a blue pinstriped tie, and matching socks. Then and only then did he sit down on the edge of the bed and look over at his wife. Her hair was lying about without clips, her face was bare of makeup, and her skin was free of smeared applications of anti-wrinkle cream. He held his breath for a nanosecond. She seemed in her sleep so peaceful, as if she were lying by a riverbed listening to Ella Fitzgerald singing out her heart from the radio in the car parked on the road above them, the way it was that afternoon shortly after they met and he had found some wildflowers and brought them to her. It was unfortunate about the poison ivy he had included in his bouquet, but then what does a city boy know about weeds? He wanted to kiss her toes, to stroke her calves, to touch just gently the place behind her ears where she put the perfume he had given her for their first anniversary. God, he was lucky she was in his bed. Did she understand that? Had he been so busy, clocking so many hours, that he had neglected to tell her, to hold her, to say to her that she was . . . well, what was she? He considered. He couldn't put a name to it, he couldn't find a way to explain it, but he knew she was a soul and that this soul was his *beshert,* his fate, his mate, his only hope. He lay down on the bed and reached for her hand. He held it without putting pressure on it, without pulling it toward him or placing it on his own chest. He just held it and waited. She slept on undisturbed, a strange sweet smile on her face as if she was dreaming of good things either in the past or in the future. Jacob startled. Am I turning her into an object? He thought. Do I like her so much because she isn't talking or demanding anything or making me feel wrong about something? Do I like her because she seems half dead? Jacob searched his mind. He looked again at Brooke's face and felt a deep sorrow. She was only flesh and blood and wouldn't last forever. She was not an object of the sort you find in the museum. She was a living person, the one he had selected out of all the others, and tonight he knew why, even if he could not have told you, not for a million dollars, and Jacob was a man who did indeed care about money.

When he woke in the morning there was Brooke by his side. She was awake. She was smiling at him. She was still without cream or makeup. She looked very young. "Jacob," she said, "do you remember when we got married and your mom and dad wanted to know if I would convert and I said never, ever?" "Yes," said Jacob, "I didn't care," he said. "It didn't matter to me. I liked you just the way you were." "I know," said Brooke, "but I've been thinking. Maybe I made a mistake." "What?" said Jacob. "I could study it for a while," she said. "I thought," said Jacob, "you weren't interested in any more mumbo-jumbo, that's what you said." "I know what I said," said Brooke, "but a person can get curious, can't they?" "Well," said Jacob, "as long as you don't make me relearn my bar mitzvah portion, what harm can it do?" Brooke looked at Jacob, at his dark eyes, at his chest with the clumps of hair sticking out from his pajama top. "Do you remember that I was a history major?" "Of course," said Jacob, who in fact had forgotten that Brooke had ever studied anything. "I would really like to know something about Jewish history—the real thing, not your mother's thumbnail version," Brooke said, looking intently into his face. "I think God wants me to do this." Would he laugh at her now? He didn't laugh. "What brought this on?" he asked. "I ran over some old guy on the bridge yesterday," Brooke said. "You did what?" Jacob jumped up and began reaching for the phone. "Did you call the insurance company? Is he in the hospital? Is he dead? Why didn't you tell me?" "Don't worry," said Brooke. "He disappeared." "What do you mean, disappeared?" asked Jacob. "I mean he was there and then he wasn't." "What has this to do with you studying Jewish history?" "I can't convert if I don't know the history and the traditions and all," said Brooke. "Yes," said Jacob, "but the man you ran over—are you sure he's all right?" "I told you," said Brooke. "He disappeared." "Into thin air," said Jacob. "Into thin air," said Brooke.

Rabbi Gedali began with his youngest students, the ones who had not yet fully changed their voices or grown to their allotted inches. He called them into his office one by one and looked deep into their eyes and told them that they were under every obligation to the entire Jewish people from the time of Abraham through that of Rashi and up to the present, and that to honor the great Rambam and to keep their minds alive and receptive to the word of Hashem, they must reveal anything they might know about the boys who were shot in the snow. There was no commandment, he repeated to his young charges, that they should keep secrets from their rabbi. He repeated this speech some forty times, as many times as years the Jews wandered in the desert, until he found Mendel Berne, who had a sharp mind and a good heart and no father at all and wanted Rabbi Gedali to care for him above all the others. Mendel had something to say, and when he had said it Rabbi Gedali embraced the young man, and there were tears on his face dripping into his beard.

"I didn't want to make you cry," said Mendel. "It's not you that is making me cry," said Rabbi Gedali. "Go now," he said to Mendel, "I wouldn't say a word about this conversation to anyone if I were you." "I won't," said Mendel, "I promise. Did I do the right thing in telling you?" said Mendel. The rabbi, who wished he did not know what he now knew, assured Mendel that he had not lost his place in the world to come.

The Imp of Disorder, the Imp of Adolescent Dreams, the Imp of Gravy Spilled, and the Imp of Dust on the Books in the Library together danced a wild imp dance. Now it would come out, now it would be seen, now everyone would know that innocence is a sham. Man is born to disgrace himself.

69

A BUSINESS DEAL
IS SEALED

Bontche Schweig looked down from the heavens, and there were tears in his eyes. Tears of rage. Ah, how good it felt to be really angry. How the anger coursed through his veins and cleared his sinuses and made his heart pump the way a human heart should. Bontche Schweig had learned some things since last he appeared in this story. He now knew that Eli and Nathaniel and his friends were members of a secret defense organization, a group that had dedicated themselves to the protection of their people, to the proactive, preemptive activity that had been so unthinkable to poor Bontche, who had always believed that survival rested with lying low, hiding in the shadows, asking little, demanding nothing. Bontche, although no longer by virtue of his existential condition able to participate in the affairs of the world, was a new member, and with a convert's zeal he wanted to see his boys on the go again. He wanted them in the streets chasing down anti-Semites wherever they might be. Samuel Linxman and his good suit and his organization with its computer-outfitted offices and his palsy-walsy way with the mainstream press did not impress Bontche. He searched all over the World to Come for Baruch Goldstein, who had shot some praying Moslems in the back, so he could give him a welcome hug and a piece of his roll, but he couldn't find Baruch anywhere. Perhaps he was alive and well in Argentina? He was pleased with all the knocking down of homes and rolling out of tanks against the enemy in Zion, and he was pleased with the fellows in Pointshrub who had taken matters into their own strong hands. You can't blame him for this.

Moderation, an Aristotelian means between two extremes, is not a natural place for any person to be. Bontche, having experienced so much cruelty in his lifetime, could only conceive of resistance as a violent act of cruelty toward someone else. To simply stand up for oneself without having to knock someone else down, at least most of the time, was an idea that might take centuries more for Bontche to master. What upset Bontche now was that Rabbi Gedali was praying in his study. Listening to his prayers, Bontche had discovered some very surprising facts that might lead to trouble for his avengers, his heroes, the golems of Pointshrub. The thought that they would be stopped, punished perhaps, made him clench his fists and grind his teeth. Time, of course, even in the World to Come, can change a person, turn him inside out and find the potential that was there all along, only hidden from sight. Bontche wasn't Bontche anymore.

Leonid and his new partner, Vladi, admired the hats they had made. They tried them on each other even though they were made for ladies. The receptionist and Vladi's assistant tried them on and then wouldn't until commanded take them off. Leonid had insisted on a softer brim, on taking the pompom off the center and moving it further forward. Vladi had written down figures on sheets of paper and then threw them into his computer and changed them a thousand times. Leonid, who had relapsed and was again smoking, was now wearing a nicotine patch. "You cannot stink like an ashtray when we go to the buyers," said Vladi. Leonid had wanted to punch Vladi in the mouth and watch his teeth fall out in response to that comment, but he had let the impulse pass. It was true, he smelled, and his teeth were yellow, so he stopped at a drugstore on his way to his brother's house for dinner and purchased a package of Crest Whitestrips. In a few weeks, he was promised, he would have a dazzling smile. Vladi went with Leonid to the MetroCity Hospital Thrift Shop. There they purchased a dark blue Armani suit and a Brooks Brothers coat and a striped tie. It was all too big for Leonid, who was wide but not tall, but Vladi had one of his workers—a man from a small village a thousand miles west of Shanghai, who nodded and nodded at Leonid as if he were a new boss, an important man—fix the sleeves and shorten the cuffs and hem the coat. Leonid bought himself a tie with cash he had stashed in his shoe box from some other dealings we won't mention here. He wanted the red tie with leopards jumping across a pink stripe down its center, but Vladi said no, the tie must not draw attention to itself. Leonid understood in an instant. In America a rich man dressed without noise and a poor man dressed loudly. Gold threads were for singers, and dark blue was the color of big bank accounts.

The two men had an appointment made by Vladi with the head buyer at Loomy's. Leonid was nervous and wanted some chewing gum, but Vladi wouldn't let him. The hats were in a box that Leonid carried in his arms. Fiona Flaherty kept the men waiting a long time. She was chatting on the phone with her younger sister about some evildoings of their older sister. Also, she expected nothing from the meeting, which she had granted because her wedding gown had been altered by a cousin of Vladi's and there had been a last-minute catastrophe that the cousin had worked all night to fix— it had to do with her gaining a few pounds in the weeks before the event. Anyway, Fiona Flaherty looked at the hats that emerged from Leonid's box. She smiled. She put one on her head. Leonid said, "Pull it down a little—more to the left." She did as he instructed and then looked in the mirror that hung on her office door. "Well," she said. "Well," said Vladi, who was not quite sure what this expression meant in this context. "Well," said Leonid, flashing his dark eyes at Fiona, who did indeed look charming in the hat.

"I'll take three hundred," said Fiona, "delivery next month." "Three hundred?" said Vladi, who did not have the capital to buy the material for twenty hats. "I don't think so," said Vladi, and was about to explain that he couldn't produce three hundred hats in a month, not without funds he didn't have, but Fiona cut him off. "All right," she said, because she was having visions of seeing her hat in other stores, "I could manage four hundred." Leonid felt faint. He did not understand that there was no money to buy the cloth. Four hundred! He had hoped she would take twenty. Vladi was very pale, but he bowed his head in agreement. "We need an advance," he said. "Of course," said Ms. Flaherty, "we do that all the time." "You do?" said Vladi, trying to keep the surprise out of his voice. "We do," she confirmed. "I would like," she added, "to keep this sample for myself. You don't mind, do you?" "Of course not," both men protested. "And what other designs do you have? Do you do anything besides hats?" "We do," said Vladi. "We do?" said Leonid.

70

THEY LOST IT AT
THE MOVIES

The older boys at Duncan Academy, some of them at least, had found their way to pot, and a few of them had tried Ecstasy, and many of them had done things with girls that their mothers, many with graduate degrees, would have wept over if they knew, which they didn't. Some of Duncan Academy's A students were experimenting with Hinduism, and some were cheating on exams, and some were sneaking cigarettes in the park. Some had bottles of scotch in their backpacks, and some were dabbling in the politics of the extreme right or the extreme left, whichever would drain the most blood from their parents' faces. They had parties on Saturday nights at which porno flicks were running in the den and Duncan Academy girls were stripping in the kitchen.

On the other hand, in a contrast as sharp as night from day, the boys at the yeshiva of Pointshrub were protected from the seductions of the secular world. They were not allowed to watch TV with all its crass materialism, its open and vulgar sex. Their heads, their bodies, were expected to remain within the community, within the approved. If rebellion reared its ugly head at all, it was expressed only in dreams or secrets so terrible they were never shared. These are not boys who would eat ham sandwiches or peek through the keyhole of their sister's bedroom. If they wished to shock their parents, they could simply carry a wallet on the Sabbath, and for the most part they did no such thing, because they believed with all their soul that God knew what they were doing and wanted them to do the right thing, the prescribed thing, the thing that kept them in the folds of the neighborhood, close to their families, as it had always been and as it would be in the generations to come.

But alas, hormones are hormones, and it is as natural for the human male in his early years to kick against the restraints of his kind as it is for beards to grow and voices to drop. So it was that Chaim found himself asking questions of Harvey, who had dropped out of the yeshiva because he was what in another part of town would be called a slow learner. Harvey had gotten a job with a bakery, and one of the men who delivered the sacks of flour to the back of the store was a black guy named Earl who had a passion for old movies. As they sat on the back steps of the bakery after the job was done, smoking the cigarette Earl offered, Earl told Chaim and Harvey stories, the likes of which they had never heard before. Chaim told the stories to Feibel, his brother. "Let's get some movies," said Feibel, putting one foot on a very slippery slope. "How?" said Chaim. Next time the truck pulled up to the back of the bakery, Feibel was there. "We want to see the movies you told Chaim and Harvey about," he said to Earl. "You need a television set," said Earl. "You got one?" "No," said Feibel. "You can get one for a few hundred dollars," Earl explained. "That all you need?" asked Feibel. "No," said Earl, "you need a VCR." "What's that?" said Feibel. Earl sighed. "You got eight hundred dollars, I'll get one for you." "And the movies," said Feibel, who was no fool. "Get us those movies, too, same price." Did Feibel have eight hundred dollars? He did not. Chaim, who worked, had saved up a few hundred. He gave what he had to his brother. Harvey chipped in. Feibel went to a few of his friends. Fifty dollars here, twelve dollars there, someone's sister lent him forty dollars believing the money was for

ANNE ROIPHE

278

the support of a yeshiva in the FSU. By the time the full eight hundred dollars was assembled, fifteen yeshiva boys had purchased a share of the VCR and the television and the movies. There was a signed contract written by Feibel and kept in his shirt drawer.

And so it was and so Rabbi Gedali heard the whole story unfold, that the VCR and the television were placed in a storeroom in the back of the bakery covered with an old piece of canvas. So it was that, never on the Sabbath, but on Wednesday nights, when the other boys were poring through books, making their eyes weak staring at fine print in texts that went round and round large pages, the fifteen who owned the equipment began to watch the movies. Earl had given them four movies. They watched them over and over. They were *Spellbound* with Ingrid Bergman, *The Bells of St. Mary's, Notorious,* and then, last but not least, *Gone With the Wind*, with Vivien Leigh. Think of the pleasure of it: a transgression more terrible than any of the boys at Duncan Academy could have concocted, a voyage out of the neighborhood, out of the people-hood, out of the America of the twenty-first century, not to mention whatever timeless place the yeshiva of Pointshrub inhabited.

Think what it did to these young imaginations, unsullied with visions of Arnold Schwarzenegger, John Wayne, Tom Hanks, innocent of Nicole Kidman and Winona Ryder and Britney Spears, never having seen the Stones or the Grateful Dead or Johnny Cash or Dolly Parton, never having heard of John Lennon, Eminem, or P.diddy. Tabula rasas they were, even though their minds were filled almost to overflowing with the wisdom of the rabbis and the portions of the week and the midrashes of the ages. Think how beautiful Ingrid Bergman looked at prayer in St. Mary's, the very spirit of God inhabiting her habit. Think how odd it must have seemed to watch the Civil War as it unfolded as Atlanta burned and think how it must have been to imagine yourself saving Vivien and Scarlett from the vile hands of those who would harm her.

To understand what followed, you must remember what it is to love truly for the first time. Because that is what happened in the back of the bakery on Wednesday nights. Fifteen young men felt their hearts captured, their sexual urges rise, their gallantry soar, their hopes for themselves fly upward in search of fulfillment. The objects of their love were Ingrid and Vivien. They soon could recite whole minutes of dialogue. They soon began to act out the parts in sync with the turnings of the VCR. They were inflamed. If they had been other boys with a different education, we might have spoken of them developing crushes, but what these boys felt was not a crush, which has about it the sound of childhood's foolery. They had a passion, a fierce and wonderful passion. This kind of passion knows only one object and cannot be shared. Which means that some of the boys loved Vivien and others preferred Ingrid, and the two camps split.

It was in this split that the *yetzer hara* found his footing. It was in this split that the disaster began.

No doubt a German hausfrau listening to Hitler at a rally may have felt love. No doubt that Paris loved Helen of Troy, and the resulting kidnapping and the whole long saga that followed began (just as with Feibel and his friends) with love. Think how much better off the ancient world would have been if Paris had hated Helen and left her where he found her. Everyone forgets that Cupid's arrow is dipped in poison.

71

IT'S ALL **HOLLYWOOD'S FAULT**, OR IS IT?

As Rabbi Gedali heard the story he felt his breath grow short. Such a thing he had never imagined, could never have imagined despite his years of study, despite his wide and deep knowledge of human nature. He stared at the young man telling him the tale as if he would bore holes through the boy's brain. "No," he kept saying, "no, it can't be." But it was.

At first the matter of which of the two actresses was more worthy, more pure, more perfect was no more than a heated discussion among friends, but then gradually lines were drawn and camps pitched. The Ingrid camp began to look down on the Vivien camp. The Vivien camp thought that the Ingrid camp was falling for images of Aryan beauty that were traitorous to the Jewish people. The Ingrid camp felt that Vivien was perhaps an evil spirit; look at the disasters that followed her about. She was dark-haired, like other demons. No matter how the Vivien camp tried to defend their heroine—pointing out, of course, that the Nazis had demonized the Jews for their dark hair—the Ingrid camp would not budge. The group watched the movies over and over, interrupting the dialogue with sighs and moans and expressions of chivalric love.

There were attempts made to defuse the tension. Feibel said it was like the school of Shammai and the school of Hillel all over again. But that just made all the boys uncomfortable and even more irritable with each other because there was an element in their love for Vivien and Ingrid that was less than holy and they knew it—how could they not? "It's like the Vilna Gaon against the Bal Shem," Feibel tried again. "It's not," said an Ingrid supporter, "not like that at all." And so it went for some weeks: the boys meeting late at night, when their families thought them asleep in their beds, watching the same films over and over, now imagining themselves inside the stories, now noticing little things, the flicker of light on an eyelash, the curve of an elbow as it bent, the slight dip of a lower lip, the hint of a hair blown out of place.

One night as snow was starting to fall they gathered as usual, but their tempers were unusually high. It became important to the Vivien camp that the Ingrid camp concede the greater value of their actress, a greater woman of valor, clearly. The Ingrid camp did not back down and growled and began to menace with their eyes. And then Harvey brought out from behind a desk in the back of the bakery a gun. He gave it to Chaim. It was there to protect against robberies. It was there because no Jew intended to be slaughtered in his workplace, because the baker, although a man with a smile for all, as a child had learned the hard way to distrust the calm of the moment. Chaim, with Harvey echoing anything he said, was a Vivien supporter. "Say it," he called out. "Say it, she is the better, she is the more perfect, she is the one you should love. Say it or I'll shoot." At first no one paid him any attention, but then there was pushing and shoving, and some fists were thrust out, and someone shouted at Chaim that he was worse than the fools of Chelm, thinking he could change a man's heart with a gun, and then there was a boy on the floor kicking his opponent, and then someone lunged for Chaim and the gun went off. The sound of the shot stunned all the boys, and Chaim, who was frightened, shot again because he didn't know what else to do, couldn't quite let go of the gun or the moment.

Someone else grabbed Chaim from behind and took the gun, and in the process more shots, random shots, rang out. There was blood on the bakery floor. There were boys lying in the blood. Chaim was shot, and he called for his mother, and then he called for Vivien as if she would appear off the screen and sweep him away. Perhaps she did. He choked and died. It was a terrible scene, and who knows exactly who did what to whom; in the excitement, the TV tipped off the table and the VCR made a screeching sound and there was just darkness. When it was over, a few boys were crying.

One of the others got a mop and a bucket of water, and they mopped down the bakery floor. Three of the survivors carried the dead and put them in the street around the corner from the bakery; it was snowing and the snow was coming down heavily, and all the world seemed magical, as if the snow could erase the past and undo what had happened and the survivors went back to their beds and Chaim's gun was placed back in the baker's drawer, where its owner might never notice that it had been used.

As for the young boy who had told all, his nose was leaking and his eyes were red when he came to the end of his tale. He had been there, included as the younger brother of one of the investors. He had hidden under a bakery cloth.

At first Rabbi Gedali was inclined to believe that the evil influence had come from the actresses and the movies and the secular world, which had lost its way and stood so far from God that no place, not even the yeshiva of Pointshrub, was safe from its corruption. But then he admitted that the boys themselves had wanted to watch the movies and that perhaps it was the gun that was to blame. If there had been no gun, then all that would have happened would have been a few bloody noses and a black eye or two. And then Rabbi Gedali acknowledged that it wasn't just the gun, not the gun alone. The shame of it overcame him, and he wept. He felt unclean, like the snow in the streets. Then he thought of the bruised and battered and dead boys in Muttonneck, and he knew that worse was to come.

Mel was on his exercise bicycle when the phone rang. He was sweating and panting and hoping that all this work would keep him alive another few years, although after twenty minutes on the bike he felt as though the end might be near. He listened to the report from the police commissioner. "I don't believe it," he said. "Are you sure? Who else knows? Are you arresting Rabbi Gedali? You can't hold him as a material witness." Mel sighed. Of course everyone else would know in a few hours. "Where are the boys who went to Muttonneck?" Mel asked. "Good question," said the police commissioner. "We have their names and addresses. We tried to pick them up, but all of them are gone, vanished, on planes to Israel, where, we are assured, they will be punished. We could try to extradite, but I doubt we'll get them."

Mel called a meeting in his office. "We can't let this city explode over Vivien Leigh and Ingrid Bergman, can we?"

72

FOOD,
GLORIOUS FOOD

What now to do for the boys of Muttonneck, who had come to America with their families in hopes of escaping the very deaths they found? What could one say to their mothers and fathers? What to do about this act of revenge on the part of some yeshiva boys that returned the city to a place of frontier justice, of lynch mobs and quick triggers, and that tore justice, real justice, down from her pedestal and left her smashed in a bloody video store? It wasn't new, this thing that had happened. The streets of the city had been witness to many beatings and murders as one group entered and piled their meager belongings into relatives' apartments. They always brought with them the smells of cooking, the sounds of accents, the color of their clothes, the alphabets of their languages, that fell on the ears of those who were already in place, or almost in place, the way a fork scrapes against the plate, or a chalk against the blackboard: unbearable that is.

If the Body Public is like a body, all parts contributing to the whole, the blood circulating through it all, the mind ordering responses, the breathing automatic, the liver with its enzymes, the aorta with its valves, everything moving together, then the Body Public that Mel presided over had developed a terrible auto-immune response, had harmed itself, perhaps terminally. So Mel thought as he considered his next move.

Mel wanted to hate the boys who had moved into Muttonneck without evidence, without thinking, who had behaved like members of an army of another country taking preemptive, preventive action, action that never preempted or prevented anything. Why had they not been good citizens who allowed the police to do their job, to wind their way to the right arrest, the right arraignment before a judge, read about the jury trial in the papers, watched the slow but steady pace of civilization repairing its rips and tears? They were gone now, these boys, out of his city, patrolling the edges of settlements far away, not talking about what had happened but carrying their guns openly, watching for the approach of shepherds and children and strangers with evil intentions. But the crowds in the streets in Muttonneck, mostly male, some women in head scarves, listening to speeches, singing songs, raising their fists, they were not going to be content until the city proved that their lives were worth as much as the lives of the yeshiva boys found in the snow. Anything that suggested otherwise was fuel for their fire, a fire that threatened to get out of control.

The translator at city hall pored over the local Arabic-language papers. "What are they saying?" Mel asked him. "You don't want to know," came the answer. "I do want to know," said Mel, "that's why we're paying you." "I mean," said the translator, "you can guess. It's as bad or worse than you might have thought." Anston Hadley called Mel. "You better do something," he said. "I'm hearing at the club that this might bring down the markets." "The markets are global," said Mel, "national. What could a small incident in Muttonneck do to the markets?" Anston said, "Listen, my friend, if there is a riot in Muttonneck, the markets will tremble, and if the markets tremble, the markets may fall. Jobs are at stake, bonuses are at stake, deals are at stake. Just take my word for it. Do something." Mel hung up. What should he do?

Moe Alter sat in the chair opposite the mayor's desk. "I don't like this," he said. "You have to be able to control these people." Mel understood perfectly, but he also understood that the entire neighborhood of Muttonneck was thirsting for revenge. They were frightened, too—what world were they in? Had this government betrayed them like every other they had ever known? They had worked hard, they had enrolled their children in school, and they knew the names of American presidents, and now the Jews were killing them. Will no one speak for them? Mel understood their fury. What to do? Bread and circuses, he thought. Wrong season for the circus, but bread is always timely.

Ina and Sergei had published two papers together. Ina had done the writing and Sergei had done the final rechecking of data. Ina and Sergei now thought like one person, at least in the lab they had moved into together. They almost didn't have to speak to each other, but they did; even in the cafeteria they leaned their heads together in a continuous whisper that made other scientists pat down their hair, straighten out their white coats, and look over their shoulders. What was it those two were saying to each other?

Mel called Ruth, who laughed. "That's what you came up with?" she said. "That's it," he said. "You got a better idea?" Ruth said, "I like yours; maybe it'll work. I'll get going." She called Ina. "I don't care what's happening in the lab—you have to come, Sergei too, and his no-good brother." "He's not so no-good," said Ina. "All right," said Ruth, "just come." Brooke promised to be there; Jacob said he would bring his staff and a few of the associates at his firm. Kim and Kelly were invited, too. In the afternoon Mel spoke to every rabbi in the city, of all stripes. He called all the leaders of all the Jewish organizations. (They won't all be listed here; there isn't enough room in all of cyberspace to print all their names.) He reached those on the political right. He tried to reach those in the middle and the left, but most of those organizations had dissolved for want of funds and disconnected their phones.

He spoke to Rabbi Gedali. "You want me to do *what*?" the old man shouted into the phone. He sighed. He consulted his heart. He agreed. Mel asked Sam Linxman to take the lead. "Cameras?" asked Sam Linxman. "Of course," said Mel. Sam agreed. He then spoke to the transit union head, to the sanitation union head. He called Anston and told him what was up. He was to be there, at Mel's side, with a contribution of his own. Anston complained. "That's too much," he said, "cut it in half." Mel agreed to 75 percent of his original request. "You jewed me down," said Mel. Anston wasn't sure if he had been insulted or complimented.

The women and girls in Pointshrub, those who had brothers at the yeshiva and their neighbors, all spent the night in their kitchens. Some grumbled, some did not. Babies woke and were nursed as pots were stirred and smells rose from the ovens. Ruth cooked her mother's kugel and wrapped it in a white napkin she used for holidays. Brooke cooked a brisket from a recipe in a Jewish cookbook. Ina and Serge were so tired from the day's work that they purchased a challah from the grocery store and put a ribbon around it.

73

EVERYONE LOVES
A PARADE

In the morning the parade began, with Linxman at the head, with Kim and Kelly each holding a bag of gefilte fish with carrot slices floating in the familiar gelatinous sauce. They walked the many blocks from the yeshiva of Pointshrub to the main street in Mutton-neck, black hats and not-so-black hats, Anston Hadley in his gray overcoat and gray leather gloves, Audrey in her mink, Ruth and Mel, Ina and Sergei pushing the baby in a stroller, Brooke and Jacob, and half the congregations of the city following. The cameras rolled, the press reported it all. It was the great apologetic walk, not to raise money for AIDS or breast cancer research or diabetes, but to insist that neighbors can live next to each other without fist-banging and bone-breaking. Leonid, who was not convinced that bone-breaking was not of use in certain difficult circumstances, came with a truck of donated dresses he had gathered from the building in which his loft was located. He handed out dresses from the back of his truck. To each dress he pinned his card, *Leonid and Vladi Inc.* The card had a silhouette of a woman's head wearing a beret with a pompom on it. The CEO of a major department store arranged for bouquets of flowers to be brought to Muttonneck and given off trucks to anyone who asked. The Wasserman Candy company had sent their executives with baskets of chocolates to hand out to all the Muttonneck children they could find. The parade broke its line and the participants went into the buildings and gave their gifts to whoever would open a door. To all who would listen, they smiled and spoke and said they were sorry. And then Rabbi Gedali made a speech in front of the market that sold curry and cumin and baklava, and Anston stepped up to the microphone that Harold had arranged to be waiting in front of the video store and told the gathering crowd of the scholarships his consortium of financial organizations was offering to members of the community, and the heads of the unions went to the microphone one by one and announced job openings, jobs that had just become available and would be reserved for members of the bereaved community, and the press shouted and asked questions, and the mayor drank a glass of wine with a man who invited him to visit his travel agent. Was this a miracle or what?

That evening, a tired Mel went to a national television studio and explained to anyone watching the news why what had quickly become known as the Gefilte Fish March had taken place and how grieved he was that violence had erupted in his city. "These days," he said, "there are many un-American activities out there, but of them all, beating up your neighbor takes the cake, the fish cake, that is." The TV journalist, an Asian American woman with hard black eyes, asked Mel, "Do you want to tell us, mayor, who is your favorite, Vivien Leigh or Ingrid Bergman?" "I admire them both," said Mel, who secretly preferred Ingrid Bergman, "but remember, they are only celluloid images on a screen, not causes to die for." "What," said the reporter, "would you die for?" Mel took the split second that you are allowed on television for apparent thought and answered, "Obviously nothing yet, since I'm still with you, but should it happen, then I'll know and then I'll die. On the whole, I think it's hard enough finding ways to live without bothering to figure out what we might die for."

The next day the mayor's poll numbers went through the proverbial roof. He was now the mayor on the roof, his tune pitch-perfect. Of course, in garbage cans all over Muttonneck gefilte fish slices could have been found virtually intact. Gefilte fish is an acquired taste. Nevertheless, the residents of Muttonneck under-stood that the gesture was well meant, even if the fish was most peculiar-smelling.

The phones were ringing like the bells of St. Mary's, sweetly on and on. Mel was wanted in San Francisco, in Cincinnati, in Chicago. He was asked to speak at college graduations and to grass-roots political clubs; there was a buzz in the air. Here was a fresh voice and a kind face, if not a handsome one. All right, he wasn't tall, and all right, he did have some minority baggage, but maybe the time had come in America to show the world just who we really are. Or so some bigwigs and money people were saying. Moe Alter was in seventh heaven. He was getting close to eighth heaven, where real power resides. "What do you know," he said to Mel, "about foreign affairs, the international arena?" Mel knew exactly what everyone else who read the *New Republic* and watched CNN knew. "We need to get you a tutor," said Moe. "I don't want a tutor," said Mel. "What are you going to be," said Moe, "an idiot savant?" "We've had presidents who are idiots," said Mel. Moe didn't laugh. "Not you," he said. "What is the capital of Sierra Leone?" Moe asked. Mel shrugged. "Which country has the great-est AIDS problem?" Moe asked. Mel gave Moe a don't-ask-me look. "Don't you want to be president one day?" Moe asked. Mel consid-ered the question. He had never thought of himself as ambitious enough for such a thing. He had never believed it when they said any American boy could be president. He knew there were qualifiers to that piece of Americana. "Really," said Moe, "think about it." "I'd probably be the first president since Kennedy to get assassinated," said Mel. "So you're afraid?" said Moe. "I am not afraid," said Mel. "I just don't think I'm the right man for the job. I'm ordinary. I'm not brilliant. I'm not Abraham Lincoln or Thomas Jefferson." "If you were," said Moe, "you could never get elected."

That night Mel woke at three A.M. and could not, despite a glass of warm milk, fall back asleep. Was ambition a sin? he wondered. He had always been ambitious, confident that he could do and win and be the king of the mountain. He wanted to be king of the mountain. He admitted that to himself. Was he worthy? Maybe yes, maybe no, but that wasn't the point. He had wanted to be mayor. He liked being mayor. He would like being president even more. The headaches would be greater, the anxiety would be horrible, the consequences of mistakes more far-reaching. Presidents were shamed all the time. Regular people loved the disgrace that fell on their leaders' heads. He considered the risks. He considered his most intimate desires. He woke Ruth up. "Are you with me?" he said. "Do you think the idea ridiculous?" "Do I have to give up my job?" she asked. "Yes," he said. "I'm going back to sleep," she said, but she didn't. Mel, on the other hand, rolled over and snored and didn't hear the alarm in the morning.

74

AWARDS AND
REWARDS

When the letter came in the mail along with all the pleas for charitable donations, the offerings of low-interest-rate credit cards, and a mammoth pile of the usual household bills, Ina sat down in her kitchen and opened it with trembling hands. It said:

Dear Ina Horowitz,

I read in the paper of your wonderful success and the award you will be receiving along with your husband. I wanted to express my pleasure in your accomplishment and to tell you that I have always known that you are a woman with a great gift who can and will make a contribution to our society. I am happy for you and for all of us that this has happened. I feel privileged to have known you.

Sincerely,

Dr. Thomas Bergen.

Dr. Bergen, her therapist, whom she had not seen for a long time, wrote her this letter. First she put it in her stocking drawer. Then she put it in the box with her pearls and her silver bracelet.

Then she put it in the scrapbook in which she kept locks from her children's first haircuts. Then she put it under her pillow. Then she put it with her passport. It was one of her important documents, after all.

It had not been one of those breakthroughs that would cure cancer or stop aging or renew a clogged heart, but it had opened a new way to look at the connection of proteins and cell change, of the collisions of acids and their probable precursors in jellyfish and then in mice, rabbits, and guinea pigs, a large number of which had been sacrificed in the process, which bothered Ina and Sergei not at all. It was a breakthrough, it was an idea that looked at known facts again and saw what everyone else had missed, how they could be piled up in a different fashion and bring about new and startling conclusions that would one day bring someone else, a scientist perhaps not yet born, to an even more important breakthrough. They went to a meeting in Chicago, where Sergei gave half the paper and Ina gave the second half, and when they sat down there was stunned silence in the audience. The paper was published in *The New England Journal of Medicine,* the one that really counted. It was translated into French and German and Italian, and it was on the Internet within hours of its publication. Ina knew that it might be years before she or Sergei came up with something so remarkable again, maybe never. Still, the victory was sweet, even if her father and mother, despite having had it explained to them at least ten times, were still somewhat vague when asked about it.

They won a prize, a major science prize that came with a few thousand dollars. The money for the prize was being put in a bank account for Ina and Sergei's children to go to private school. It would get them through January of first grade. Their photos were in the paper. Moe made sure that the coverage was good and that Ina's maiden name was repeated again and again. "Daddy's Girl" was the caption of the photo of Mel kissing his daughter in the lobby of the Bloomberg Hotel, where the prize had been awarded at a black-tie dinner. Leonid and his new, very tall Jamaican girl-

friend, a much-in-demand model named Althea, attended the dinner sitting at the table with the Rosenberg family. Leonid had a
new haircut. He had on a fine new (not rented) tuxedo. Not only
were the hats he had designed selling across the country, but the
jacket that he next designed was mass-produced by a factory in
China hired by Vladi for the purpose and had sold so well that
Leonid had bought a large apartment downtown and Vladi would
soon move to the suburbs with his family.

At the dinner Leonid asked his brother to come outside with
him. In the lobby of the hotel they found a far corner with deep
chairs and sat down. Sergei, who was very happy and had drunk two
glasses of wine, which was a lot for him because he wasn't a
drinker, was suddenly anxious. What could his brother want now?
Money, the prize money? Leonid said, "Sergei, I am your loving
brother, and so I am giving to you this," and from inside his jacket
pocket he pulled out an envelope. Sergei opened the envelope and
turned pale. "But this is so much," he said. "I am a rich man," said
Leonid, "and you, you will have whatever I have, because you are
my brother and you brought me to this country when I had nothing, because you believed in me." That was not quite true. Sergei
had not believed in Leonid. Ina had not believed in Leonid. They
both had thought he would end up serving a twenty-year jail term,
but family is family and Sergei had loved his brother despite thinking the worst of him. "But," said Sergei, "this check—do you
understand how many zeroes you have put here?" Leonid laughed.
"Buy an apartment big enough for your family," he said. "Buy a
house at the beach if you like. I am designing dresses for big chains
next spring. I am buying real estate." "But," said Sergei, "perhaps
the business will one day slip." "Don't worry," said Leonid. "Vladi
and I know how to stay on top." He clapped his brother on the
back. They hugged. Ina said, when Sergei whispered the news to
her, "We can't accept." "I did already," said Sergei. Leonid stood
up at the table and lifted his glass, "God bless America," he said,
"and God bless capitalism," he added, "and God bless the women

who buy the clothes we make." Everyone lifted their glasses to that toast. Leonid added, "And God bless my brother and his wife. I adopt them as my personal scientists forever after." Everyone drank to that. Leonid went on, "I am going to design a new dress for the Statue of Liberty. Why should she wear such an outdated shmatta?"

"Make her a hat," said Mel, "a hat with a red pompom." Along the sides of the room the mayor's usual police escort stood stony-faced, staring out into the crowd. At the entrance to the banquet hall there were two more security guards, gifts of the government to those who were running for national office. The Imps of Misfortune tried to blow a fuse in the hotel's cellar, but a backup fuse went right to work. They tried to trip up a waiter carrying all the tiramisus on a large silver tray, but the waiter caught himself at the last minute, kicking an imp right in the small of his crooked little back. The Spawn of Lilith tried to start a fire in the kitchen, but the sous chef put it out. Some days nothing works.

That night Althea rubbed her coffee-colored cheek against Leonid's chest. "I don't want to convert," she said. "Don't," said Leonid. "I'm a pagan," said Althea. "Me too," said Leonid, "a Jewish pagan." "Brooke can say the blessings on the bread and wine in Hebrew," said Althea. "I can't," said Leonid, and went right to sleep.

That night, just before getting into bed, Ina took Dr. Bergen's letter out from its hiding place and replaced it again. She didn't have to reread it. She had memorized the contents.

75

THE BELL
TOLLS

By the time the following Thanksgiving came around, even more
security men were following Mel and Ruth about. "No cameras," said Ruth. "This is a private family matter." "No cameras," Mel said, "and no reporters, either." Ruth put out her silver
candlesticks that weren't really silver because the originals had
been pawned in order to pay the obstetrician when Jacob was born.

It was possible to purchase the entire meal from the takeout
department of a large food store, but that seemed ugly to Ruth, a
slap in the face to the generations of women who had labored over
stoves, rubbed and rolled, wiped their hands on aprons, pounded
on boards, snipped and stuffed and sliced and chopped. It was a
fine thing that women could now do brain surgery and sit on the
Supreme Court, and it was an especially fine thing that her very
own daughter had won an important science prize, and she herself
was pleased that she hadn't yet quit her job but had only taken a
leave of absence, but it seemed disrespectful and unkind to let Mexican and Guatemalan workers prepare the food for Thanksgiving.
This was not, she was quick to explain to her daughter-in-law,
because she didn't respect Mexican and Guatemalan workers and

their right to make a living. In fact, Ruth harbored no sentimental visions of her mother in the kitchen. The lady was exhausted, worked to the bone by the time every holiday meal was served, and then there were the dishes, the endless dishes, and while the men felt the festivities warm their faces (or was it the wine?), as they joked and told stories the females rushed about clearing and washing and wrapping leftovers for the guests while backs ached and ankles swelled and hands smelled of detergent and spices in some disagreeable combination. Ruth preferred to make her own Thanksgiving food not because she courted disaster or was a masochist in any sense of the word but because she believed that if you don't use your own arms to beat and stir, then the moment, the emotion of it all, becomes too easy, too quick, too easily forgotten. It's all very well for women to use their minds, but if they don't remember about their hands, they will be cut off from the way it was, from the human need for food and cleanliness, and that would be a great loss. So she had Ina make the stuffing and Brooke make the sweet potatoes with marshmallows, and she made the turkey and two kinds of pies.

The afternoon of Thanksgiving the family gathered around the table. Moe Alter was there. His children were with his ex-wife. Leonid arrived with Althea, now his fiancée. Harold had come in a beautiful pink suit that Leonid admired. Kim and Kelly were prepared to read the Declaration of Independence before the meal. Kelly's hair was long and Kim's was short, and you could see that they had different ideas about things. Kim's face was no longer ashen, and her eyes were bright. She held her mother's hand under the table.

The room was hot. The windows were open, but the steam from the kitchen permeated everything. Ruth wiped her forehead. She took a deep breath. There didn't seem to be enough air in her lungs. She felt a pain in her chest, a slight pain. She stood up, wanting privacy, needing to be alone, just for a moment. Then she was down on the floor. Mel stood over her. "Ruth, Ruth," he yelled into her ear, as if the problem were a sudden deafness. Moe whipped out his cell phone. Jacob pulled his from his pocket. Ina and Sergei bent down over Ruth, listening for a heartbeat. Kim and Kelly began to cry. Ina and Sergei's little girl, Anna, put her head in her father's lap and her hands over her ears. The paramedics arrived and lifted Ruth up on a stretcher and carried her out. The security men raced into the street to follow the ambulance. Was she still breathing? Ina wasn't quite sure. The paramedics disappeared with Ruth into the back of the ambulance. Mel wanted to ride with them. But the security guards insisted on coming along, and they all wouldn't fit in the ambulance. The hospital was close by. The family would follow. Mel, shocked into silence, his own heart pounding, was pushed by the security guards into their car. Ina, who had never been quite sure if she really loved her mother, was sure now. The food remained on the table and the candles burned down; the lady hired to clean up was not sure if she should wait or pick up the dishes, but the Thanksgiving had ended before Mel made his speech praising America with all its checks and balances, all its brilliant laws designed to blunt the natural cruelty of man. Now they were all back in the real world.

Ruth was dreaming, if a person who has lost consciousness, whose heart is leaking, can be said to dream. She saw herself on a long journey, with a backpack and the red sandals she had worn in college. She saw the swirling dust of the desert and the long line of people walking and walking. In her dream she wasn't worried. She wasn't sad. She was on a journey, which was the way it was sup- posed to be. You weren't expected to arrive, but you were expected to move forward. Ruth understood this. She understood that she was going to die, and she wasn't all that surprised. She wished she could go back and comfort her family, but she realized that com- forting her family was a habit a person could unlearn. No one soul is really necessary in this world. She had done her part. The sojourn in the desert had a purpose, even if she couldn't figure out what.

Mel was sitting in the waiting room. Jacob and Ina were there. Moe was talking on his phone to the city editor of the *Metropolitan Herald,* demanding a front-page obituary. The children were asleep on the chairs, half-empty soda cans resting against the wall. No one seemed to want to leave. No one seemed to know what to do. The Imps of Misfortune and the Spawn of Lilith were weeping despite themselves. This was not what they intended.

76

A STORY NEEDS
AN ENDING

Think of the pages of the calendar flipping past, the way they used to in movies made more than a half century ago. Over the numbered pages with the names of the months on the top, as they quickly appeared and disappeared from view, the audience could see leaves falling or blossoms growing or snowdrifts piling high or bells ringing. Time is passing. Time has passed. How long? Just the right amount to bring us to the place we are now.

We are in a room with a makeup woman brushing powder on Mel's nose. The full cast has assembled here with him: Ina and Sergei and their children, Brooke and Jacob and their children, and Leonid and his new wife, who, for reasons of multicultural appeal, has been asked by Moe to stand at Mel's right hand when the time comes. Rabbi Gedali was there to stand with Mel, or rather stand discreetly behind him, to provide the proper religious note, to indicate God's approval of the party's choice. "You're our Queen Esther," said the rabbi in a whisper in Mel's ear. "Not surprising, then," Mel answered. "I have the support of the transgendered." Fortunately Rabbi Gedali did not quite catch his words. Don't blame Rabbi Gedali for not comparing Mel to King Solomon or

King David. By now the rabbi knew Mel too well for that. Also, in his rabbinic heart he did not believe in Jewish kings. In fact, he did not believe in kings. "Isn't it exciting?" Jacob said to Kim. "Oh, phony baloney," she answered, but was bouncing up and down just the same. "You look fine," said Ina to her father. He grinned his grin at her. "Are you sure?" he asked. "What would your mother say?" "Mom would say you're a ham," Ina said. "I *am* a ham," Mel said. "I do like a crowd." "You have a big one tonight," said Moe, "not merely the hundred and forty thousand in the stadium but with the prime-time national hookup you might say the whole country is all ears." Audrey Hadley and Anston were in the front row of the balcony. "I wouldn't have believed it," Anston said. "My father wouldn't go duck hunting with one of those people, and now look—the top job is within his reach." "I don't think Mel duck-hunts," said Audrey. "He doesn't even play golf," said Anston. "Have you ever heard of an American who doesn't play golf?" "Ruth should have been here," said Audrey.

Balloons were cradled in nets above the audience, ready to fall; camera lights were flashing; music was playing. "The speech," said Moe, "stick to it, don't try to wing it." Mel grinned. "What I'm good at," he said, "is winging it." "Not tonight," said Moe. Jacob looked at his father and sighed. There was no question now that he wouldn't be able to outstrip his dad, that he himself would be a mere footnote in history, unless of course this was the beginning of a dynasty. Even in America there were dynasties. That thought brought lightness to his step as the whole entourage walked through the underground passage with the camera operators walking backward before them up to the stairs that would take them to the elevator to the platform, and then the crowds would scream and yell, "Tell 'em, Mel," "Tell 'em, Mel," "Rosenberg lives," "Rosenberg lives"—so the chant went. They meant this one, not the other one, who in the excitement of the moment had been forgotten by all but a few grouchy talking heads who found the name ominous.

Soon Maddie would say into her microphone (she was covering the convention for a major network), "Here they are." Ina would have tears in her eyes because her mother really should have been there, and Mel would wave the crowd into silence, which would take a long time, and the balloons, red, white, and blue, would be falling and falling, and then the former mayor would say to all assembled—those in the stadium, those in their living rooms, those with radios in trailer parks, those staring up at the TV over the end of the bar, and those with flat-screen TVs that stretch more yards than a cruise ship—to all he would say, "My fellow Americans . . ."

ABOUT THE AUTHOR

ANNE ROIPHE is the author of seven novels, including *Up the Sandbox, Lovingkindness,* and *The Pursuit of Happiness.* Her nonfiction books include National Book Award nominee *Fruitful: A Real Mother in the Modern World; 1185 Park Avenue: A Memoir;* and *Married: A Fine Predicament.* For more than three decades, she has illuminated the complex realm of women's lives with provocative insight.